EMMA MORGAN is a w
bestselling debut novel, *A L*
was published by Viking in 2
Polari First Book Prize. Emma
WriteNow scheme and she
Writers' Award for Fiction.

BEGGARS WOULD RIDE

EMMA MORGAN

NORTHODOX
PRESS

Northodox Press Ltd
Maiden Greve, Malton,
North Yorkshire, YO17 7BE

This edition 2025

1

First published in Great Britain by
Northodox Press Ltd 2025

Copyright © Emma Morgan 2025

Emma Morgan asserts the moral right to
be identified as the author of this work.

ISBN: 978-1-915179-75-3

This book is set in Caslon Pro Std

This Novel is entirely a work of fiction. The names, characters and incidents portrayed in it are the work of the author's imagination. Any resemblance to actual persons, living or dead, events or localities is entirely coincidental.

All rights reserved. No part of this publication may be reproduced, stored in a retrieval system, or transmitted, in any form or by any means, electronic, mechanical, photocopying, recording, or otherwise, without the prior permission of the publishers.

This book is sold subject to the condition that it shall not, by way of trade or otherwise, be lent, re-sold, hired out or otherwise circulated without the publisher's prior consent in any form of binding or cover other than that in which it is published and without a similar condition including this condition being imposed on the subsequent purchaser.

Printed and bound by CPI Group (UK) Ltd,
Croydon, CR0 4YY

PART ONE

Nat

At home she cuts up a quick line on a hardback Dylan Thomas. Always thought he was overrated. The taxi driver's an Evertonian but she's got the echoes of a headache and can't be arsed to argue. The entrance to the student dive is patchworked with posters for stuff she's not much interested in.

She scans the room for Popper and finds him easily enough because he's hanging onto the edge of the bar in an air pocket that no-one wants to breach. He looks like someone on one hell of a comedown, possibly with a knife in his sock. Junkie, she knows people are thinking, junkie nutter. Were she to need one, she couldn't get a better bodyguard.

She pushes her way through the crush to his side, but he's so far gone that he's oblivious until she's right next to him.

'Nat, Nat. Alright mate, alright mate.'

He plucks at her sleeve like a kid desperate for change to go to the sweet shop.

'Alright?' she says. 'What you drinking?'

'Thiss.'

'What's that?'

'Peach sschnappss.'

'Why you drinking that shite?'

'Jusst fancied it like. The bottle looked pretty.'

'For fuck's sake. You should have gone for the blue curaçao

while you were at it. Eh,' she says to the bartender. 'Get rid of this and give us a couple of Bushmills.'

She searches in a pocket and finds the Valium that she keeps on her for days when he gets like this, just in case, the way parents keep spare inhalers for their asthmatic kids. She gives him three of the pills. When she presses the glass of whiskey in between his clutched hands, it gives her a flashback to Petey holding the goblet with the communion wine in front of the altar. She hates Catholics. The adoration of agony is their quiddity. She has always wanted to say that line to someone. He coughs up most of the whiskey over the bar. The tattooed lad swipes at it with a dirty tea towel. That's what she loves about good bar staff, that seen it all, mopped all of it up complacency.

'Another one, then. And a water. Tap. And an espresso while you're at it. And you can keep the change.'

A woman with the floppy fringe of some Brideshead aesthete leans her arms on the bar next to Popper. Her silver bracelets jangle.

'Two glasses of white wine please,' the woman says, in the standard southern middle-class accent which always puts her back up, no matter how many times she hears it, 'oh and a piece of carrot cake. Would you like anything, Popper?'

'Nah.'

'You're reading, right?'

'Yeah, I am. Yeah. Gonna read. Yeah.'

'You'll be great. You always read really well.'

'Need a hand?' she says.

The woman looks at her.

'Erm… yeah. Over there. Thanks.'

She pats Popper on the back, picks up the woman's drinks, and follows her as she threads her way through the crowd. Too old to be a student, could be a post-grad though. Or another one of those so-called digital nomads who thought they'd slum it up north because it's cheap.

The woman takes a seat and for a moment she wishes she could sit down next to her, take the weight off her feet, slip her arm around the woman's back, and tell her the line about quiddity.

'Thanks,' says the woman.

'No worries,' she says. 'Alright?' and she tilts her chin at the woman's friend who she recognises from round where she lives. Used to be a party girl back in the day. Quick mental inventory. Ever slept with her? No. That's OK then.

'Hi,' says the friend.

She makes her way back to Popper and the bar.

Gwen

She watches the tall woman with the confident smile move away from her. She's not reading this evening, has written nothing new, and she's glad of it; it's been a long day full of children who refuse to sit down and who refuse to be quiet. She's got a headache.

'Lola?' she says, 'Do you know her?'

'Yeah,' says Lola, who is also watching the woman's departing back. 'She's a friend of Popper's?'

The woman is standing with her front to her now, next to Popper at the bar, and she wonders what their relationship is. The woman, tall and broad and beautiful in black jeans, black boots and a black bomber jacket, Popper, little and wiry in a grimy t-shirt.

'Gwen?' says Lola.

'Yeah?'

'Don't even go there. That isn't a place you wanna go.'

'Why not?' she says, looking at Lola now.

'They're starting,' says Lola and puts her finger to her lips.

She drags her eyes back to the front where the little stage is, but this room is no longer a neutral place to be in; it's a room with a possibility in it now. Her curiosity has got the better of her. What's so wrong with that woman?

Nat

She stands near the bar holding Popper tightly by the back of his t-shirt, so that he doesn't do a runner. If he pulls any tighter, she'll be strangling him. It's like having a dog by the scruff of its neck, a dog that is likely to bite someone. She discounts the bloke who's up on the stage after about twenty seconds, although she'd like to get a look at the pieces of paper he's perorating from. She bets there are no capitals or punctuation on there. None at all. The lanky MC in an ugly checked shirt gets up again.

'Thanks Mike. Well, next on tonight we have an up-and-coming local star with his own inimitable style. Good to see him back here again. Ladies and Gentlemen. I give you - Popper.'

She pushes him in the direction of the stage, and he somehow makes it up the step without falling; he sidles up to the mike, holding onto both sides of his shaved head, having forgotten how to blink, his eyes all pupils, his face all eyes. For a couple of seconds that feel like a couple of minutes, he just stands there, and she is grateful that the room is dominated by people who don't drink lager. Then he starts to slur into the mike like a 3 a.m. drunk, slow enough to be painful, all sibilants and spit.

> *No fish on Fridays*
> *So come let us go whoring*
> *For red satin suspenders*

Beggars Would Ride

And tight black lace bras
In the fish pools of streetlamps
They lurk with no knickers
No elastic between us
They sell cunt by the yard
In the cold streets of this city
Where the girls are so pretty
They add to their dole fees
By selling their sex
They'll wear fishnets
We'll shrimp them
For sure it's a Friday
Take a cold pint of Guinness
And get out your net
They'll wear rubber
And us too
And together
We'll rub down
We'll make friction in parked cars
And dark alleyways
It's better than wives kid
For whores its upfront with
Don't you know it's the truth
That in time
We all have to pay.

The poem takes all of thirty seconds and after he finishes, there's a silence in which you could hear a pin drop and then a big grateful round of applause like a collective sigh of relief. He stands there for a moment doing a good impression of 'The Scream' and then legs it for the door. She goes after him and finds him on his knees in the Men's, throwing up into a toilet.

'Christ!' Vomit is one of the few things she has never been able to handle. 'I'll wait for you outside.'

She stands in the narrow corridor, leaning against the dirty wall, the pine cleaner they use in the toilets reeking the place out, thinking that this is fucking typical. She needs a cigarette. Maybe she should just leave Popper to it. Would serve him right. What a state to get into. The southern girl comes down the corridor towards her and she smiles and switches herself back on. Yeah, she thinks, yeah, yeah, yeah.

'Is he OK?'

'He's throwing up.'

'Poor Popper. I know he gets really nervous, but he's normally OK once he gets on stage.'

'You a friend of his?'

'Well, I wouldn't say we're friends. I see him at these kinds of things sometimes.'

'You a student?'

'No.'

The woman crosses her arms over her chest. Nice chest on her. Somewhere soft to lay your weary head of an evening.

'It's the accent,' she says.

'Yeah, I know. And the clothes. Sorry, just I get it a lot. Especially from taxi drivers. Not a student no, I'm a teacher.'

'Of what?'

'Five-year-olds.'

'Whereabouts?'

'Why? Have you got a points system?'

This makes her smile.

'Maybe.'

'I work in Bootle.'

'Nothing doing, should have said Allerton.'

Popper staggers out of the Men's, face nearly as white as the wall he now lays his head against. He is still twitching, and he mumbles into the plaster.

'Popper, I can't hear you lad if you talk to the wall.'

She takes him and turns him around. The runt of the litter if ever there was one. His manky t-shirt reads 'The Pixies' and it's so wet it's dripping onto the floor.

'Why are you all wet?' she says.

'Bottled it, didn't I?'

'Not entirely.'

'Twat.'

'I think the one you did was called "Fucker",' she says.

The woman laughs. Popper makes a sudden move towards her with teeth bared and she backs away from him, shocked.

'What you want?' he says.

'Popper,' she says, and puts her arm out as a barrier across his chest. He crumples back into himself like a damp paper bag.

'Sssorry. Sssorry Gwen. Sssorry. Bit wound up like. Sssorry.'

'I think,' she says, still holding on to his t-shirt with one hand, 'that Gwen just came to see if you were alright. Christ Pop, I could wring you out onto the floor,' and she lets go. 'Please tell us that's just water.'

'Yeah. Yeah, I am. Alright. Yeah. Been ssick like. Threw up. Ta. Ta Gwen.'

'It's OK,' says the woman. 'We were just concerned about you. But that poem you read; I really liked it. It was a good performance. Didn't you hear all the clapping? People thought you did that on purpose. Maybe it's the way forward. Just the one poem.'

'Ssstupid.'

'No, not stupid. You just got freaked out. I get like that.'

'Yeah?'

'Yeah. Always. You've seen me. Only I throw up before, not after. It's fine. Come back in. I'll buy you a drink. I'm sure Si wouldn't mind if you wanted to go up again.'

'I dunked my head in the ssink. That's why I'm all sssoaked.'

'Go and wring yourself out in the sink then, lad,' she says. 'You're getting Gwen wet.'

'Do you want a tissue? I might have a tissue,' says Gwen, and she feels around in her pockets, looking at the floor while she does so. Sweet daft girl, she thinks, he needs a change of clothes, not a bloody tissue, but her hands are distracting her because she wants to put her hands in Gwen's pockets too. Or better still, down the back of her jeans.

'No, sorry, can't find any.'

'Ss'OK. No worriesss.'

'Maybe you should go and take your t-shirt off. I think I might have something in my bag you could wear. I'll go and get it.'

And off she goes back down the corridor. Back views of girls. Better than front views of girls? Nah, not better. Just different.

Beautiful.

She leads Popper into the Ladies. She strips his t-shirt off him and makes him stand under the hand dryer while she swishes the t-shirt around in a sink full of cold water. There's only a sliver of soap, but she has a scrub at the t-shirt with it, anyway. Jesus, the stuff she has to do. Popper is crouched under the dryer, face turned up into the blast of hot air.

'It's supposed to be drying your jeans, not your hair. You've got no hair to dry.'

'Feelsss nice. Hot.'

Gwen comes in, carrying a plastic bag.

'Should Popper be in the Ladies?' Gwen says.

Which makes her smile, that adherence to rules. She bets Gwen went to private school. 'Probably not. I'm Nat, by the way,' she says.

'Gwen,' says the woman, and holds out her hand. She wipes her own on her jeans and then takes hers. The handshake is firm, but Gwen's hands are much smaller than her own and her nails are bitten to the quick. Nic would despise her for that, but she finds it affecting – the childishness of it. The dryer stops suddenly, and Popper finally wakes up to the pheromones.

'Ssshe writess good ssstuff,' he says, looking from one to the other.

She turns back to the sink and starts to wring out the t-shirt, watching Gwen in the mirror. She has her head down, looking at her trainers, rocking on the balls of her feet, not seeming to want to look her in the eye.

'Oh yeah, I've got this,' says Gwen, looking up. She pulls a green t-shirt out of the plastic bag, like someone doing a conjuring trick. 'It'll be too big for you, but at least it's dry. It's even new.' She pulls off the tag from the label. 'I only bought it today.'

She gives it to Popper, who puts it on. It's far too baggy for him. He holds the bottom of it, trying to read it upside down.

'I can't say that fits very well,' says Gwen, 'But at least it will be dry. Stop you from catching cold. It says, "Mason's Premium Quality Veg". I don't know why. I just liked the colour.'

'They're not a band then?' says Popper.

'No, not as far as I'm aware.'

'Do you wanna do a swap, Gwen?' she says, holding up the wet t-shirt.

'No thanks. Here, have this plastic bag.'

She takes it and the ends of her fingertips brush Gwen's.

'Suits you Pop,' she says. 'What you wanna do now, then?'

'Go home,' says Popper, still staring down at the t-shirt.

'Yeah?'

'Yeah, but you're alright. I'll sssort mesself out.'

'You're no good. Where'd you really wanna go? Home? Mine? Cracke? Phil? Grapes?'

'Phil.'

'Wanna come, Gwen?' she says, looking at her.

'Thanks, but I'm with people.'

'OK. Well, we'll be up the Phil if you change your mind.'

'OK.'

'Thankss for the t-sshirt Gwen. I'll wassh it and give it back. Promisse.'

'Let's go,' she says and opens the door for Gwen who goes through first. In the corridor she stands with the plastic bag containing the wet t-shirt in one hand and Popper grasped in the other.

'That was the world's worst wet t-shirt comp,' she says. 'Bye Gwen. Thank you.'

'That's OK,' Gwen says. 'Bye Popper. Bye, nice to meet you,' and she flicks her eyes up at her, and then she walks away so fast she's almost running.

Shite. She wasn't a bad-looking girl. That might have been alright. She's tempted to cuff Popper round the back of his head.

'Ssorry Nat,' Popper says, looking so miserable he might cry.

'You stupid fucker,' she says, and she takes hold of the back of his neck again to manoeuvre him down the stairs because enclosed spaces bring on his claustrophobia.

Gwen

She watches poetry for an hour, an hour spent tearing up beer mats and picking at her nails and pulling at bits of her hair.

'Right then,' Lola says, and puts her bright red leather bag on the table and paws around in it to find her bright red lipstick, which matches her bag and her expensive red shoes. She slicks some on without the use of a mirror, the skill of which always amazes her. Then Lola pulls on her jacket, which is also red and leather and expensive, like all of it came together in some designer Barbie doll set.

'Come on,' says Lola.

They go down the stairs and out onto the street and head towards the bus stop. On the way Lola tells her the stuff she wants to hear, or maybe the stuff she doesn't want to hear.

There are men outside the pub over the road who leer at them, but Lola ignores them, doesn't even flip them the finger. It's hard to keep up with her because Lola is moving so fast. How do you do that in heels?

'And if you're still interested after all that then there's no hope for you,' Lola says, after she has given her the lowdown without pause for breath.

'I don't want to be interested.'

Which is true, no, now she's heard that she wishes she'd never glanced at that woman in the first place.

'But you are. That's OK. Everyone is. She has that effect. Question is: are you more interested now or less? 'Cos if it's more, then you're in deep shite.'

They reach the bus stop. Lola steps over the pink of a spilled milkshake.

'Why are people so disgusting?' Lola says and turns to her. 'So, Gwen, I have two proposals for you.'

'I imagine you're going to tell me them whether I want you to or not.'

'Listen. One: Think with the upper part of your body. It'll never go anywhere or get you anywhere, there is nothing long term ever, and it might make your life difficult 'cos her locals your local now. Two: Think with the lower part of your body. It'll never go anywhere etc., but you might have one really, really great night. Or so it's said. And if you can accept that for what it is, i.e., a bit of fun, and still look her in the eye next time you see her, then that's fine then right?'

'That's very black and white Lola.'

'Yeah. 'Cos it is very black and white. I am very black and white. I'd take option two. Go find her. It's gonna nark you now otherwise and you might as well get it over with rather than mooning round annoying me. You're living in my neck of the woods now; it's practically a rite of passage. When I said don't go there, I didn't mean she's an arsehole, 'cos she's not at all, and I try not to hold it against her that she's so bloody good looking. She's a nice woman. She just isn't your knives and forks type. Don't expect anything past a couple of orgasms and you'll be fine. So why not? Think of all the calories you'll burn. Better than that librarian you were with before. Bet she showed you a good time.'

'She wasn't a librarian; she was an educational research fellow.'

'Gwen, love, honestly, did she ever make you come?'

'Once. I think that was an accident though. I'd spent the afternoon watching a film with Penelope Cruz in it.'

'Oh, well then. If Penelope doesn't do it for you, you're probably half-way up the morgue. Where'd she go? Did she say?'

'The Phil,' she says reluctantly.

Lola takes hold of her arms and kisses her on both cheeks.

'Go electrocute yourself, sweetheart. If she keeps you up long enough, buy us some croissants for brekkie on your way home.'

Lola pushes her in one direction along Renshaw Street and she walks off in the other.

'But what if I said I preferred the other option?'

'Then you'd be lying,' says Lola, over her shoulder, still walking.

'I don't want to do this. I much prefer Arctic explorers,' she says, her voice getting louder.

'Do you know any of them?' says Lola.

'I do actually. Her name's Marcella. She's only got eight toes left. No, really, I do.'

Lola stops and turns round.

'Gwen?'

'Yes?'

'This is a bank holiday weekend. What else you gonna do? Write lesson plans?'

Lola walks off again.

'Can't you at least come with me then? I can't go up there on my own!' she shouts at her departing back.

'And I'll want to hear all the gory details!' Lola shouts back. 'Word on the street is that she gives the best head this side of the Runcorn Bridge.'

Halfway up Hardman Street, she stops dead and almost turns round. She could get the bus home from here. Surely that would be more sensible? But she can't not go up there now, she's compelled as if by some magnet sucking her in. Yes, she'll go in quickly and then leave. She'll be able to tell Lola she couldn't find her, which will be the truth, and hopefully that will be that. That seems like a reasonable plan. She breathes out and continues up the hill.

Entering the pub doesn't feel safe at all to her, no, it feels downright dangerous, a place full of risk. She tunnels her way through the crowd to the bigger room and has a quick look around, but she doesn't see either the woman or Popper. Maybe she has already left then. Yeah, she's not here she thinks, she'll have gone on by now, and she relaxes into disappointment but yet also relief.

She feels a hand on her shoulder, breath on her neck, voice in her ear, but she doesn't turn around. The hand is heavy on her, and she can feel it burn right through her coat, where it alters the feel of the blood rushing through her shoulder. She shouldn't be here. The voice says, 'I'm taking him home now. He's drunk himself into a stupor. Come back to mine? We'll drop him off first.'

She turns to look at her. Nat must be six feet at least, so that she's only up to her shoulder. She is beautiful, stunning would be the word, but yet there is also something reticent about her. She's not out there with her body on a plate for all to see, she is quiet in her clothes and is wearing only minimal make-up. Her red brown hair is pulled back in a high ponytail, but she can't help wondering what that hair would feel like on her face. They both wait.

Nat

She sizes her up. The light brown sulky posh boy hair. The round pink-cheeked face of a country girl out of Thomas Hardy. Not the heroine. One of the milkmaids. Her big pale green eyes fringed by lashes that are barely there. She's not wearing any make-up, and she likes that in her. A brave woman to come looking for her all by herself.

'To do what?' Gwen says.

'Talk shite?'

'Fine.'

'Let's go then.'

She finds Popper, once again hanging onto the edge of the bar, but this time more out of drunkenness than panic, and pulls him towards her. Then she shepherds them all out of the pub, although she doesn't touch Gwen again. She is enjoying the anticipation now.

She more or less has to carry Popper up his stairs to his attic flat, where she pulls his trainers off and puts him to bed on the mattress on the floor. He's still wearing Gwen's t-shirt. She goes and switches the heating on and puts the wet t-shirt from the bag on a radiator which is nearly falling off the wall, bloody hell, all it would need is a screwdriver, it would only take a couple of minutes. The likelihood of Popper having a screwdriver is nil though. She considers getting a knife from the kitchen but then she remembers the girl. She'd almost forgotten her for a moment; she's a bit drunk too now, although she can hold her drink much better than Popper. She's going to have to come in here again and give him a hand clearing up. She wipes the cold sweat off his face with a dubious towel, then she tucks him up inside the duvet that he nicked from

John Lewis, fuck knows how, he won't let on, and puts a glass of water and a bowl for an ashtray on the floor next to him.

Behind Popper's head are the piles of his books, the best cared for things in the place. He won't read anything but hardbacks, says he doesn't like the way that paperback spines fall apart. She takes a book off the top of a pile, it's 'Treasure Island', and puts it between his arms like a kid's teddy. She makes sure there's nothing he can fall over on the way to the toilet, makes sure there's nothing lit that shouldn't be, and then she looks out of the window at the black cab waiting far down below and feels an uncustomary moment of hesitation, a temptation to just stay here, sit down on Popper's sagging armchair and spend the rest of the night reading. What is wrong with her tonight? She runs back down the long stairs. The girl is looking out of the window of the taxi, shoved right over to the other side of the seat.

'Sorry to keep you waiting,' she says as she gets in.

'I like this part of Liverpool,' Gwen says quietly, as though to herself, as the cab turns a corner. 'All this decaying grandeur. Do you live in a mansion then?'

'Decaying? Nah, not quite. Just a flat. What? You think I look like a lady or something?'

'You look like someone I shouldn't be going home with.'

'Then don't. Where do you live? I'll drop you.'

'It's OK. I trust you.'

'You shouldn't.'

'Shouldn't I?'

'No. You shouldn't.'

'Will you hurt me?'

'That's not my thing.'

'What is your thing?'

Gwen

Nat smiles at her now, a full-on smile. God help me, she thinks.

But it's not true - Nat does live in a mansion, although hers is one of the smaller ones, in a wide street of three-storey houses in various states of repair. And it's tempting to relate them to their inhabitants because some of them are looking alright, like their ordinary residents get up in the morning, have a cup of tea, and go to work, and some of them have skips in the garden and scaffolding up against their walls, 'being tarted up for hipsters,' as Nat would tell her if asked, but the odd one looks completely unloved, the people in them not ones you would want to visit, probably not even ones you would want to know.

As for Nat's, there are no lights shining out, and she doesn't like it as they go down the overgrown drive in the semi-dark to her house. She's not sure if she wants to go any further. Now they are at the base of the steps leading up to the front door and the outside light suddenly flicks on and she feels rabbit in headlights, almost stumbles, almost grabs hold of Nat but doesn't. Because she was right, she thinks, she was right, she's not to be trusted, and her mum would be saying what an earth are you doing child, get out of there right now, go on, run, run.

'These places, they're just so solid,' she says, and Nat stops halfway up her steps and turns towards her.

'Built to last. Merchant houses.'

'This one looks like Miss Havisham lives here. Who's your gardener?'

'It's an artistic statement. I'm going the Chelsea Flower next year. Come head.'

And so she does, and most of the reason she does, when she thinks about it later, is because Nat is not the kind of woman you disobey when she gives you an order, however mildly that order, that instruction, might be couched.

Nat

In the little hall of her flat, she hangs up their coats and sits on the trunk that once belonged to an uncle who was a merchant sailor and slips off her Chelsea boots while Gwen heels off her Converse.

'You'll ruin your shoes doing that my dad always said,' she says.

'Yeah, I do,' says Gwen.

Then she pushes open the door to the front room. She likes to leave all the doors closed before she goes out, it's a thing she has. A wall of books greet her and Gwen goes straight to them. She likes that in a person, it doesn't happen often enough.

'This is a nice room,' Gwen says, and she can still hear the nerves.

'Ta.'

'I like sash windows, there's something romantic about them. They always make me want to open them and lean out.'

She has a picture in her head then of Gwen leaning out of the window and her standing close up behind her, pulling down her jeans. Jesus. She's in one of those moods now.

She sits by the side of the big table in what she thinks of as 'my' chair, although all the chairs are hers, stretches her legs out, and starts to skin up. It's only early. She tries to imagine what a woman like this can find out about her from this room. It's not a bad flat, plenty of space, the light's good up here in the eaves, she likes that it's high up and she can look down on the street. Private. She painted all the walls white himself. Did the skirting boards white and all the woodwork too, she did a good job, even their dad said so. Does it look like a woman lives here? In her experience, most women have things with flowers on, don't they? She should buy some cushions for the sofa, perhaps. Why is she thinking about this shite? And this girl, this girl she's brought home, what's she doing bringing a girl back here, she thought she'd given that up, this girl is touching her books and flicking through them. That always makes her feel slightly exposed, especially when it's someone looking at them who's been to university. She doesn't like to admit that this makes her feel something like inferior. Should have pulled her finger out then. It's her own bloody fault.

Gwen's only about Popper's height, but, unlike him, everything about her is deliciously plump and rounded. Why does a girl built like that wear that scruffy gear? She should be wearing whatever a milkmaid wears. What do they wear? Her jeans, she notices, are grass stained at the knees. She's what her friend Jack calls 'a winter warmer', someone to come home to on a freezing January night and lie down on to take the frost out of your hair.

'What you doing here anyway?' she says.

'Talking to you.'

'I meant in this city.'

'What do you want me to say? It's always been my dream to work with lice ridden slum children and give something back?'

'Because that way when they're grow up, they'll at least be able to fill out their Housing Benefit forms neatly?'

'Why do people ask me that all the time? It's like you have some sort of immigration policy. This is just a city; it's not a mission statement. People ask me why I'm here like it's the edge of the known world.'

'It is the edge of the known world. You weren't up tonight?'

'Not in the mood.'

'What mood do you have to be in?'

'Combatorial.'

'I think it's combative.'

'I prefer combatorial. We could go to bed now, couldn't we?'

She suppresses a smile. There's a silence between them like an unsheathing of knives.

'Will you tell me a poem?'

'What kind of poem?'

'One you don't read in public.'

'One I don't read? Pffff. I don't know. There's all kinds of rubbish.'

'Tell me one that you never tell anyone.'

Gwen finally turns round. She's back to thinking about taking off her jeans. She does so like a girl with big legs.

'The thing is…' Gwen says.

'What?'

'I do want to go to bed with you, yes. That's why I came right? That's why you asked me back, isn't it? Or were you just going to ply me with coffee? Recite me sonnets? But I'm finding this… I don't normally do one-night stands and you see… I've been warned about you.'

'What did they say?'

'Enough.'

'Gwen. Come here. Please. Please come over here.' Gwen crosses the floor and stands by her chair. 'I'm gonna be straight with you. I only do one-night stands, more or less. So that makes this problematic. And what you've heard is probably true. Well, most of it. I make no apologies. I am who I am. It's not big, and it's not clever but that's the way it is.'

She pulls Gwen towards her, and she slides onto her lap, puts her arms up around her neck and her face into the crook of her chin. She feels Gwen's heart beating hard through her jumper, she feels the softness of her chest and the way she was feeling anyway, the insistent thump, thump, thump inside her is cranked right up. She smells like… there is no analogy maybe… the closest thing to say is that she smells like clean hair and warm woman. She puts her arms around Gwen's back.

'We could just do it here in the chair,' Gwen whispers.
'We could.'
'Or on the floor. On the sofa. Table.'
'We can do it anywhere you damn well like girl.'
'The bath?'
'Yeah. The bath.'
Their 'A's do not match. Barth, she said. Barth. Parth. Graass.
'Bet you didn't have no coal cellar.'
'No, we had a wood burning stove.'

She puts her mouth very softly against Gwen's neck, feels her pulse move under her lips.

'Or I could just get up now and go home. Would that make me a tease?' Gwen says, and she can feel the vibration of the words in her throat. 'If I get up and go home now, what'll you do?'

'Go back out maybe. Or have a smoke and go to bed. Could do with an early night.'

'It's two.'

'That's dead early for me.'

She hugs her harder then, her arm around her waist. She makes no attempts to get under her clothes. She strokes her hair, and it feels like she had expected it to. Soft. Would her skin under her clothes feel the same way? And what about the inside of her?

'On nights like this,' Gwen says, 'anything could happen. Have you got a pen?'

She reaches across the table for one, dipping her.

'Have you got any tattoos?'

'Yeah.'

'How many?'

'Just the one.'

'LFC on your bicep? Mum? An anchor?'

'Just this,' and she pulls up her right sleeve to show her. Gwen traces it with her fingers, which are ever so slightly, almost imperceptibly, shaking. Framed by wings the black tattoo says:

every angel is terrifying

'What's that from?'

'Rilke.'

Gwen carefully rolls up her left sleeve all the way to her shoulder, and it gives her goose pimples. She rearranges her in her lap. All the possibilities. What she wants to do most of all, right this moment, is put her tongue into every fold she has. Gwen takes the pen and writes on her arm.

'Wait,' Gwen says and licks her thumb and rubs out some of what she has written.

The firm press of the pen while it draws the words onto her skin does remind her of the needle, although it doesn't hurt like that did. She was only nineteen when she had that done. Twelve years back. Another life. The feel of Gwen's thumb on her skin. The saliva on her lips. She wants to put her fingers into her mouth. She's getting to the oh fuck this point, she can feel it rising in herself like anger. Not that she can't be patient. She is naturally patient and sometimes she has waited all night long just for the kick of it but she's too tired to be patient tonight. Gwen's fingers are black. She has ink on her lips, on her tongue. She is using her sleeve to clean up her arm. Finally, what she's written runs from shoulder to wrist.

'What does it say?' she asks.

'You'll have to read it in the mirror.'

Something in her cracks, and it must have been the tiredness she says to herself later because she never cracks. Fuck it, she thinks. Let's just get on with this. She pulls up Gwen's t-shirt and puts her hand on her breast and she is as soft as she thought she might be, hoped she might be. She slips her other hand between her legs, feels the warmth of her through her jeans, hears the way her breathing goes, feels she has her, in every way, in the palm of her hand.

'You smell like summer,' she says, which is what she does smell of she realises now, and she unzips her jeans. Soon she will be in the place in the world where she feels most at home, in the soft, wet refuge of a soft, warm woman. Her favourite, favourite place. She pushes her hand very gently over her belly and down inside the cotton of her knickers. She cups her, doesn't do anything else, just cups her until she feels that her breathing is exactly in time with Gwen's breathing because she knows that breathing counts; that if she breathes slowly enough, her pulse will be Gwen's pulse, her blood will almost be her blood; she will forget that they are separate, and that is a wonderful thing, the opposite of terrifying whatever that is, the best release of all the releases, not the oblivion that drugs give you, but something else, a stillness that is the best way to forget she knows.

Gwen puts her hand over hers.

'Nat?' she whispers so close to her ear that her lips tickle.

'Yeah?'

'No.'

And before she knows what's happening, she hears the front door of the flat slam, hears Gwen running, running fast, down the stairs.

Gwen

She runs all the way home, and she's no runner, but she's got to get away. Completely out of breath, she arrives panting on her front doorstep. Because it was a mistake going there and she knew it would be one from the moment she first set eyes on Nat. But sometimes you do that, don't you? You know something is really wrong for you, but you go for it, anyway. A form of perversion. That or stupidity. Even though you know it will end badly. But she didn't stay and so is this maturity? She unlocks the door and climbs the stairs to the flat. She opens the front door and goes in as quietly as she can. Lola's bedroom door is closed. She hopes she doesn't hear her; she can't cope with any questions right now and Lola will probably want a full-on discussion, no, a dissection in minute detail, despite the time of night.

She slips into her bedroom and pulls the door to, and lies down on top of her duvet, fully clothed with her Converse still on. She realises that she ran here without lacing them up. That was stupid, wasn't it? She could have gone flying. And then what? She imagines the grazes she would have sustained if she had fallen. And although she did the right thing, she knows she did, it doesn't stop the longing that has opened up inside her.

Nat

'Good?' says Popper the next night, after she has spent a day out of kilter because of that woman and hating it.

'What?' she snaps.

'Gwen.'

'I didn't.'

'Thought sshe wass your type.'

'What is my type?'

'Sshe's like you.'

'How is she like me?'

'Don't get narked. You know. Wordss. Clever like. And sshe's got big legss. Thought you'd go for it.'

'Well, I didn't.'

'Alright. Not my fault iss it?'

She hardly speaks all night. She's home by three. She's been wearing a t-shirt with long sleeves, and she takes it off now to look at the marks on her arm in the bathroom mirror. She finds her pen but no paper, so she uses the inside cover of a book and slowly transcribes what Gwen wrote. She sits on the couch reading it and smoking a spliff. She's a sceptic. It's in her bones. She's a cynic about people. She believes in blow and Baudelaire. But not people. She's seen what they can do. For fuck's sake.

> *On nights like this*
> *Anything could happen*
> *Everything I fear the most*
> *Could come to pass*

Beggars Would Ride

The way your mouth
May feel on mine
Might well destroy me
Like a bomb
Waiting inside me
Tick tick
It would say
Tick tock
If I stay here you will
Initiate me into something
Other than myself
Into some other person
That alone I would not
Know how to become.

'Those line breaks aren't right,' she says into the air.

She puts her t-shirt back on and wanders around the flat. Paces. Stands in the kitchen looking out into the dark garden. She likes that it's overgrown, a mess of buddleia and bramble, but maybe she should sort it out since no-one else in the building has ever bothered. Make a lawn to lie down on maybe. But then she'd have to get a mower, and that seems so suburban, so Sunday afternoon. It would make her feel old and too much like their dad. Fuck that.

She skins up again. Wonders if, for next winter, she should get bigger radiators. Thinks that their dad would be disgusted by the fact that she has never, ever had her windows cleaned, although they would have a job getting a brush all the way up here. Have to use a crane maybe. She likes the idea of a washing line. Christ. What next? Croquet hoops? She never chases, doesn't have to. Only if it's part of the whole evening game, the night game. But this. Fucking hell. She left. And it wasn't because she wanted her to come after her. No, she'd heard what she'd said and called her on it. She rings Popper's mobile. He's awake. Of course.

'Gwen's number? What's her number?'

'Dunno. Dunno it.'

'Well, where's she live?'

'Why?'

'Because.'

'Sshe ussed to live in town but I think sshe sshares with that girl now. You know. That girl.'

'Brown girl? Not bad looking?'

'Yeah, her.'

'Lola.'

'Yeah. Lola.'

'Where does Lola live?'

'I think sshe lives near youse. On Praise street.'

'Christ. What number?'

'Dunno. Never been there.'

She switches off her mobile and leaves it on the table, puts her jacket on and goes out. Five minutes' walk. For fuck's sake. She thinks of their mum telling them off for swearing and making them put money into the cardboard swear box Petey had made. He'd drawn a wonky picture of a dragonfly on the front of it for some reason best known to himself. Then their mum taking the box and emptying it into the plate at Mass. It gave a whole new meaning to the phrase, 'From your mouth to God's ear'.

As she walks down the street she thinks, as she has done so many times, about how you measure distance. Because this is only miles from where she grew up, but it might as well be Brazil, might as well be another planet. All this decaying grandeur, all these great, solid piles built in the days when Liverpool was the rich kid, now carved up into flats for the lairy crowd of so-called bohemians who hang out round here. It's the in-between bit of her city. Certainly not rough. Not 'nice and quiet' either though, which was their mum's highest compliment for a place. Cool? There are people who think so. What does that even mean? It means somewhere between cold and warm. She hates the misuse of words. But she likes it round here. Beautiful, becoming more expensive by the day, less and less falling apart. Bet Gwen could get a poem out of that. Bet Gwen could make up words to describe it. How great to be able to do that. That invention. And her sitting on her lap with her softness.

She feels powerful for the simple reason of being the only one awake. There aren't many cars at this time of night. Now she is here in the street where Gwen lives. Apparently. A shorter street than hers, the houses tall yellow Victorian terrace. Not a cut through so hardly any traffic. What is she going to do now? She hasn't thought it through, but now, when it comes down to it, there only seems to be the one option. She's going to do a Mum. Oh well. Keep it in the family. This is Liverpool after all, night's full of trauma, the city can cope.

'Gwen!' she shouts out, disturbing the street-lit silence. 'Gwen! Gwen!'

She stands still in the middle of the road since there's nothing coming to mow her down. Werewolf howling in the street. She looks around for the moon but it's dark up there beyond the greyish orange glow of light pollution. She has the moment of peacefulness that she only normally gets inside girls or books. Maybe she's more stoned than she thought. She sits down on a wall. Oh well, it was worth a try, wasn't it? She gets a packet of cigarettes out of her jacket pocket and lights one. She takes a deep drag. It was always unlikely that this would happen. Better left alone really. But still, she's glad she came out, it was the trying that seems important although she's not sure why. She gets up and starts to walk back up the middle of the street. Then she hears fast footsteps hurtling down the tarmac towards her.

'Sorry,' she says, turning around.

There's a furious woman with a big black jumper on, red tartan pyjama bottoms, and trainers, who marches straight up to her.

'What?' Gwen says. 'My flatmate just woke me up. Says some

lunatic's shouting my name in the street. And it's you. What the hell are you doing? It's four o'clock in the morning!'

'You didn't leave a phone number.'

Gwen looks like she's going to punch her. Then she sneezes.

'And you wonder why? Go home!'

'Or what? You gonna black my eye? Look.'

'No, you look. I wasn't leading you on yesterday. And I wasn't playing by those stupid girl rules either to get you to chase me. I didn't want this. I don't want you. The fact that you're some big fish does absolutely nothing for me. And you don't need me to add to your probably very extensive list. And yeah, come one step nearer to me and I will black your eye. I'll break your nose too. I'm a black belt.'

Bloody hell, she thinks, who knew that a woman that looked that soft could get this angry.

'I read the poem.'

'Good for you. I was being stupid. I was showing off.'

'Didn't know you lived round here too. How come I've never seen you?'

'Because you're a vampire and only come out after dark?'

'More like a werewolf.'

Gwen turns and marches away. She follows her, keeping a few steps behind in case she does take a swing because you never do know. Gwen turns around and glares at her, crossing her arms over her chest.

'Look. I can't. I don't,' she says.

'Can't?' says Gwen. 'Don't? You aren't being your suave self this evening. Aren't you a bit inarticulate for a Liverpudlian tonight? Will they send you to live on the Wirral?'

Eyes hammering her. She makes her want to laugh. She wants to hold her. Kiss her. Do her right here, up against the wall.. But she's not making the same mistake twice.

'Don't let's do this,' she says.
'What?' says Gwen.
'The gun fighting.'
'We could use dictionaries.'
'The OED?'
'I prefer Collins.'
'Look Gwen. I've got an offer for you. Cut you a deal. Are you up for it? Come back with me now. I'd be grateful for whatever you're prepared to give me, considering the mess I've made of this. Stay the night. Have tea and toast with me in the morning. Stay and talk to me. There's a compromise in here somewhere.'
'Are we talking about a sleepover here?'
'You've got the pjs already. Gwen?'
'Yes?'
'Is Gwen short for Gwendolyn? Were they into Oscar Wilde?'
'No,' says Gwen so quietly she can hardly hear her. 'Guinevere.'
'A King Arthur phase then?'
'Yes. We could be penfriends instead.'
'Or we could be heroes. Do you eat toast?'
'Marmite or no Marmite?'
'Is that your deal breaker?' she says. 'Who's your football team?'
'I didn't have one but Lola's red so now in theory I'm red too or she'd scalp me even though I don't get football. And you didn't answer my question.'
'Only the Marmite tribe ever ask that question. I'm on the side of the righteous. Come head then.'

She holds out her hand, and Gwen takes it. Her little one in her big one. It reminds her of taking Petey to school.

They say nothing as they walk home but she can feel the heat in Gwen's hand which she is grateful for because by the time they reach the flat they are both shivering. She leaves her in the hall taking off her trainers and goes in the bathroom to put the shower on; when she comes back, she takes Gwen's arms in her hands.

'Look, I've put the shower on. I need to get warm, and I am gonna wash this off. Do you wanna come in with me? No funny stuff. Warm us up. Or if you prefer, I'll tuck you up on the sofa with a blanky and make you cocoa. If I had any. I'll put brandy in your tea.'

'OK.'

'The shower or the sofa?'

'The table. The floor. But not the bath.'

'Ain't got no barth girl. Ain't got no coal hole neither.'

She gets her by the hand and takes her through into the dark bathroom where she takes all her clothes off at once and stands in front of Gwen.

'Can I undress you?' she says.

'If you like the body of a woman who likes cake.'

'Yeah, I do.'

She pulls off the pyjama bottoms but then Gwen backs out of her hold and pulls her jumper and her pyjama top up over her head in one big tangle. Gwen wraps her hands around her breasts, and then unwraps them and puts them behind her back. She steps backwards into the light so that she can see that there is writing on her belly.

'When did you write this?'

'Before I went to sleep, before you woke me up.'

'Why?'

'It was like blowing out candles. Making a wish. Turns out it's hard to do you know. Write on yourself upside down. So it's wonky. And it was a spur of the moment thing and so I used a Sharpie as well which was really bloody stupid, wasn't it? I'm scarred for life now.'

She comes towards her and touches the writing with the tips of her fingers.

'I don't know it.'

'It's from Rilke. "Letters to a young poet". Expect it's not his, it's the young poet's and I can't remember his name which is stupid because I love that book.'

On her sweet, rounded belly is written:

> *Because I want so much to pray sounds*
> *That my hot mouth cannot find*

She kneels in front of her. Holds Gwen's hips in both hands, puts her hot mouth where it says, 'hot mouth'.

Gwen

She wants to stay here, into some far-off future, pinned to the sheet by Nat's weight. Nat's breath on her neck. Nat's voice in her ear.

'Guinevere,' Nat says, and her voice is as if it's coming from the bottom of a well. Nat has stroked every bit of her skin, from foot to forehead, she has brushed her hair back gently from the back of her neck and bitten her there. She has licked her nipples and they are hard and wet with saliva and pressed against Nat's chest.

'Yes?' she says, and it comes out as a gasp.

'You feel good,' Nat says.

'Thank you,' she says.

Nat kisses her so deep that it's like drowning.

They sit up in bed, eating toast. She tries not to get crumbs on the duvet, but the honey has dripped down her forearms and she has to put her plate down on the bedside table to lick it off. Nat is watching her, and she feels fixed there, in the pressure of her attention, unable to move.

'Sorry,' she says.

'Why?'

'I'm making a mess of your bed.'

Nat smiles but she feels shy. This is always the shy time. Nat takes hold of her arm and licks it from elbow to wrist. Then she does the same to the other one.

'You taste nice,' Nat says.

'Thank you.'

'I didn't mean the honey,' she says, and Nat pushes her face down under the duvet.

She can't seem to go home. It's 6 p.m.

'I'd better go,' she says. 'Lola might be worried.'

'Ring her.'

'I haven't got my phone.'

'Are you sore?'

'No, I'm OK.'

The prosaic rubs against her. She has been lost in a dreamy haze of nakedness, lack of sleep and orgasm, a combination that has made her feel enervated. If she's going to leave then she needs to get out of bed and go and find her clothes, but she feels too shy to do that in front of Nat because she might look at the cellulite on her bum and think she'd make a mistake. She feels self-conscious, almost embarrassed at the shape of her body which unlike Nat's is far from perfect. Surely Nat must not mind her lack of perfection though, considering the things she has done to her. But, apart from anything else, right now she really needs a wee. She has an idea.

'Have you got a dressing gown that I can use?' she says.

Nat gets out of bed where she has been leaning against the bed head with her arm behind her head and goes to the wardrobe, still naked. She opens it. Then she turns back to her. If I was God, she thinks, and I had to make a woman, this is the woman I would make. And I'd make her first this time.

Nat laughs now, a sharp laugh like a bark.

'I don't know why I'm looking in here. I don't have a dressing gown. Would a t-shirt do you?'

'Yes.'

Nat gets a t-shirt out of a chest of drawers and, while the drawer is open, she sees that there's not the expected jumble in there but neat piles. She wants to go to inspect the rest to see if they're all as tidy. Nat stands next to the bed and gives her a plain black t-shirt. She pulls it on. It is too big and reminds her of Popper wearing hers. She's probably not going to get that back. Nat puts on a t-shirt and trackies over her beauty.

'Tea?' Nat says.

'Yes please.'

She waits until Nat leaves the room and then goes to the bathroom and finds that her clothes have been put into a neat pile with her socks balled up on top. She doesn't want to take off Nat's t-shirt now, it smells of her. Would she miss it? She will pretend she's forgotten to give it back, but will that make it some sort of serial killer souvenir? She doesn't think she'll need one to remember this night-day. She doubts if she'll ever be able to forget, it's likely to be fixed in her erotic imagination like a butterfly on a pin in a Victorian gentleman's collection. She puts her pyjama top on over the t-shirt and then her jumper and her pyjama bottoms and her socks and goes to the kitchen. Nat is standing by the open kitchen window with her back to her, looking out over the back garden and smoking a cigarette. She surprises herself by going to her and wrapping her arms around her waist and leaning her face against her t-shirt. She immediately realises that this is overfamiliar and that she shouldn't have done it. She steps back and Nat doesn't turn round but continues smoking.

'I've changed my mind about the tea,' she says, embarrassed now. 'I'd better go.'

'OK.'

'I had a nice time.'

'Good.'

'I'll see you then.'

'See you.'

Nat doesn't turn and so she leaves the kitchen with the very start of what might be evening after shame but then, as she is pulling up her socks, she hears her call out, 'Gwen' and is relieved. Nat comes into the hall where she is standing with one Converse on and one off.

'I'll drive you home,' says Nat.

'It's only around the corner.'

'You're in your pyjamas.'

'I've seen people in pyjamas in Tesco.'

'I just want to make sure you get home safe.'

'It's broad daylight still.'

'Still. Let me drive you home.'

It's a nice gesture, kind, she thinks. She puts her other shoe on, and Nat slips her feet into trainers. She follows her downstairs. She is feeling tender now, both inside and out, small, childlike. Better to just get home and get back into her own bed and hope to avoid the Lola interview.

In the street Nat has a silver car. Inside it's very clean and smells of leather. Nat drives her home. It only takes a minute which makes her smile. Nat stops the car where she directs her but leaves the engine running.

'What number flat are you?' Nat says.

'Four,' she says.

'Hang on here a sec then,' Nat says and unbuckles her seatbelt and gets out of the car without turning off the engine. She goes up the door where she rings the buzzer. She doesn't move, just as instructed. She hears Nat say into the intercom, 'Lola, I've got Gwen with me,' and something incomprehensible comes out. 'Right,' Nat says.

Nat gets back into the car.

'Lola's got a mouth on her,' Nat says.

'Yes.'

'So Gwen,' Nat says, still looking straight ahead out of the windscreen, 'here's the Rubicon.'

'What is?'

'You can go back in there and I'll see you around. Or.'

'Or?'

'You stay over again.' She would laugh but something deep inside her does a jump and she loses her breath. 'I'm sorry if that's sounds pressurising. I didn't mean it to be.'

'Again,' she says in a voice much smaller than the one she meant to use. Nat puts her hand out and strokes her fringe back.

'Alright then,' Nat says. 'Going to need some proper scran down us first though. Keep our strength up. Egg and chips do you?'

Nat grins at her.

Nat

Well, that's a first she thinks. Never done that one before. She has surprised herself. Keeping that girl here, like she was a prisoner. But there was something about her, past her sweet vulnerability, past her polite middle-class ways, some, she will have to class it as a hunger that went way past the way she wolfed down her chips. She likes a hungry girl, especially one who doesn't look that way straight off. The surprise of it. Once Gwen's finally gone the next morning, she sits at the kitchen table smoking. The curve of her hip. Her inner thighs. The body hair as opposed to the normal lack of it. The way she tasted – warm salt. Should keep her going for a while that one.

Gwen

She met Lola on a training day. They had to say hello and produce an interesting fact about themselves. So, they're trawling around the dullest of circles, with her thinking, oh God this is going to be the longest day, until they get to this pretty woman with her hands placed elegantly in her lap, this woman dressed like a hummingbird in turquoise, yellow and purple.

'I love giving head, but they have to be washed first. That's why I keep liquid soap in my handbag. There aren't enough bidets in this country in my opinion,' says the woman, and the teacher trainer had to appeal for quiet, especially from her because she had gone into hysterics.

Before Lola became a teacher, she was a dancer. As in Go-Go. 'Not lap, laps for muppets, more money yeah, but you have to fondle toads, and I don't like toads.' Lola told her this within the first twenty minutes of meeting her, after they'd been kicked out of the classroom. 'Not up to being no ballet dancer see but what I don't know about poles not worth knowing. And we're not talking your Eastern Europeans here.' And she took off her shoe and showed her the scar on her foot. 'Fucking five-foot-eleven drag queen with a four-inch spike heel. Three bones broken. Kaput. My dancing days were over. So, I had a think about stuff, stopped taking so many drugs, remembered I had A' levels and a brain and went to college.'

And this was how she was delighted to discover in Maria de los Dolores Jones Garcia what she believes to be one of the world's all-time greatest cultural mixes: the Liverpudlian Andalusian – a human firecracker. She's now engaged to the drag queen who broke her foot, 'He carried me to the hozzy, the love, and I fell for him over the drip,' and Lola sports a big canary yellow diamond because when he's dressed as a man, Lee's a wanker. 'Sorry,' Lola says, 'banker, whoops got mixed up again.' Lee's one flaw is that he's a Mancunian. But then you can't have everything

'Well, that one I'd never have got,' Lola says to her now. 'Should have gone down Ladbrokes and put some money on it, would have made a frigging fortune. What've you done to her?'

'Nothing. This is not like… it's not like… you know. I'm not proud of it. It's not.'

'You've been gone all weekend. Or did you not notice? Can you sit down?'

'So delicate Lola.'

'Yeah, that's me. I'm so sophisticated I'm thinking of emigrating to Paris. I've always wanted to be one of those ladies who only wears monochrome and has a whole wardrobe full of scarves. I could have one of those little poodles what fits in my handbag. My Prada handbag.'

'Prada is from Italy.'

'How do you know that?'

'Because you told me. What are you doing here anyway?'

'I've got to wait for the rest of my masks to dry. I'm resting my hair-dryer 'cos otherwise I think it might burst into flames. Is it that good?'

'Is what that good?

'It's just as well coy suits you.'

'This isn't coy. This is what goes on tour, stays on tour.'

'Did you learn that sort of stag night crap off of her? 'Cos that's just bloke talk for "I fuck strippers".'

'So delicate Lola. I'm going to work. Don't burn down the flat.'

'Course I won't burn down the flat. My house insurance is two weeks out of date.'

'Good to know.'

She gets up from the table and takes her mug and plate to the sink and leaves them on the draining board. She should wash them up but Lola's got her back to her and so she leaves them. Lola switches her hair-dryer back on and sniffs at the blast of hot air. She goes to her bedroom to get changed for work. Her head is muzzy, her body is exhausted. She hasn't had nearly enough sleep. But it was worth it. It was, in fact, wonderful. She goes back into the kitchen.

'What's Lee like then?' she says over the sound of the hair-dryer. Lola switches it off and looks up.

'I'm sure you had a great time Gwen and no, I don't want to know the gory details, but...'

'But what?'

'Finite. Remember that word? Finite. Now eff off. And Lee's amazing. He's got a cock the size of the Ark Royal. The first time I shagged him I couldn't sit down for a week.'

In the classroom it is so hard to concentrate. She keeps having flashbacks to skin on skin, mouth on mouth, which make her shiver and gulp.

'You alright Miss?' says Jason Matthews. He has snot on his upper lip. Nothing like snot to ruin a fantasy.

'Yes, thank you,' she says, 'why don't you choose another book?'

On the way home on the bus, she thinks about one-night stands. She has always found them banal, although there is often pleasure to be had, some lack of connection that means you never properly interact with any true honesty, no matter how often you come. You walk away in the morning and appreciate the freedom of relief at never having to ask a stranger who has seen your every physical flaw for toothpaste again. But she doesn't feel like that today. She feels like there is a rough rope connecting Nat to her and she has reeled it all the way out and now it is spinning back in, tighter and tighter, until sometime later there she will be, standing next to her.

She is lost in her erotic thoughts again, the bus bumping along until she reaches her stop. She hesitates when she gets off. It would be so easy to go one way when she should be going the other. She could go up to Nat's flat, see if she's in, make believe it was a casual spur of the moment kind of thing. Maybe she is a vampire who sleeps by day. What would Nat say to her? What would she do? Would she kiss her again? She hadn't known that sex could do this to you, had thought it was just a metaphor about knees going weak but there is a peculiar combination inside of her – of lack of energy, coupled with the adrenalin rush every time she remembers something they did. Whoosh. It makes her want to giggle. She kind of wants to tell Lola everything about it in intimate detail, just to be able to relive it, but she's not that sort of person, too shy. She starts to walk in Nat's direction, the rope pulling back in, and then she stops. No, she absolutely mustn't do that. You don't just turn up at someone's door unannounced like that, it makes you look needy. She dithers. This is so unbecoming. She turns and goes home. Perhaps it would help if she ate something.

Lola hasn't burnt down the house which has to be a good thing.

She finds a white envelope hand addressed to 'Gwen' on the tiles of the hall. Weird. She opens it.

Dear Gwen,

I cannot write as you do, am often the victim of qualifying clauses, and therefore what I write may well seem awkward to you and it is – in comparison to your lightness, my darkness, in comparison to your not inconsiderable gifts, my falling weight.

I wanted to tell you only one thing: that I admire you. May I admire you? Would that be pleasant for you, or would it be a burden?

Have you ever been in the park after dark? I hope that, being the good girl you are, you never have. If you would like to though, then why don't you come down to the pub after nine and we will slip away. I have something to show you.

Emma Morgan

Natalie Shaw

Her heart feels like it has suddenly become solar powered, glowing bright

'Alright?' Lola says when she gets into the kitchen, 'I was going to cook some carbonara. You up for it?'

'Yeah. But I've got to go out later.'

'OK. I'll do it early. Where you going?'

When she doesn't answer, just tries to hide the enormous smile that is seeping out of her pores, Lola looks at her and then raises her eyebrows.

'Oh God,' Lola says. 'Here it starts.'

'What?'

'"The anticipation of tears."'

'Is that a quote?'

'Yeah, from my mum. She would say that to me every time I had a new boyfriend.'

'And was she right?'

'Mostly.'

'Until you met Lee?'

'Pretty much. But you know what?'

'What?'

'I know nothing I can say will make any difference. You look like a fish that's just been blown up by dynamite.'

'Thanks.'

'Kind of like this.'

Lola opens her mouth and crosses her eyes.

She has to laugh, and Lola laughs too.

'Oh well,' says Lola. 'Better get some carbs down you then.'

'She's not my girlfriend,' she says, picking at her nails.

'Nope.'

'She's just someone I met the other night.'

'And can't stop thinking about?'

'Yeah,' she says and feels stupid.

Lola comes up to her and grabs her arms near the elbows.

'I'm not getting at you,' Lola says. 'Do what you gotta do. Fry us some bacon though first.'

She can't concentrate all evening and Lola must know that but doesn't say anything else, which she is grateful for. She tries to do some marking, tries to read a book, wishes she smoked. She spends half an hour watching TV with Lola, twitching her foot where it's crossed over her knee until Lola pushes her off the sofa. At nine fifteen she goes down the road to the pub. She hopes she won't have to scout around for her, but she sees Nat at the bar straight off. Part of her wants to turn round and walk away because Lola's right, there must be, there has to be, the anticipation of tears. But then Nat turns around and that grin she has when she sees her lurches her heart up her throat. 'Fuck,' she says under her breath, 'fuck, fuck, fuck,' and walks towards her.

Under the trees in the big park, in the very frightening darkness, a darkness of which Nat does not seem to be frightened at all but is merely alive to.

'I'm scared Nat. In fact, I'm very scared.'

'I'm here. Nothing's gonna happen. Trust me.'

'I do. I am trying to. But I really don't like the dark. What did you want to show me?'

'Not exactly show.'

'Tell then?'

'Not tell either.'

'What then?'

'This,' and Nat puts her hands up to her face and kisses her in a way that allows her to get lost in the dark cave of her mouth. It is the best kiss she has ever had in her life. Nat's mouth, her tongue, her lips, her teeth, the taste of her, the darkness, the smell of leaves, the sound of the wind in the trees, Nat's body up against hers, the cotton feel of her jacket, Nat's hands on her face, and the way her heart feels, feels full of delight and tenderness and warmth, belonging and rightness, and everything else she has ever experienced in life, wonderful as many of those things have been, falls away from the gentle excitement of this kiss. For some time, some indefinable period of time, there is nothing else for her in this world, apart from this woman, and this woman's mouth.

Nat

She's at the bar. She turns round and sees Gwen and smiles. There she is. In her baggy jeans. She has always preferred a not dressed up girl. She has been unusually preoccupied by her own thoughts. Even Popper must have noticed but hasn't said anything. She can see him though, watching her out of the corner of his eyes, and would almost be embarrassed, that is if she did embarrassment. Is that even true? No, it isn't. The fact is that their mum sometimes made her feel embarrassed, though she has never told anyone that, not even Nic. Least of all Nic. She needs to ring her, but she doesn't want to think about that now. She would prefer to take this woman into the park and kiss her under the trees and try not to calculate any further ahead than taking her back to hers and fucking her again. Calculation is her day job, her night job. But surely even she's allowed a night or two off? Can't she make up her own rules and not be stabbed by the error of her ways? The way that honey dripped down the length of her forearms. Bloody hell.

Gwen

She thinks that it's not just the sex, though the sex has her spinning out of her own head half the time, it's the way Nat looks at her every time she sees her, as though she is somebody she had always wanted to meet and is glad to have found. It's the conversations they have when they're not in bed, the elation of finding someone you not only fancy, not only want to sleep with, but want to talk to as well. In fact, there is no-one else right now she would rather talk to, rather see, family included. But is this all a very bad idea? Could it easily turn addictive? She senses that it could, but it would be so difficult to break it at this very moment, fragile as it is. No, she'll leave it, see what happens, and pretend it's only the most casual of encounters, not something that has completely knocked her off course. She is careful not to make any demands on her at all. She doesn't even have her phone number which is mad. They are still communicating by letter, like this is another century. She spends time on them, using her best handwriting and even her ink pen. Nat writes in sharp pencil, and she is pleased by that fact, the solidity of it matches the solidity of her. She pushes the envelopes through Nat's letter box and runs away, as though what she's delivered is sordid. But it's the opposite.

Dear Natalie Shaw

How are you today? I hope you have enjoyed the sun and been to see the cherry tree blossom in the park. I admired it yesterday as though I was Japanese. I wanted to sit down and have a picnic under the tree, but it was too cold, and that Mersey wind was blowing down the collar of my shirt. So I merely strolled underneath, blissed up by the pink and the white.

Gwen Robertson

She hasn't worked out how to sign off yet. Everything sounds too formal. What she wants to write is 'yours' because, although she knows it's a terrible idea, and knows that Lola continues to watch her with increasing concern, that's how she feels. She is grateful to work for distracting her. You can't fail in your concentration when thirty small faces are looking your way and waiting for your next word. She wakes up in the morning, in her double bed which so dominates the room she has to slide out of the bottom of it, Nat laughed when she saw it, as well she might, and her first thought is a memory of something they have done together, of something she has said. Nat has a bigger vocabulary than hers. She doesn't tell her that this surprised her. She wonders about her level of education. Has she got many GCSES? Has she got A' Levels? She doubts she's been to university but that is just patronising. Maybe she has. Maybe she's got a degree in rocket science and in her spare time practices nuclear fission.

Nat

She stands in the doorway of her bedroom watching Gwen who is oblivious to her. She's got her head bent over her phone.

'Hello,' she says.

'Hello,' says Gwen, looking up at her and smiling. She smiles back, puts the toast and tea on the bedside table.

'I think that 6 down is "abyss",' says Gwen.

'Yeah, I think you're right,' she says.

Gwen puts the answer into her phone. She sits on the bed next to Gwen and puts her arm around her shoulders. Gwen leans her face into her neck.

'I think that 8 across is cunnilingus,' she says, and Gwen laughs into her neck.

'How do you spell that?' says Gwen.

Gwen

At the back of Nat's house, Nat pushes her up against the brickwork so that it's hard against her back.

'This is OK really,' she says. 'I was worried it might be really dark. But I think I'm quite inebriated.'

'You are such a cheap date,' says Nat.

'Is this a date? I must say this is the strangest date I've ever been on.'

'Never really been on a date,' says Nat, kissing her neck so that she gets tingles.

'Who was the first girl you ever kissed?'

'Properly kissed?'

'Yes.'

'Dunno,' says Nat, stopping kissing her and placing her hands on the wall either side of her head. 'I practiced on a pillow. I remember that much.'

'Where's the weirdest place you've ever had sex?'

'Define "weird".'

'Well, tell me where you've had sex and I'll pick one.'

'No.'

'Are you shy?'

'Houses.'

'Whose house? Your house?'

'You're the exception, not the rule.'

'Where else?

'I don't think we should talk about this.'

'You don't have to enumerate them one by one. I'm just

interested. Please.'

Nat sighs and moves away from her, putting her back against the wall and already she misses her warmth. She looks up at the sky. No stars. Why are there never any stars here?

'Houses,' Nat says. 'Gardens. Sheds. Schools. Graveyards. Cinemas. Cars. Pubs. Clubs. Toilets. Shops. Bus shelters. A furniture warehouse. Echoed strangely. Raves. Stairwells. Lifts. Parks. The Playhouse. Lewises. Uni library. That was interesting. Churches. In the orchestra pit in the Phil. In a field. The odd phone box. Central Library. Tried in Paddy's Wigwam just to be blasphemous but just couldn't somehow. But the Anglican yes. Cold in there. This is in no particular order. Steps. Benches. Otterspool. The ferry. And other places I can't properly recall because I was a little off of it. You?'

She can't begin to take this information in, it swirls around above her head in the night air. Eventually she says, 'I'm a bit overwhelmed by the extensive nature of your list.'

'Well,' says Nat, 'let me take your mind off things then,' and resumes kissing her neck.

Nat

She is on top of Gwen in Gwen's too soft bed. They are both very quiet, very contained, Gwen perhaps because Lola is in the next room; her because she likes it like that sometimes. She stops and starts to laugh. She lifts herself up on her hands as though doing a push-up and hovers there.

'Bloody hell Gwen. Where did you learn to do that?'

'I didn't learn it; I've never done it before. It occurred to me during an erotic fantasy I had about you on the bus home from work. I find bus rides very inspirational. And then I thought of this too.'

Gwen whispers into her ear; her lips tickle.

'Hang on a sec,' she says and rolls away. She reaches down the side of the bed to where she left her mobile on a wobbly bookstack and makes a call.

'I'm gonna be late. Dunno. Eleven? Yeah. OK.'

She replaces the phone on top of some book.

'Could you run that by me again please?' she says to Gwen.

Gwen

Nat won't go in the Catholic cathedral, the one they call 'Paddy's Wigwam', which is an accurate description she thinks for a round building with a hat of spikes. She's tried to make her go in. The light, she says, is great in there. The windows. But she won't. No way. No fucking way. So she goes down Hope Street with her to the café under the Everyman theatre and has a drink instead.

'Are pubs and bars your churches?' she asks her.

'Dunno.'

She knows that look in Nat now. It is her off switch. She has never met anyone before whose off switch is so effective. It leaves her full of questions that she never voices.

She sits there thinking that there are moments of change, of redemption, in life, but we do not remember them. They flick past us with the alacrity of presentation slides. One life ends and then the next life opens up and the transition is almost seamless. It is only looking back that you realise where the join was.

'Do you think that we were meant to meet?'

And Nat looks at her straight and leans towards her, arms on the table, and says it's a good question but one she can't answer, having been brought up as she was with God and Lenin ruling her destiny, she no longer wishes to ascribe anything to lightning strike, that it's all too burning bush for her liking, all too Finland Station. But she says this, that it's not the good stuff whose beginnings you can pinpoint, but the negative epiphanies, the moments of nausea, visceral, immediate in our memories, where you fucked up completely or were fucked up by something over which you had no control. We are branded with our mistakes like scars she says, and then she looks away.

She really wishes she hadn't asked.

'We rewind and rewind and it doesn't make no never mind,' Nat says. 'Let's go the Walker.'

They walk down the hill past a mishmash of buildings, some of them boarded up, and she wonders again why the pavements here are filled with wonky paving stones and she smiles then.

'What you smiling at?'

'Is "wonky" a good word to describe this city?'

'Nah,' Nat says, and smiles with her wonderful smile, '"rambunctious", this city is "rambunctious".'

They make their way through the middle of the city, past the Adelphi Hotel in its faded splendour, past pubs and the station, to that strange island of classical architecture, great dirty edifices of culture, the library, the art gallery, the museum, surrounded by lanes of rushing traffic.

Nat loves the Walker; she loves Pre-Raphaelite for some reason she can't get. It's a bit overblown for her but she likes that she likes it, likes the peace she sees in her when she sits in here on a wooden bench and looks up at angels, at Dante watching Beatrice pass by, at the dragon and Andromeda. Nat's arm around makes her feel safe. Maybe that's what Nat feels in here then. Safe. Private. Not watched for once.

Nat

They're in some bar. It's how she maps her city out – by clubs and bars, not by the name of streets. At least that's the official version. Sometimes she maps it by sex acts. But she'd rather keep that one to herself.

She doesn't particularly want to be here, she was a bit busy with stuff to be honest, but Gwen asked her, and she doesn't seem to be able to say no to Gwen. That isn't a good sign, she's well aware of that. This thing, this woman rather, is turning into something she has never had any hunger for – a relationship. She has always thought that word to be a drag on you, like a collar attached to a leash and you'd be off, raring to run, and yank, you're back with some woman who's nagging you about shite you're not interested in. But being with Gwen isn't like this, which is interesting in itself. It's more like a pleasant activity, like a hobby you've just got into, although she hates that word, and is taking up too much of your time, but right now you can't seem to make yourself care about that. All her walls, all her distances, she doesn't feel that bothered for once. It's weird.

Turns out Lola has some lungs on her that are good for something else apart from opining vociferously on a range of subjects. She should be annoying perhaps but she just finds her funny. Too mouthy for her though.

Lola and her friend Amy are up on the tiny stage in front of them. There are only about thirty people in here but not many more would fit anyway. There are lamplit tables and a lamplit bar and she rather likes it in here, it has a speakeasy feel. She once... but she's not going to go there. She has her hand on Gwen's knee and is aware that it isn't for a feel-up, but rather it's a proprietary hand, a this is my girl hand. Hmmm. Maybe that's not good. She moves it, but Gwen is caught up in the music and doesn't seem to notice.

Sort of bluesy, sort of jazzy, although sometimes Lola sings in Spanish and could be saying anything at all. Her bandmate, Amy the pink dreadlocked tattooist, is strumming her guitar while sitting on a stool but Lola is dancing with hand turns like a Hindu goddess, throat circled with a black choker and now she is starting to do those soft claps that flamenco dancers do and stamp her feet in time, without breaking the beat, and the very good charlie she did earlier kicks in and she feels it course through her. Her mobile vibrates in her pocket and knocks her back into reality. That will be Popper. She sighs. There is no respite. There is no let-up. This is the game. She pats Gwen on the leg, and Gwen caught up in the music, half turns to her.

'Gotta go see a man about a dog,' she whispers into her ear, and she can feel, for the first time, the displeasure radiating off Gwen, a pheromone of disappointment, and it irks her. Lola stops singing right then, which is a mercy, and the room is full of applause, and she kisses Gwen softly on the cheek and gets up and slips out of the room.

Outside the air is a shock, no longer soft and sleek, but traffic fumed and loud. She wishes she was back in the little room with Gwen, for a moment, a very brief moment, she wishes she was a different kind of woman altogether.

She pushes up the volume button on her phone and presses redial.

'Yeah?' she says.

Nat

She's standing at the bar in The Grapes in Matthew Street, waiting to get served, when the back of her neck prickles. She turns to one side and it's Nic, she hasn't seen her for months, they've never been separated that long since she was in prison. She stays quiet, doesn't want to spook her, and yet all she wants to do is take her in her arms and hold her tight, even if it would be mostly bones that she's hugging. She's way too thin. Their dad would hate to see her like this. That's not the first thing she should say, but she says it anyway.

'You seen Dad lately?'

Although she knows she hasn't. Their dad rings her once a week, regular as clockwork on a Sunday, and he always says the same thing, 'Have you heard from your sister? She won't answer the phone.' Sometimes she rings her herself and gets the same ringing out. Nic never answers texts so there's no point in that either. The odd time she's been round her house and stood by the railings and considered ringing the doorbell. But what's the fucking point?

Next to her, Nic puts her back against the bar now and looks at the room and is looked at in her turn. It's not just her looks, it's some scent she gives off, an availability which she doesn't have and is relieved she doesn't. She is more of the 'Will you fuck off?' type rather than the 'Will you come over here?' She looks around, there's a man coming towards them, but she stares him down and the man diverts his course, pretends he was going outside. She ventures a hand towards Nic's elbow, but Nic flinches away.

'Is it true then, Natalie? That you're seeing some girl?' says Nic.

'How do you know that?'

'Fuck. Never would have fucking believed it. So when am I gonna meet her?'

'With a mouth on you like that? How about never?'

'For fuck's sake, you sound like our mum. Who is this girl? The fucking queen?'

'No. She's a teacher. Gwen.'

'Where from?'

'Down south.'

'Oh aye. Posh girl then?'

'Do you want me to do a socio-economic analysis?'

'Don't be getting up yourself Natalie. Just 'cos you think you know more words than me. What does her daddy do?'

'No idea.'

'Liar. It'll be the first thing you asked. Does her daddy hate you?'

'I don't want to discuss this Nicola.'

'What makes her so special? Can't believe this. Surely you haven't stopped?'

'Have you?'

'I'm not talking about me.'

'Well, I am. When you gonna stop? You said you was thinking about it last time I saw you.'

'Fuck off Natalie. Leave me be. Let me meet the girl. Ask me to tea.'

'Nah, no way, not putting the poor girl through that shite. You'd give her the third fucking degree.'

'I won't. Promise I won't.'

'Don't believe you Nic. It's not worth the hassle.'

'I thought it was about avoiding the hassle.'

'Yeah, hustle, not hassle. It was. It is. She doesn't hassle me none.'

'I'll promise on our Petey.'

'Really?'
'Really.'
'Dunno how to do this. Take some girl to meet my sister. Dunno how to do any of this if the truth be told. Dunno if I want her meeting you, or you meeting her.'
'Natalie?'
'Yeah?'
'Stop being an arsehole. Show me the girl.'

Nic gets her own way. She's the only one who ever does with her. No, that's not true, their Petey does, and Popper sometimes does. And Gwen does. Yeah, Gwen does a bit. Oh shite. She can't work out if this is a bad idea or not, but at least she'll get to see Nic again and that's something. She lets her choose the venue, that's how lenient she's being. She can sense that under her curiosity there is something about this must be hard for her.

So they're sitting in some dolled up place, steel bar lit up with blue spotlights, fucking horrible, minimalist pretentious shite, out to prove that it's hip, cool and metropolitan, too much fucking metal and mirrors, like a sort of nightmare dentist's, nasty sub Francis Bacon slashes of paintings, bar staff who look like hairdressers, the kind of place Nic thinks is glamorous. Just to be annoying she asks for a Laphroaig and is annoyed when they have it. And charge her a fucking arm and a leg for it too.

Gwen

Nicola is looking at her, eyeing her up and down, weighing and measuring her in a way that she recognizes from a holiday she once had in Rome, and the way that the men in the street there would strip you down with their eyes. She has never had a woman assess her in the same way. It is alarming, provocative, and very intrusive. But then she is Nat's sister. Nat's twin. And Nat is perfectly capable of looking at you in exactly the same way, although her stare is somehow deeper and quieter. And seeing them sitting next to each other is a wonder. They are not identical, but she does look like Nat: grey-green eyes, although hers have gold flecks in and are made up to some sort of professional standard when Nat only seems to go for a lick of mascara, fair skin, a few freckles, killer cheekbones, a much smaller nose but still slightly aquiline. Her hair is red brown like Nat's but highlighted so that it has gold bits and reddish bits and is long and smooth, piled up on top of her head in elegant disarray. She is Nat's height, more or less, skinny as anything, possessor of legs you would kill someone to get, long beautiful legs, lathed to perfection, she sits with them tucked demurely to one side, knees touching, but when she sways her way to the bar in her ankle breakers you can feel the room sway to the same rhythm as various men turn around to admire the brevity of her skirt. She is wearing a short-sleeved gold silk blouse that looks as if it was tailored to fit but no jewellery apart from the thick gold hoops in her ears. She doesn't exactly need the adornment. Nicola is immaculate and there is something about her beauty that is intimidating in a way that Nat's isn't.

Next to her she feels very, very shabby. She should have showered, she put some lipstick on, but she forgot to brush her teeth, maybe her breath smells, and she shouldn't have worn these jeans they're too tight. She's wearing a girl's top thing in an attempt to look halfway decent but looking down at her cleavage she can see it looks cheap, which is probably because it was, she got it off a market stall, and the green beads on it are already falling off. Obviously, Nicola does not buy her clothes off market stalls, she buys them in those scary shops where the shop girls look at you like you're some sort of cockroach, and why-oh-why did she come here in trainers? She feels grimy and sweaty and childish and exposed. Grubby. She feels grubby. She tries to hide her bitten nails under the table, but she sees that Nicola has even noticed that she is doing this. Just like Nat. They notice everything.

'I really like your hair Nicola,' she says.

'Ta.'

'How do you get it to stay up like that?'

'Dunno.'

'It's lovely. I wish I had hair like that.'

'Ta.'

'Nic. Cut it out,' says Nat.

'I couldn't get your sister to tell me anything about you.'

'Oh aye. I like your hair.'

And without asking for permission, Nic puts her manicured hand to her face and entwines her fingers in her hair, pulls a little too tight. It's a very intimate gesture, too intimate, and if any other stranger did it, she would draw back immediately but she doesn't do that now because she is looking at her mouth, that beautiful Nat mouth but red lipsticked so it shines. How strange to see them next to each other. One dressed so elegantly and one not and yet both the most beautiful women in the room and together an assault on the senses.

'Soft,' says Nicola, withdrawing her hand. 'Thought it would be soft. To be honest love you don't look like the kind of girl who's that bothered about hair. Don't mean to be rude or nothing.'

'You are quite right. I just chop bits off when it gets annoying.'

'That's weird. That's what our Natalie does too. Are you sharing nail scissors?'

'Same again?' Nat says.

'It's my round,' she says.

Nat

When Gwen's gone to the bar to get the next round in, she turns to her sister.

'Stop being a bitch,' she says with force.

'I'm not. I like her. She's funny. Is she good?'

'What the fuck has that got to do with you Nicola?'

'Just asking. And it's not really a question, is it?'

'No. Of course it's not a fucking question.'

'I'll give you my fucking take then. She's got nice hair. Sweet face. Beautiful eyes. Big juicy legs like what you like, nice arse on her, everybody needs a bosom for a pillow, got dressed in the dark in some poor lad's hand-me-downs, and obviously knows her way roundabout your body Natalie or you wouldn't be bothering. Like that, don't you? You always did. They look one way in the street and act another way in your bed. I can see she's a good girl. Clever like. I'm glad for you. You could be doing a lot worse. I'm pleased for you. Gotta go. Give us something for the journey.'

'What? What do you mean gotta go?'

'I'm working.'

'Ah Nic. Phone in. Stay.'

'I've got work. Eh Gwen,' and she picks her vodka tonic out of Gwen's hand. 'Gotta go, it was nice meeting you love, and you're alright, you can chill, you've passed. See you soon,' and she kisses Gwen's cheek softly. She leans into her and then she walks away, and they watch go her with her vodka in her hand, watch a man open a door to let her leave.

'Does she normally take her drink with her?' says Gwen.

'Yeah. She likes to take one to go.'
'I thought she worked in a shop.'
'Stock take.'

She feels something akin to despair. She should have grabbed her and held onto her, not that she would have let her. But now she's gone and that's that. Too late now.

'Why'd she go? Didn't she like me? I mean, it's OK if she didn't, she is something else, she's competition for your good looks Nat, blimey but she's sexy.'

'You think my sister's sexy?'

'I think she's dead sexy. And she looked at me like she would eat me there at first. It was terrifying.'

'She's gone to work.'

'At this time? Are you going to tell me about her now? Now that I've passed apparently. Where does she live? Does she have a husband, boyfriend? Kids? What does she do?'

'She lives near town. She has a boyfriend. No kids. What does Nic do? Good question.'

'Doesn't she work?'

'Yeah Gwen, she works. Wanna know what our kid does do you?'

She stands up.

'Are we off too?'

'I'm going to the toilet.'

She leans down to her, wipes Nic's lipstick off her cheek, takes her chin in her hand.

'Where the fuck have you ended up Guinevere Robertson? How the fuck did you end up with the likes of me?'

But Gwen just smiles.

She goes to the toilet and when she comes back, she takes her by her elbow. It's a warm night and she leads her out into the street, hustles her along until they come to a jigger, she takes her down it, to a place which is dark but not dark enough, quiet but not quiet enough. She presses her up against a brick wall still warm from the sun.

'You're a lovely girl, did you know that? And I'm dead glad Nic liked you and now I don't wanna talk about me sister no more, you hear me, there's other stuff I'd rather be doing.'

'Are you going to give me an example? Or do I have to guess?'

'No, I'm gonna show you, close your eyes now, I know you don't like the dark.'

Gwen

On the way home in the taxi, she rests her head on Nat's shoulder, thinks about her sexy sister and her beautiful mouth.

'Can I ask again now?' she says. 'Now I've exhausted you for a brief period.'

'It wasn't that brief.'

'It wasn't brief at all.'

Nat pulls her onto her lap and kisses her, strokes her face.

'You have beautiful eyes, our kid said so too.' And then to the taxi driver, 'And you can keep your eyes on the road mate.'

'What does Petey look like?'

'Our Petey? A sweet lad. Shy though.'

'Just as well one of you is. I am having a good time with you. Did you know that? A really good time. That's how I ended up with the likes of you. Because you show me a really good time. You have impressed me. Or impressed yourself on me.'

'Good.'

Nat smiles at her.

'Nat?'

'Yeah?'

'I think I'm in love with you.'

Nat puts her hand up to stroke her hair again and then looks out the window. She looks back.

'Your mum know about me?'

'I told her I was seeing someone, yes.'

'And what did you tell her I do?'

'Marketing.'

'Good one.'

'I'm sorry that I just said that.'

Nat looks at her straight, just as Nic looked at her before. Those same eyes.

'My sister? Our Nicola? My sister's in entertainment. Like I'm in marketing Gwen. I think you're great I do but what the fuck are you doing?'

'I'm sorry. I didn't mean to. Can you just forget I said that? It just came out my mouth.'

She slides off her lap.

'I think I'll drop you off at yours, alright? I've got some stuff to do.'

'Is that the brush off?'

'Nah. This is the heads up. I make my living off the sale of illegal substances, Nic's boyfriend's a junkie who I wouldn't piss on if he was on fire, and my sister makes the most of her looks by fucking men for cash. She's a hooker. So frankly girl, I think you may be in the wrong film. Pull over here mate.'

The driver does.

'The lady's staying on.'

Nat gives the driver some cash, gets out of the cab, and walks off, leaving her alone.

'Where to, love?' says the cab driver.

'Er,' she says, trying to ignore the tears that are pricking at her eyes.

Nat

She's not used to feeling this out-of-control rage, and she's not even sure why. She walks back to her flat but turns round when she gets to the front door of her house and goes back out again. She ends up in a club in town, off her face on a nice bit of MDMA she's kept for herself for emergencies. She's so near the speakers she's virtually got her head in them, and the bass is bumping up her spine. The pill is helping but not that much. She goes to the toilet to do some charlie but the cistern is filthy and so she does it off a key instead. On the way out, she bumps into someone she knows, someone she remembers as being a very good lay.

'Alright Nat?' says the woman, leaning into her, all perfume and long hair.

There is a moment then, a suspension of time which she breathes into hard, it feels like when you're running, and you've nearly reached the top of a hill but you're not sure you're going to make it.

'You got anything good?'

She goes back into the toilets with her. Patricia. That's the woman's name. She never did like that name. They do some more coke, and the woman goes to kiss her, but she backs off.

'Sorry,' she says, 'not tonight.'

'Oh right,' says Patricia, insulted. 'Seeing someone?'

'More or less.'

'Oh! Didn't think you were into that sort of thing.'

And then she doesn't want to be here anymore.

'Gotta go,' she says.

She walks home, although that is generally not advisable at this time of night. If anyone comes for her though, they're going to regret it. She's not in the mood. And all the time half of her is thinking, you've fucked this up, you've gone and fucked this up and the other half is thinking, thank Christ for that.

PART TWO

Gwen

She sits at her sister Rosa's cheery Calamine pink kitchen back home in Somerset, with her head laid on the long pine table that used to be at Veronica and Harry's house, the one they'd scored their initials into one day after supper when their parents were otherwise occupied. Now Rosa's kids Hector and Cassandra have done the same thing. She wonders if they bit their lips with the effort as she did, she remembers the way they had to grip their protractors, the concentration that was on Rosa's face that must have been on hers too, they'd gouged them in, it was like digging, it felt very, very naughty and very, very good. And then Harry came in and just looked at them and said nothing. They sent themselves to their rooms and went to bed. They were never punished in their household, just made to argue their corner, and consider the consequences of their actions. They might end up having the most boring thing imaginable "the family meeting". Rosa learned pretty young just to act contrite, take away her own privileges, and she taught her to act the same. As teenagers they even curfewed themselves for throwing up simultaneously on the hall carpet after way too much cider. As a tactic, it worked very well.

Cassie has added a striped fish beside her name. Hector a wonky tractor. At least she thinks it's a tractor. She bangs her head gently against the table and stamps her bare feet on the cold slate floor.

'Stop doing that. You'll give the kids ideas,' says Rosa.

'I'm the auntie; I'm supposed to be giving them ideas. Anyway, they're in bed. Did you ground them? Or did they ground themselves?'

'They can sense bad behaviour through walls even when they're comatose. And I draw the line at head banging unless it's to Metallica. No, of course I didn't ground them; I told Cass she now couldn't get her ears pierced for another ten years and she cried. I told Hector he wasn't getting a Game Boy for his birthday after all. And he raged down the garden and kicked his football over the fence and then Cassie joined him, and they pulled all of the daisies out of the lawn. All of them. It took them about an hour. Then I gave them raspberry ripple ice cream because I felt strangely proud of their response. You'll love parenting sweetie; it makes you completely irrational. And anyway, we did it first, didn't we? I didn't have a leg to stand on.'

Her sister sighs. She looks tired. She looks knackered.

'You look knackered Rosie.'

'No shit Sherlock. So fess up. What's happening? Job shit? Money shit? This stupid government shit?'

'Job good. Tough but good. Money fine. I'm sharing with this girl now I met on a course. She's a star. She reminds me of you. Bossy. Her flat's great. So now I live in the hippy bit of Liverpool.'

'Good girl, I knew you'd find it.'

'Yeah, I've got a homing instinct for joss sticks.'

'How could you not?'

'You should come up. It's a good flat. Good road. Big houses, not like that terraced back-to-back Northern thing. God listen to me.'

'Nothing like some stereotyping. So bar the government slowly inciting us to anarchist uprising, which woman is giving you gyp this time?'

'That implies they all give me gyp.'

'It's in the job description.'

'Your husband is an angel of virtue.'

'I trained him army style.'

'I don't even want to go there. Help. Help. Help me please.'

Rosa sits down at the opposite end of the old table and stretches her arms down its length. She reaches out her hands too and their hands nowhere near touch but at least their hands are the same size and at least, like starfish wanting to mate, they are reaching towards each other. There's something to be said for the familiarity of family, for years of shared history, for bodies that aren't alien to yours, for gestures that must be your own too. This must be how Nat feels with Nicola. It must be so weird to grow up a twin, so full on. Oh fuck, fuck, fuckity fuck. Natalie Shaw.

She picks up a salt cellar shaped like Postman Pat's cat and bangs it on the blue china plate with a fish on that she bought Rosa as a wedding present.

'Stop trying to break my things.'

She looks at Rosa's nose stud, at the way her short light brown hair frames her face. It's her hair too if she could be bothered to get hers properly cut, her face too, round, with a pointy chin like a pixie. She looks at Rosa's rows of earrings, remembers Rosa and herself piercing each other's ears with needles. How they'd drunk red wine stolen from their parents' wine rack before they'd felt tipped the dots on where the earrings should go, how they'd ice cubed their ears, pissed, giggling together in Rosa's bedroom, decked out with hangings and drapery like a gypsy's den, which to her, two years younger, always seemed like the best place in the whole wide world. And now she lives in the wide world and sometimes she wishes she doesn't. Sometimes she wishes that she'd never moved away or that she'd picked a nearby uni and then worked her way back through the south-west of England like Rosa did. She wishes that she walked through fields of long grass in the hot summer sun every day, getting grass seeds all over her jeans, and turning round to see the trample she had made behind her. She wishes that she had picnics on riverbanks with Hector and Cassie and told them stories of Mole and Rat, and that she jumped into cold rivers just as she has done today. She wishes she always had Veronica to sit on the sofa with and read poetry to, and that everyday Harry pulled up carrots as though it was a conjuring trick and grated them to make carrot and raisin salads for her because he knew she couldn't use a grater without loss of flesh. Sometimes she wishes that she could just be herself all the time again, that she didn't live in a city, an alien city. Sometimes she just wishes she was home.

'I'm glad you're you. Veronica looks well.'

'I'm glad you're you too you little bugger. Yeah, she does. The old bat.'

'Hardly little. OK. Met woman. Very unwise choice of woman. Seeing woman for several months. Argued with woman. Woman not speaking to me. Came down here.'

'Describe woman.'

'Beautiful like you wouldn't believe. Clever. So clever and erudite and brilliant and wonderful and amazing.'

'Sex?'

'Have you ever had to ask the person you're having sex with to please stop now because you've had so many orgasms it's starting to hurt?'

'Unfortunately, no, not that I can remember. But Marcus and I once got into a position so painful that we had to book emergency back-to-back chiropractor's appointments. So clever and beautiful and terribly sexy. And? Catch? Why haven't you told me about this one before?'

'Occupation.'

'Mmm. OK.'

'Dealer.'

She is expecting a strong reaction, but she gets none and this makes her slightly disappointed. Was she expecting to shock? Was she wanting to show how mature she is now? How she's out with the big kids. But Rosa shows nothing on her face, she's so neutral she could be Nat.

'Mmm. OK.'

'You're supposed to disapprove,' she says, confused.

'Uh huh. That's why I'm ten minutes away from my nightly spliff. You just think it'd make it easier if I went off on one. Admit it.'

'Oh bollocks.'

'You've already said that. What is the real problem? Is she some kind of gangster?'

'Well, not really. No. I don't think so. She has cachet round our way. I don't know. She's not in a gang. She doesn't carry a gun, but she might have one, I guess. I don't know. I don't ask. No one has ever said anything bad about her, the opposite actually, a good deal kind of thing. Everybody knows her. You know that sort of person that everybody knows, and everybody likes and respects and if they don't then nobody's saying.'

'What does your friend say about her?'

'Well, she told me not to go there and she told me about her reputation and then she told me to go there and get it over with but that would be it, one night and that's that. Except it hasn't been. It's been two months now. I know that doesn't seem like a very long time and it isn't, but it's got to me, she's got to me, I don't know why. And Lola's nice when she comes round; we have supper together and stuff. It's not a problem but I know she doesn't approve really. Not that she doesn't like her. Just that she thinks that me liking her as much as I do is a terrible idea. Which it is. It's been so quick. It's taken me by surprise. I didn't know I could feel like this.'

'Oh shit. That sounds bad.'

'Yeah. Who's your drug dealer?'

'Neil Evans.'

'From my year? He was such a wuss.'

'He still is. Only now he's a wuss with a wankery beard and low-level connections with some nice boys in Bristol. And besides weed?'

'Pills. Coke. Speed. I have no idea where she gets any of it from. I don't ask. Would you? That's it as far as I know.'

'Are you sure?'

'Never heard anything else. Of course she could but I don't think she would. Does that make sense?'

'Yeah. OK. I'm with you so far. So what's the prob'?'
'I fucked up.'
'Mmm.'
'I told her I was in love with her. I told her I was in love with her Rosie after we'd just been to meet her sister and it turns out she, well, she's a prostitute apparently, not that I care, not that it has anything whatsoever to do with me, and I don't know, she seemed like she was suddenly ashamed of it, yeah, ashamed, I think, of both of them and what they do and I told her I loved her and she didn't reply, which I didn't expect her to, not really, she's not that sort person, Lola told me that she wasn't from the start you know, she was always promiscuous, she told me that the first night I met her, and now she's seeing me and that is totally out of character and I don't know.'

Rosa lays her head down on the table.

'I can no longer maintain this conversation without stimulation.'

She finds wine and two wine glasses made out of blue recycled glass. She finds a ready rolled spliff in the book sized wooden box of ready rolled spliffs that's high on a shelf.

'I love it that Marcus does this for you.'

'I love Marcus because he does this for me. It's why I married him. Well, that and the shagging.'

She sits next to Rosa and hands over her wine. She watches the way something gives inside her sister, like she's located the off switch. She thinks about the kids in her class and the way their off switches are stories and crayons and gluing and their fumblings to make marks on paper that approximate words. Puddles work for them too. She strokes her sister's hair. Rosa yawns.

'When was the last time you jumped in a puddle?'

'What?'

'Never mind.'

'It's not that I'm not taking your problems seriously sweetheart, it's just that compared to motherhood every problem seems somehow minor. Stealth bombing? Try getting two kids up for school in the morning. Deforestation crises? Try making them do their frigging homework. I don't mean to belittle you honest I don't but it's fairly clear cut, isn't it? You are in love with. What's her name?'

'Natalie. Nat. Natalie Shaw.'

'I like the name. You are in love with Natalie the sexy drug dealer. Is she in love with you? You don't know. Get back on the train tomorrow. Go see Natalie. Ascertain this.'

'That easy?'

'No. Probably not. But I don't think you've got any other option.'

'This is why you are a manager and all-round genius in the field of social care.'

'Oh yes.'

'You mean I have to ask her if she loves me? It's pointless.'

'Could you remind me why you are with this woman? Is the sex that good?'

'Yes, actually it is. I'm with her because when I'm not with her, I'm not right anymore.'

'Oh dearie dearie me.'

'If I ask her any more stuff, I'm scared she'll just look down her nose at me as though I'm a stupid little girl.'

'I don't like her.'

'She's lovely Rosie. You'd love her.'

'No. I don't like her. She's usurped me. That's my job. She won't do that you daft thing. And if she does, she's an idiot, and why would you want to be with her? Yeah, yeah, the sex. Go see her and sort it out or I'll take Marcus and we'll run away and leave you with these two monsters of destruction and anarchy. Not to mention the cat with the runs. Have I told you about the cat with the runs?'

'Do you have to?'

Rosa frowns and Gwen thinks that were she to purse her mouth and cross her arms at the same time, it would be full-on Lola.

'This is my life, Gwen. It's not about romance and sex. It's about mad panics in the morning and bumper packs of loo roll and cat poo and separating fighting children and not enough sleep and too much work.'

'Are you saying I don't work hard?'

'No, of course I'm not. That's not what I'm saying at all.'

'Then what are you saying?'

She pulls back from her, but Rosa takes her hand and sandwiches it between her own.

'I am thirty-two Guinevere. I am married and I have a stupidly large mortgage and a lovely husband who I see only to pass out with in bed at night and two wonderful children who run me ragged and a job that I don't really have the energy or the patience for anymore. Make the most of not having all of that sweetie. Appreciate it.'

'Thanks for the lecture.'

Rosa ruffles her hair with affection

'Go sort this out. And then bring her down here and I'll give her the once over. Have you told the ancient bodies?'

'Yeah. Sure. Veronica, I'm seeing a dodgy woman who deals drugs and possibly has a gun in a cupboard. Oh yeah, and she has a sister who's a prostitute. I told them she worked in marketing.'

'Brilliant.'

'I thought so. Oh bugger.'

'I'm going to make you clean the oven with your tongue if you say that again. Sort. It. Out. Sister.'

Rosa hugs her.

'Shall we go next door and get mad Milly to read the tarot for you?'

Gwen laughs. She wipes her eyes on her sleeve and goes to find her bag and fishes in it.

She gets out some tissues and a zip lock bag full of weed. She throws the bag to Rosa who opens it and sniffs the contents. Gwen blows her nose.

'Please marry her.'

Nat

She has been off her head all week, in a speed and whiskey blur, so much so that she hasn't had time to have a comedown or a hangover. She hasn't been this out of it since she came out of nick. What the fuck is going on? This is just avoidance. She needs to slow down before she gives herself a heart attack or gets cirrhosis. She's even slept at Popper's on his dirty crack whore mattress and woken up to see Popper curled up in his armchair. This has got to stop.

She sits up.

'Popper?' she says and then rolls off the mattress and gets up to go and shake him to wake him up. Popper comes to with a grunt.

'What?'

'The time has come.'

'What?'

'Get your Marigolds on.'

It takes all morning, them both scrubbing and dusting. Popper doesn't own a hoover so she has to brush up with a brush and pan which seems very old fashioned. She chases the dust mice from out of the corners in the bedroom and the wardrobe door swings open.

'Popper?' she shouts.

He comes in, dirty and sweaty. But that's hardly unusual.

'Why is your wardrobe full of coats?'

Popper comes over. He fingers one of the mothy old coats.

'Where'd you get all these then?'

'Charity shop.'

'I hope you paid for them.'

'Yeah, I did. I thought…'

'What?'

He opens the wardrobe wide and gets in. He sits cross legged under the coats with them draped over his face.

'Is it a Narnia thing?' she says.

'Just feel safer in here.'

'Fair enough. Now get out and do the washing up.'

She feels better afterwards. Cleaner. It's the sort of day when it might be good to be out on the river, head up in the clean salt air. Maybe she should go take the ferry. Or maybe, just maybe, she should sort her fucking life out first, stop behaving like a lightweight.

Gwen

She falls asleep and wakes up drooling with her forehead clammed to the train window. It's a shitty day with rain coming down outside, and everything is grey. She is glad she is not wearing sandals. She wonders what it is like to have a house that backs onto a railway. She watches back gardens flashing by in their infinite variety of lawns and garden sheds and climbing frames. The odd abandoned bit of furniture. Why do people abandon furniture at the bottom of their gardens? Do they go down there to sulk on their soggy sofas? And do you get used to the noise? Do you stop noticing it? Or do you time your life by it? Can't go to sleep 'til the ten thirty has gone past. Next stop Runcorn. Next stop Liverpool. The adrenalin that rushes through her at that announcement makes her feel slightly sick. The bridge, the streets seen backwards, like on rewind.

She thinks about the who is your favourite Beatles question. She's only ever met one person who's gone for George. The oddball choice. The show-offs go for Ringo, just to be contrary. The good hearted, the sweet ones for Paul. In her mind it's not even a question and it's never been one because it's so obvious. Nat just raised her eyebrows when she asked her, and she laughed. But to sleep with? Stu, she thinks. She's talking to Nat in her head like she does all the time when she's not with her now, saving up stories for her, making up words, as if things, events, people only become meaningful and real if Nat hears them. Thinking them without saying them is a very, very poor substitute but it passes the time. She wonders if people shag in train toilets. Yuk. It's not appealing. But if she was here, would she? Even though she's not here. Might not be here ever again. Oh shit, shit, shit, and she bites her lip. She has not seen her since last Monday night. And today is Sunday. And tomorrow is work again. And being at home for the weekend has only made it worse. How is she going to go to work like this? With a big Natalie Shaw shaped hole in the middle of Liverpool, a hole like a bomb crater.

She almost clung to Veronica when she left; she pretended she was crying because she was sad to go. This was what Lola was on about. Why didn't she listen to Lola when Lola is always right? This is just a shadow of how much this if going to hurt now. It is going to crush her. She's going to have to move. See if she can get out of next year's contract. But how is she going to forget? How do you forget this? So stupid. She is so fucking stupid.

The truth is she came here because she didn't much like London where she went to uni; she didn't much like Loughborough where she went to teacher training and then worked, and when she was doing a couple of months of travelling in South America, she'd have a look on the net when she had a chance, and there was a job here. She had no idea about the city, had never been, didn't know much about the north if the truth be told. So why did she pick it? Sitting in a mouldy café in Caracas with a moulting green parrot in one corner saying pieces of eight, hola, hola, pieces of eight, she, with great difficulty considering the slowness of the connection and the age of the computer, managed to fill in an initial application form online. She thought it would be a challenge she supposes. Be hard. Inner city school. Difficult kids with difficult problems. She would be doing something meaningful. Give it a year. Give it a go. And the truth is she likes it. It's really hard. She likes that it's really hard.

No, she won't do this; she won't give this up this easily, fuck it as Nat would say. Fuck it. Right. She's got to try to sort it out, at least try, but she's scared. She doesn't want to have to see her; she doesn't want to have to not see her. Nat hasn't phoned or texted. She hasn't even written. She's had to bury herself under a duvet of an evening to stop herself going round to hers, although she was so scared of going round to hers in case she got there, and she didn't answer the bell. In case she was standing up there looking down at her but didn't answer the bell because she knew it was her. She'll just walk away; it's what she does, isn't it? Walk away. Shut the door. One and then another and then another. Maybe she already has. Oh God. Oh God. Maybe she already is the past, already gone.

She stands with her bag, stomach jolting around, waiting to jump out of the train, run down the platform, get a taxi, get to her flat, tell her she's been an idiot, she's so sorry for saying that; she didn't mean to. There is a queue. Overwrought woman with grizzling snotty child. Short man in blue t-shirt. She wants to push through or climb over their heads, but she doesn't. Instead, she stands there counting to ten. And then to ten. And then to ten. Then she's out. She hoists her rucksack onto her back, and marches as quickly down the platform as she can, fumbles for her ticket to get through the barrier and then out into the concourse, and then she sees her. Nat with her hands in the pockets of her bomber jacket. Nat with her neutral watching look. The best-looking person in the whole concourse. She puts down her bag. Nat's not smiling, and she is trying to stop herself, hiding her mouth with her hand.

'Lola told me the train,' says Nat.

She doesn't come towards her, just stands there, ten feet away.

'I'm sorry,' she says.

'No, I'm sorry.'

She doesn't move towards her because, if she does, she thinks that she might grab hold of her and cling on like a baby marmoset.

'I wasn't trying to put any pressure on you; it just came out of my mouth. So stupid.'

'No, not stupid Gwen. Coming from your mouth really good to hear. But I can't. I'm sorry about that but I can't.'

'It's fine.'

'Tell me straight. I like your straightness. Is it fine?'

'Yes, it is. You are fine and your sister is fine, and I don't care, not about any of it, I don't. I just. I like you. The rest of it is nothing to do with me. It's your work and her work, what's it got to do with me?'

'Nothing. I overreacted is all. I had a proper kick off. It's normally Nic who specialises in that kind of door slamming shite. I'm sorry. I made an assumption about how you would be seeing us if I told you that and I got myself into a nark about it without even giving you the chance to say anything. I misjudged you as I thought you might misjudge us. But you didn't, did you? You don't. You're a fine, fine girl and this week has been shite. I've had some things to think about, I'm sorry for being such a tosser.'

'You're not a tosser, not least because "tosser" is a truly awful word.'

'There's something I want to tell you. Another thing. If you want to hear it that is. I mean you don't have to talk to me at all if you don't wanna. I can leave now. I just wanted to say sorry.'

'Now?'

'Better now, yeah.'

Nat gestures for her to sit on one of the metal benches and sits down next to her but doesn't touch her. She wants so badly to rest her head on her shoulder but instead, she sits upright, attentive. Nat stares up at the departures board and doesn't look at her when she says, 'I did some time. Two years, taken down to eight months or so.'

She tries not to betray her shock. She folds her hands around her elbows and looks up at the board too.

'For dealing?'

'Well, that was the charge, but it was because someone didn't like me, not for something I specifically did. Although I have been dealing since I was about fourteen. And when I was in there, I was with someone. Evie. It started off a prison thing but then… I don't talk about this stuff. You can send me to live on the Wirral if you want.'

She is curious now.

'What happened? With Evie?'

'She got out before me, and she got killed.'

'Oh, I'm sorry,' she says, and puts her hand on her sleeve. Nat looks down at it and then places her big hand on top and she is so relieved then, to be touched, that it takes her surprise away.

'Yeah. Me too. You would have liked her, I think. She was a forger by trade, but she was an artist really. Should have gone to art school in a just world. She did that Van Gogh copy in the flat. Got a lot of drawings too, in a box somewhere. And she did my tattoo.'

'It's a good tattoo.'

They are quiet for a moment, the hustle and bustle all around them, the announcements blaring out.

'Do you miss her?'

'Less now. I'm telling you this because…'

'You don't have to explain why.'

'Yeah, I do. Because I want you to… I want to be as upfront with you as I am capable of because I would like you to come and live with me.'

'What?'

She takes her hand from under hers and draws back so she can look at her properly. Nat's looking at her in the eyes now, with her stern stare.

'Yeah. Crazy right? But I think it might work. Could work. Give it a go? Give me a chance, eh? I can't believe I'm asking you this to be honest, but I've not seen you for a week and my bed's all empty. You can bring your books. Bring everything. I... I'm not always home. I'm not home a lot. But you know that. I've got my stuff to do. If you understand that. I want this. I want you. "Come live with me and be my girl and we will all the pleasures prove."'

She's made a mistake. It should be "love" not "girl". Except it's no mistake because that word has never crossed her lips. Maybe it never will. But isn't this as good as? Isn't this as good as, better than, words? She looks around her, wondering if anyone has been listening in to their conversation. She's heard some good conversations in train stations herself, but this outdoes all of them. Prison. Girlfriend who died. Invitation to move in. All in the space of a minute. She tries to get her head together.

'I've never lived with anyone before,' she says carefully, to buy time.

'Me neither. Well, only my family. If that counts. I dunno if I can. But I wanna try. I dunno why. Well, I do. I've got no-one to talk to.'

She wants to laugh then, puts her hand over her mouth to hide her smile.

'Is that technically possible? That you can stop verbalizing?'

'Verbalisation.'

'Verbiage.'

'Verbid.'

'What's "verbid" when it's at home?'

'Look it up. Look Gwen...'

Nat stands up now and steps away from her and put her hands in her pockets. I'm in love with you and I love you, she thinks, and these may now be words I will never say but what does it bloody well matter? Her heart is twittering around, a frantic bird trapped in a too small cage.

'Look at what?' she says.

'I didn't mean look. I dunno if I can like. But I wanna try. I dunno why really. Well, I do. Shite. It's only you girl what makes me this aphasiac. I didn't mean look.'

'Then you should say what you mean.'

'And mean what I say? Yeah, I should. I missed you. I really missed you. Fuck, I'm soft. Don't tell no-one. I'm not a great person Gwen, I'm not, which is serious litote, and you're… sorry… shit… bad idea. I tell you all this and still think you might want to. A nice girl like you. God. If you still wanna speak to me, it would be a fucking miracle. Are you still speaking to me?'

'If I can get a word in. It's very quick.'

'Yeah. It is. But it's what I want. Would you like it? Nic would give me a reference I expect.'

And Nat is grinning.

'I'll ring her,' she says. 'Yesterday Natalie Shaw, I will come and live with you yesterday.'

Nat grabs her and lifts her up, buries her face in her breasts. She is laughing, laughing. The people around them stare at them but she doesn't care. Gwen in the sky with diamonds. This is the rashest decision she has ever made in her life. Nat puts her down again and picks up her bag from the seat. She takes her hand and starts dragging her along the concourse at a speed she has to call running although she's running while Nat is striding.

'What's the hurry?' she says, getting out of breath already.

'Stop talking. Run.'

'Where are we going?'

'To talk shite.'

'Have you ever done it on a train?'

'Only caught the once.'

'And?'

'Ticket Inspector liked me, so it was alright.'

'You had sex with the Ticket Inspector?'

Nat

The most ridiculous idea she has ever had. She didn't think she was this impulsive. Maybe when she was a kid yeah, but that was a long time ago. Now she normally considers everything. It's how she makes her living, how she keeps safe. But she was eating toast, after she got home from cleaning Popper's, and she thought, you know what this is? I miss her. This is what this is all about. I miss her. And I'm fucking terrified about it. I got into this, but now I don't know how to get out. I should be able to, but I can't. Not yet. Why not then? Why the fuck not? If you don't try, you don't know after all.

The long nights she has walked into, all the hedonistic excess. She's bored of it, the repetition, the dark rooms with unknown women and the tired morning afters. She has never admitted that to anyone before. Not even to herself. Would it expose Gwen to any danger? She considers this. No more than can be helped. For years she's been sheltered by Jack, and she doesn't think that that's going to change. Rash? Daft? Probably. But why the fuck not? All things said and done it can't be any worse than living with Nic. At least she should be able to get in the bathroom of a morning. She laughs. Yeah. Yeah, yeah, yeah.

Gwen

Nat is the most elegant woman she has ever met; she has yet to see her do an uncouth thing, make a movement that is ungainly or extraneous. From putting on her socks to skinning up she does everything easily, with economy. Compared to other women she seems finer, never clumsy, never stupid, even her sweat smells good.

Nat leaves the door of the bathroom open while she's in the shower and she sits in the hallway cross legged and watches her dry herself, framed by a wall of tiny azure tiles, tiles that are rough and uneven and which she seems to like to stroke, tiles that she did herself. She watches the way she combs her fingers through her chin length hair, brushes her teeth, puts on some moisturiser and a bit of foundation and some mascara. And that's it. The mirror is her friend, she thinks, but not her soul sucker, she is not vain, and what a lovely thing that is in her, to be so beautiful but so basic. Nat doesn't look at her watching her either, she is not preening in her gaze, she hardly seems to notice.

Then Nat leaves the bathroom, and she follows her down the hall and into the bedroom and watches her put her clothes on. So straightforward. Like an army kit. Plain black knickers and bra. Black jeans. T-shirt. Socks. Grey cashmere jumper if she's cold. Black cotton trousers if she's warm. That's it unless she's going for a run or down the gym. It's a uniform. Next, she will go into the hall, she's seen her do this enough times now, and she will get her black boots or her black trainers out of the trunk there and sit on it to pull them on. She will reach up to get her black jacket off the hook if she needs it. Her black wool winter coat is hung up in the wardrobe on a proper hanger, a wooden hanger, she won't have wire.

She doesn't seem bothered that her wardrobe is being crowded out with all her scruffy crap. Sometimes, she finds her in the bedroom with a spliff in her mouth hanging her stuff up because it's falling off the hangers. She has assigned her a drawer that now, unlike hers, looks like a jumble sale. Nat holds up a pair of combats now that are so ragged that they look like they have been used by the SAS for night manoeuvres across especially rough terrain.

'You need to fix these. Can you sew?'

'No. But I'm good with safety pins. Have you not noticed that most of my clothes are vintage early punk? Why? Can you sew?' There is a silence. 'Seriously?' She is amazed. 'You can sew?'

'Our mum taught all three of us. Don't know why, maybe she thought it might be useful. I'm shite at it though but Petey's not half bad. And Nic, she's amazing. Can turn her hand to anything. If you asked her nicely, she might fix some of this stuff for you. Or make you something even.'

'Your incredibly glamorous sister would be willing to sew up clothes that she would probably only think suitable for dish cloths?'

'Maybe. Maybe not. She's hard to predict is our Nicola. She might just tell you to fuck off. Or she might be into it. Anything is possible.'

'That's such a weird suggestion. No, I couldn't take the shame. I should just throw most of it away. Nat?'

'Yeah?'

'Why does she, you know?'

'What?'

'You know. Why? Couldn't you try to?'

Nat turns away and picks up a shirt that is so worn it's as thin as tissue paper.

'Put this on,' she says.

'Now that does need to be binned. Look, it's transparent.'
'Exactly.'
'I'm sorry I'm so chaotic.'
'Don't matter to me lovely girl.'
She goes to Nat and unzips her jeans.
'Sometimes when I'm with you I can't decide what to do,' she says.
'Meaning?'
'I get overwhelmed by you and I can't decide what to do. Like a kid in a sweetshop. I can't cope with all this decision making, I'm greedy about you, I want to do everything at once.'
'I think it's rubbing off on you.'
'What is?'
'This place. Everything's too much here. We're the kingdom of overwind. But there's a way out of this.'
'Enlighten me.'
'Start local. Think global. It doesn't matter where you start, just start. Just keep on doing what you're doing, and we'll work our way on from there. Don't have to make no choices because sooner or later we'll crack on with all of it. Why do you think we're so into our amphetamines? We're not into stopping that's why. Don't matter if it's a party or arguing the party line, we'll keep going for days.'
'Can you keep going for days?'
'Is that a serious question?'
Nat backs her towards the bed.
'I like this city,' she says.
'What's that got to do with anything?'
'Don't know.'
Nat lies her down and kisses her and kisses her.
Nat's city, not hers. But she's been adopted or is being adopted bit by bit into her new mad cap, 'Do you smoke a weed?'; 'Alright girl?'; 'Chin up kidda it might never happen,' family. Scousers.

They can out talk anyone she has ever met. She thought she liked to talk, was full of words herself, but she's teaching her to talk all over again, right on through the night, talk and not let up, until your jaw aches and your tongue's tired and your brain hurts, and you've turned yourself inside out.

Everyone knows Nat. She doesn't know if that's a good thing. Here they lay in heavy with the charm and the blag. She watches the men walk, not walking really, more like bouncing, moving like featherweights in that optimistic way they have, a cheerful walk, a going to see a man about a dog walk, come on if you think you're hard enough. She watches the women in packs, tottering along in their heels. Nat on the other hand is solid. She walks and stands like he means it. She wouldn't fall over if pushed, she believes that. She always knows how to handle herself, never gets into fights. There is some sort of buzz she gives out like static, it's a force field that people get pulled into and she's seen its effect many times now, watching people, even the very off their heads, the very difficult and demanding, become calmer in her presence, and it makes her feel safe, held in this place where she is always looking out, always watching, never scared, held in her firm gaze, a gaze that is as beneficent as her hands. Ah, Nat's hands. They should be insured.

But then, annoyingly, there is Popper – skinny little speed freak Popper. Might get his name from Iggy as he is prone to taking his t-shirt off in the last of the night and exposing his very visible ribs to the dance floor. Or it might be from the poppers. Which he loves for some reason. Poppers, way too much speed, coke if Nat will spare it, half a handful of MDMA. Cider. Whisky. Lager. Draw of course but almost always skunk so strong it's hallucinogenic, and he likes his best in bottles. But not ketamine, because Nat wouldn't take that if you paid her or sell it either. And not crack. Not heroin. None of this unpredictable mixed up stuff people deal now and no pharmies outside of the Valium Nat keeps for him. She can see that even he has to stick to the rules. Nat's rules. She only deals the classics. And the best of the classics at that. She is the Bronte sister of local narcotics.

'I don't like them. No, in fact, to be entirely accurate, I hate them,' Nat says when she asks her about it, because now and then, she does manage to ask her something.

'Who?'

'Skag heads. Crack heads. Wankers who've got so many anxiolytics and benzodiazepines in them they don't know their arse from their elbow.'

'You're a dealer who doesn't like, sorry, hates, druggies.'

'That's about the sum of it, yeah.'

'Could you elaborate please?'

'There are party drugs. There are mellow drugs. And then there's the stuff that'll do for you. That'll turn you into an unbearable robbing, thieving piece of shite. And I don't want anything to do with that. It's my business ethic.'

'It's your manifesto.'

'It's my unique selling point. Don't sell what you won't take yourself. Just as well I'm not a dog food manufacturer.'

Nat has her arm around her waist, standing at the bar, sipping her Bushmills. She likes her on the whiskey, it brings out even more of the Irish in her, the charm, the lyricism, it exaggerates her natural friendliness.

There's someone Nat knows, knows well it seems, that even she, naïve as she is, has heard of. Jack Sands, he's kind of famous, but not in a good way. There are rumours about him that she doesn't want to think about. So she ignores it. Is that the best way to deal with it? What other options does she have? And who would she ask? Lola? Lola would look at her and tell her it's best not to know. Popper, but Popper hates her now it seems. He can be a nasty bastard, Popper, which is hardly surprising with the intake he has. She's hardly ever seen him straight; she doesn't often see him eat, unlike Nat who can not only put it away but also cooks. Now that she's around Popper more she can see that he's a nasty little shit. A nasty little fucker with a twist in his tongue, a twist in his tail. Dancing tiptoes in his trainers, manically whirling his arms in the air, reaching for something he's never going to get hold of. Dancing like there's no tomorrow, like tomorrow isn't even a place. Sulking very quietly with his black metal rimmed glasses on, reading something that he hopes you're going to ask him about. "Fear and Loathing in Las Vegas." "The Heart of Darkness." "A Season in Hell." You have to wonder if he is actually reading them or just pretending to read them. She expects he has the Cliff Notes.

If Nat is the General, then what does that make Popper? The bad lieutenant? When God made Popper, he forgot to set the overload function. He never knows when enough if enough. You'd think he'd boil dry eventually, but he never does. She'll say that for him, he's got stamina. Nat has stamina but hers is that of a marathon runner. Popper's is that of a rabid dog. And she's a lightweight.

Sometimes she feels like she's David Attenborough watching the hungry animals eyeing each other, Popper a hyena, Nat a lion or a wolf, ears up, sniffing for something she hasn't got the sense to smell.

They stop to do speed off a key in a side street. Half of her share ends up down her front. She's a drugs incompetent.

'No worries girl, it was surplus to requirements anyway, there's way too much sugar in it. The dented cans. Stock control. Have some more if you want.'

'It'ss like ssniffing fucking sssherbet.'

They're coked up, but she declined. Nat crossed his legs when she said no and said nothing. She knows she doesn't like it and so she didn't push. Popper did. Popper always pushes.

'Oh go on Gwen. Have ssome. Go on. Why not? Why not?'

'Because I don't want to.'

'Why not? Why not? Go on. Have a ssniff. Go on.'

'Leave it Popper.'

'I'm jusst messsing. Only having a laugh. Go on Gwen. You do wanna really, don't you?'

'Popper, I said leave the girl alone.'

Popper is the one who leans into her when Nat goes to the loo and boasts about the size of his cock and what he would do with it if she fancied it like. She knows he means none of it, it's just his challenge to her, because he feels usurped, it's to get her to know her place, remind her she's just a girl. Just some expendable girl. So she doesn't take him seriously. Nobody does. He's Popper.

'It's huge. I could be in films. When Nat's out like, go on, jusst a change girl, jusst a bit of a change.'

'Fuck off,' she says, and he laughs.

'I won't tell if you won't. I'd give you a good sseeing to.'

But then the demons get into her, the city demons that spit and swirl in the hard breeze here and she moves right into him, almost as close as if she might kiss him, her breath on his cheek. She can smell that funky smell he has, part unwashed, part iron filings, part skunk.

'I'm not…' she says.

'Not what?' he says, and his mouth is so near her mouth they could suck the same lollipop.

'I'm not, not one little tiny littlest bit remotely interested.'

His teeth bare into his hyena snarl. He leans away and laughs at her, but his eyes are even harder than usual, if that's possible.

'And when you laugh, you look like Gollum,' she says, and he stops laughing and stares at her with his big druggy eyes. 'You really do.'

'And you girl,' he says, tipping right back in his chair like the baddest kid in school, 'you look like the princesss of the bleeding pea. And don't you fucking forget that you have no fucking idea about nothing.'

'No,' she says, 'I fucking don't and I like it like that.'

'The sstuff I could tell you,' he whispers, and the whisper is like hard rain on her skin. His voice is like razor blades, and he wants her cut. Cut or cut out. Probably both.

'It's the stuff I don't need to know.'

'Needss musst when the devil drives/ needss musst where the demonss thrive/ Who'ss city is thiss then?/ Mine 'cos it'ss me birth right/ Coming over all menace/ When the temperature dropss.'

'Yeah,' she says, 'yeah.'

In the Ladies she does a little more speed. And why not? It's a Friday. She rubs a bit on her gums. It is like sherbet. She's getting amphetamine brain. Blagger's tongue. She looks at herself in the mirror, at her eyes. Not that she hadn't done drugs before, but theirs is a different way of doing drugs. This is an endurance test that takes drugs out of the occasional bender or the festival binge, out of the spliff now and then with the glass of wine at the weekend and into every day. Scousers on speed. Speaking as fast as Formula One. Popper on speed and coke is the fastest talking blagger of them all. The king of blag. The king of gab. He bounces like one of those space hoppers she had wanted as a kid.

'Popper, did you have a space hopper when you were a kid?'

'Did I have a what? A sspace hopper? Hear that Nat? Girl wantss to know if I had a fucking hopper. Yeah, a Denniss hopper. Op, op, oppa, bop, bop, boppa, pop, pop, poppa.'

'Shut it. Go shift some gear.'

'Bop, bop, boppity, hop, hop, hoppity, jusst like a rabbit, bounce, bounce, under the table, over sshe goes, rabbit hutchess, rabbit holess, down the rabbit hole with Alice, go assk Alice

I think sshe knows, that's a ssong issn't it, ssing, ssang, ssong, ssand, ssandcastles, moatss, sstoatss, goatss eating grass, grassss, emeraldss, ssasperilla, ssaperilla, caterpilla, caterpilla with a hooka, how much iss that hooka in your window, mushroomss, mushroomss, magic musshroomss.'

'Why are you still here?'

'Going bosss. Already gone bosss. Bye Gwen. Bye bye Gwen. Bye bye.'

'How do you cope?' she asks Nat.

'It's too much sugar. He has a bad reaction to it. Shouldn't have let him have any more of that speed. Stupid.'

'So it's not the speed, it's the sugar in the speed?'

'Yeah, you should see him on coke. As in the drink.'

'He has the drug intake of Uruguay, and he has a problem with Maltesers?'

'That's about the sum of it yeah. He's very sensitive.'

'But doesn't he drive you round the bend?'

'Nah, he drives me up the fucking wall. But I ignore it because he's very, very good at his job.'

'We are talking about Popper here?'

'Yeah, Popper. Cos even when he's completely off of it he's never lost nothing, never been robbed off or done over, never, to the best of my knowledge ever robbed off of me, no backhanders, no nothing, he always knows what's where, and he never forgets a thing. He's as mad as a box of frogs but he's a model employee. Kiss me.'

'Why?'

'Because I like the way you kiss.'

She kisses her now, full on, in public, ignoring the wolf whistles behind them, Nat holds her up against her so tight she can hardly breathe, Nat puts her hands in the back pockets of her jeans and she knows that if they were anywhere else but here, standing at the bar, she'd put her hands down the back of her jeans and this thought makes her heart grow bigger in her chest, it makes her throat tighten and she snakes one leg around the back of hers, higher, higher, now she can hear the catcalls, the shouts of 'Get a room Nat,' the urge not to stop is stronger in her than it should be, behind her back she feels the edge of the bar and she could, she could right now haul herself onto it and sit there, and wrap her legs around her waist and just keep going. Where would she stop? Would she stop? She takes her mouth off her, trying to catch her breath.

'Nat,' she says, 'are we giving a floor show?'

Nat lets her go and turns around, puts her back up against the bar, leans back, elbows on the wood, looking at the room. Her face like nothing is happening. Nobody is looking now; they all have their heads down. But when, out of curiosity, the faces start to turn back and look at them, she lifts her chin. And then the chairs scrape on the floor, and the room, slowly at first, and then all at once, empties. Even the bartender disappears. Nat turns back to her, puts her hands around her waist and lifts her onto the bar. She parts her knees with her hands and pushes her way between them, she slides her hands down the back of her jeans.

'I'll come anywhere with you girl,' Nat says quietly, 'anywhere you wanna go.'

Nat

And there is no going back now, all of it hurts, she thinks, but it is the past and you have to take some solace in that. It gets better or at least softer. Doesn't it? Not really. You just get used to living with it and sometimes it is distant, and you feel almost at peace with it and sometimes it comes right up and bites you and you might just as well be there again, in the howling dread of it, the cold fever of it crawling on your skin.

And it doesn't make no never mind.

Kidda.

Gwen

She sits on Nat's chair and watches the patterns the leaves from the trees outside make on the wall in the morning sunlight. Then she drags the chair, which turns out to be surprisingly heavy, to the window into a sunny patch and opens the window and puts her feet up on the sill. The air smells washed. She has woken up far too early and surprise, surprise, Nat isn't here. She thinks about the word "chirm", the chirping of birds, and wonders if she can get it into a poem without sounding full of it. 'Full of it.' She is gaining words off them. It is catching, the Scouse. Is it like a disease then or just a habit? Will her A's go hard and flat like smacked heads? Will it make Popper like her more or like her less? Less she thinks, but then everything she does seems to make him like her less than he once did. Did he ever like her? Once, maybe, before all of this. He was friendly enough to her then when she stood next to him at open mike nights, trying not to categorise him, a man like him, in places like this. A little hard nut among the wine bar crowd. She admired him really, for having the balls to do it, because although she knew nothing about him then she imagined he must be out of her comfort zone. But did she always judge him? Did she always think 'council flat, comprehensive'? No, of course she didn't, she went to a comp too, even if it was full of hippy middle-class kids, and Nat laughed when she told her that, and she could tell that, almost against her own will, she had got points. Nat is council house too. But she's not chippy. Popper is as chippy as ground up stone, as chippy as chip shops. She has noticed that

Popper always stands too close, but then that's a Scouse thing, she thinks they often stand too close, a bit too in your face, or maybe that's just her, maybe for them she stands too far away. Stand offish. Distant. Posh. Do you always have to wrestle with this boring shit? Yes. Here you do.

She misses home. The ease of it. Sometimes she feels like the enemy. A paid-up member of the bourgeoisie. But maybe that's just Popper. It even almost makes her miss London, where nobody gives a shit who you are, where you come from. Whereas her origins are marks she bears here. Stigma. Stigmata. Is it that they are lapsed Catholics that make them so rebellious? So determined to live it up. Nat says so.

When she's not with her she misses her body like… on the bus to work she tries to come up with similes, but they are ridiculous and tawdry. Like wine during Lent? Like deserts miss the rain? Like meat misses salt? No, she misses Nat like she misses Nat, there is no simile.

Nat

If Gwen hasn't seen her for more than twenty-four hours, she'll ring her; she'll be sitting in a bar, in a club, at Popper's, in the house of someone she knows, wherever, and her mobile will ring, and it will be Gwen and it's like her heart is a lamp and someone has just switched it on. She comes up behind Gwen now in the kitchen and buries her nose in her neck.

'Have you got enough clothes on Gwen? It gets dead cold,' says Lola, who is standing next to the window smoking.

'I've got loads of clothes on,' says Gwen. 'You're really good,' she says to Petey who is sitting at the table drawing. 'I love that one in Nat's bedroom that you did of avocets.'

'Our bedroom,' she says.

'Our bedroom,' repeats Gwen with a smile.

'Thank you,' says Petey. 'I like birds. Do you wanna have a look at my sketchbook?'

'I'd love to.'

Petey is doing his A' levels in Chester where their dad lives with his second wife, and she is hoping he will get into John Moores to do art. There is something fragile about him, always has been, but she tries not to worry. She knows that Nic worries too. She hasn't seen her since the night she had that argument with Gwen. She isn't expecting to see her any time soon either although she has rung her to no avail. Petey passes Gwen his sketchbook, and he wishes Nic was there to see it. She has disappeared again, back into her twilight world. She was hoping that Gwen might interest her enough to make her keep in contact, especially now she must know they're living together, but it seems not. It hurts her more than normal.

'Lola's right girl, it gets freezing. Are you gonna be warm enough?' she says to Gwen.

'Stop it. This is like some parental outing. Yes, I am wearing enough clothes. Do you want me to go and put a vest on?'

'We're being serious here Gwen. You'll freeze your tits off if you don't go proper wrapped up. You'll get pneumonia, don't think we're joking. No, don't look at me like that, like you're humouring my overprotective sensibilities. Lee, come in here love and see if you can slap some sense into this girl, 'cos I can't,' calls out Lola. 'We're going the footie not the opera. Step away from the mascara wand.'

And here's Lee. Kinda chunky. Bald. Fake tanned to treacle toffee. But with a face like a kid's drawing of a happy kid. He rolls down the sleeves on his Ralph Lauren.

'Right. Sorted. Here I am my little jellybean. All present and correct.'

'Gwen needs insulating.'

'Have you got a vest on Lee?' says Gwen.

'I am wearing a vest yeah, it's a sporty little number from Mr Thomas Hilfiger. Now shut up, go get some more clothes on and then we can go. This is a seminal occasion. And socks. Have you got some decent socks on woman? Wool. You need wool at the very least. Have you got any cashmere? Look, come with me, show me your room, I'll get you kitted out. Did I tell you how beautiful you look today, Lola my darling? You look fucking gorgeous. I love you in purple. Right Gwen, let's be having you.'

'You are so clever Petey. I wish I could draw like that,' says Gwen as Lee manoeuvres her out of the room.

'I keep telling him he should give up the money game and go into Ladies Fashions,' Lola says. 'I'm gonna buy him a couple of

Barbies to dress up for Chrimbo.'

'Is Gwen alright?' she says.

'Alright like what?'

'Alright living with me.'

Lola raises her eyebrows.

'Well, your shift schedules don't seem to coincide that well, but yeah, apart from that, she doesn't seem to have gone off you yet which, I would like to point out, is because you have completely lucked out.'

'I know I've lucked out Lola; I don't need to be told that.'

'Good. But I'm telling you anyway.'

'He's nice to live with,' says Petey, not looking up from his drawing.

'Yeah? What was so nice about living with me lad?'

'You make good gravy. And you taught me how to climb trees.'

'I'll put that on my business cards.'

'And you looked after our mum.'

She goes over and puts her arm around Petey's neck and kisses him on the top of the head.

'I tried.'

Gwen shuffles into the room with a penguin gait, followed by Lee.

'He just stuffed me in stuff,' says Gwen grumpily. 'And he made me put on your socks Nat because he said that mine would shame Primark. But they're huge and now they're falling off. And I'm boiling, and I feel like I'm going to suffocate.'

'Then our Lee has achieved his mission. Better suffocation than frostbite in your fanny. Are we finally ready now?' asks Lola.

'Thanks Lee, you did a good job. You look lovely girl, like you've been inflated. Better suffocation than permafrostisation.'

'Better suffocation than coming fifth,' says Lee, grinning.

'I told you I'm not gonna do this with you if you start,' says Lola. 'I don't want you getting mashed up and neither do you.

Do you like that pretty face of yours? 'Cos I do.'

'I know, I know, I've taken off my eyeliner, I'll not say nothing to no-one, honest Lola I won't, I'm safe as houses me. Honest. Just taking the piss.'

'Thanks for the job you did on my girl. I owe you a pint. But Lola's right.'

'I know mate. Lola's always right. I take that as read. I'll behave myself Lola, I promise. Won't even laugh when we score. Again. Honest I won't.'

And Lee claps his hands together with considerable glee, like a man who's just won a tonne on an outsider.

'Right my hearties. Everybody warm enough? Then Anfield here we come.'

Gwen

Nat takes her arm, and she's grateful for that because she feels frightened of being toppled over. She is fragile here, a shell-less chick in a crowd of aggressive cockerels who has no idea what to do or which way to go. She is frightened and clings onto her arm, but Nat doesn't seem to mind and leads her until they find their seats and they can sit down. Everyone else seems delighted by the whole thing, as if they have caught the excitement of the crowd around them and it's now fizzing like champagne through their veins. Meanwhile all she feels is fear. She cowers in her seat.

'Are you OK Gwen?' Lola says. She is on the other side of her, and she grips onto her hand now as well as Nat's.

'Yeah,' she says, and Lola somehow manages to hear her, despite the noise. Either that she can lip read, who knows, Lola has all sorts of unusual skills.

She still wants to turn around and leave the stadium but there are far too many people to attempt that and so she tries to take in air.

'You're not having a panic attack, are you?' says Lola.

'No,' she says.

'You sure?'

'Yes.'

'Well, you look dead pale. Don't worry. It'll be better now we're in our seats.'

The noise doesn't abate and, when the players come on the pitch far below them, it rises to a screech that almost deafens her. But that's nothing to what happens when the match starts. There is shouting behind her and in front of her and to both sides.

She has never been a witness to this level of swearing before, not to mention the chanting and the singing. At first, she wants to put her hands over her ears but, after a while, it starts to have a physical effect on her that's not just the accelerated heart rate of fear. She was not expecting this at all. It feels like something is taking over her body so that she no longer has control of it. She can't see what is happening on the pitch very well from up here and she doesn't understand it at all because for her it is still only some small figures of men kicking a ball around but everyone else around her understands what's going on and so perhaps that doesn't matter. Everyone else is filled with a passion in this one moment in time that will never come again. Life is so fleeting and yet here they all are together, sharing in something that is much bigger than themselves and which has taken over not just their minds but their bodies too. She gives up trying to defend herself against it. She feels that she is right here and right now.

And then Liverpool scores a goal, and the noise level rises so much it feels like her eardrums might burst. Everyone jumps up at the same time apart from Lee and she is carried up with them. All she can hear is the word 'goal' being screamed. The only thing she can compare it with is MDMA – it pulls your insides out so that you are at one with everyone around you. It feels amazing.

Liverpool beats Manchester City. The score is 2-1. The people around her are ecstatic. She'd like to have a football team to call her own now. The fact that she hasn't had one before seems ridiculous. It's not the same as seeing it on TV, not at all. It's a completely different world – one charged up with emotion and excitement, with adrenalin and despair that can immediately turn into elation. She has seen joy now on thousands of faces all at once and it was electrifying.

Nat

They've made it through the crush at the turnstiles, and are walking away from Anfield, the crowd streaming out behind them under an overcast sky.

'Can I have a drink in the pub to celebrate?' Petey asks her.

'You can have a coke,' she says.

'Did you like it Gwen?' says Petey.

Gwen stops dead in the street.

'It was like… it was like… I don't think there's a simile. It was like nothing else I've ever seen. All those people going one way in the street like one big monster spreading out, and then the way in, all squashed, and then coming out into all that space and light, more people together than I've ever seen, and the noise, I didn't expect all the noise, and the excitement, and then after the game started the… I can't think of the word.'

'The passion?' she says.

'I've never been interested in football. But when you're there, and everyone is focused on these small men kicking this tiny ball around it's so different. And all the singing and the shouting and the swearing and how everyone went completely mad when they scored the first time. I nearly went deaf. And then they moved, they all moved towards the pitch, they pushed up. All that energy. All that intensity, that was the word I wanted, all that intensity. It was amazing. Absolutely amazing.'

'Have you just had a Damascene moment, Gwen?' she says.

'I loved it. I absolutely loved it. When can we go again?'

'Don't sulk Lee Dawes,' says Lola. 'It's unbecoming.'

Lee stands to one side of them all, shunning their happiness.

'Appalling, we played like blind donkeys in mud. Like drunk, blind donkeys in mud.'

'And we played brilliant,' says Petey.

'I'm renouncing the faith. I'm giving up. Never again.'

'I love Anfield,' says Gwen.

'We played brilliant,' says Petey.

'Get me out of this living hell!' says Lee, and he starts to jog along the street away from them while they all laugh.

It was a good day, she thinks, a great day in which my girl got it and how good is that. Shows you how you shouldn't underestimate southerners.

She makes it home. She goes out a lot. Always has, it's what she does. If she's been out all night, Gwen leaves her notes when she goes to work, poems on the table for when she comes home, torn out pages from her notebooks, sometimes she draws on them and puts them next to her things in the bathroom cupboard.

Dear Nat, I miss the smell of your skin and I miss your arms round my waist and your face in my hair and I have gone to work, and the washing is in the machine and I miss you.

Lovely Nat, I will sit looking out the window and think about your mouth. It is only seven. You are still up and out and at 'em. I am drinking tea. If you should be here when I get home from school, I will expect you to put your hands down my knickers.

What to do with them though? What she should do is tear them up or burn them in the ashtray because they are written to a person who she has problems acknowledging. Someone who has a shared domestic existence. She is making her way up the stairs at four a.m.

and trying to remember if there is milk, not for her tea when she gets up, but for Gwen's Cocoa Pops. It worries her. She keeps the notes in an envelope underneath her socks in the drawer.

And Gwen doesn't complain when she isn't there, if she doesn't shop, if there's no milk, when she doesn't come home. She makes no promises to her, tells no lies, well, no direct lies, but she has a counsel to keep, and she keeps her separate from most of it. Business is business and Gwen is Gwen, and though she sometimes comes along for the ride, she knows she doesn't really get it. Of course she doesn't. She's a soft girl and that's how she wants her to stay. The only corruption she wants her to see is the corruption they can get into together. That dirty smile on her face. Fucking hell.

Sometimes she is sitting with a drink or in a taxi. Sometimes she is off her face at the end of the night. She'll get this thing – she has named it mouth memory – and she can actually remember how the inside of her mouth feels, she can recall with some accuracy the shape of her teeth, the texture of her tongue. Nobody notices unless Popper is with her, and Popper will look up from whatever he is fiddling with – roaches, wraps, bits of poem, the strange origami twiddles that he likes doing but which being Popper, he makes out of porn mags, and says, 'Where? Where's the sskirt? Is sshe sstacked?' It makes her laugh; he looks just like some kid would, if you told him that you'd seen an ice cream van. Popper is ridiculous of course, but useful, and his company helps her keep her mind on the things in hand and keeps her awake to the world they live in. Because if she isn't careful, she could lose it sometimes, really lose it. And she has, now and then.

The stupidest night she was in the back of somewhere, and she took off all of a sudden, literally ran out the door. And she's four streets away before she knows what she's doing and slows down to a walk. Then she stops and gives herself a good talking to in the midnight street, with her hands on her hips, breathing hard. She looks up into the drizzle falling lightly onto her head, sees it falling through the yellow light from the streetlamp and then she ignores what she's just said to herself and takes off again, a little out of shape but not too bad, counting down the streets, jogging through the night like some lunatic. Just to get home to her. The madness of the long-distance runner she calls that night.

What she needs is one of those things for dogs, one of those electric things that gives them a shock if they try to stray past their fence. Yeah, she needs one of them. Or she needs to nail her feet to the fucking floor. She hasn't done that again, but it doesn't mean she doesn't want to on a regular basis. So she surrounds himself with people, hangs out with Popper, takes a few more risks, stays out more. She's hoping Gwen'll complain but she doesn't.

She walks in, Gwen's doing the washing up, and she wraps her arms around her waist and Gwen rubs her cheek on hers and tells her the word of the day, tells her about what her little kids have been up to at school, what books she's been reading to them. Then Gwen turns round and puts foam in her hair, tries to make her a soapsuds crown.

'It's so good to see you lovely Nat,' she says and they spend the rest of the evening lying on the carpet listening to Massive Attack and snogging like teenagers, watching 'All about my mother' and eating cold spaghetti that they cooked two hours earlier and then forgot about, having gotten into something or other that involved a position that she hasn't been in for years, but now she is looking at her in it, has become her favourite, and is something she will ask her for again and again. Again, Gwen, again and again and again, a position that Gwen seems to have thought up for herself while she was waiting for her to come home. Or maybe on the bus back from work. Who knows what that girl thinks of on the top deck? She'd do her on the top deck.

She'd do her anywhere.

But sometimes, like tonight, the fact that she's here, in her flat, in her bed, comes as a surprise to her, she's wiped her so completely from her mind while she was out. Here she is as she stumbles into the bedroom, looking at her by the light from the hall. She doesn't want to wake her up; she likes the way she looks while she sleeps, pink and white and innocent, her hand over her face or curled around her neck.

She pulls the covers back softly to see all of her and it's a striptease but not like the old slappers in the pubs with the veins in their legs and the mazzy under their eyes, and it's not like the young ones in the strip clubs with their tight skin and their fake breasts hard on their skinny little chests. It's Gwen wearing her trackies rolled up her legs and some nasty old t-shirt of hers that got shrunk in the wash. And it's Gwen's arse in her trackies and she pulls the t-shirt up to see the smoothness of her back and then she pulls the trackies down just a bit to see the soft cushion of her hip and the line of her belly and the curve of her arse. Fuck knows why she wears this manky gear to bed. But she knows why, she wears it to keep herself warm when she's not there and to have the smell of her around her and she almost feels something then, something other people might call remorse, but she has no remorse. You can't stay sharp if you have regrets.

'Je ne regrette fuck all,' she hisses into the air, and realises she is too off her head for this yet.

She goes into the living room and sits in her chair and gets the whiskey out and rolls a reefer. She takes off her socks. She rolls another, smokes half of that, takes her jeans and her bra and her t-shirt off and leaves it all on the floor and walks back to the bedroom, glass in one hand, ashtray in the other. She leans against the chest of drawers and lights some of the candles on top. One of them's a Gwen candle, bright red, an arty candle. She only buys the plain ones himself. Church candles. Just to say fuck them.

She is slightly stoned now, not much drunk, the coke just coming through, giving an edge to it all.

'Alright?' says Gwen, turning onto her back and half opening her eyes, her t-shirt ridden up so that she can see her pubic hair, the patch of her belly above it where she likes to rest her head, which she will always associate with the words she wrote there. That she never shaves or waxes that hair is good. That she isn't dyed or messed around with. That she goes around bare faced for days, even out of the house, even out at night, like no other woman she knows ever would.

'I'd rather be seen dead than go out without my eyeliner on,' Nic used to say, 'it looks like I've got no eyes.'

Her sister was spot on about it, she does, if she had to make a choice, like the ones who aren't so obvious about it, who aren't so very out there beautiful. And she likes that when she walks down the street with her, that this makes her private, for her alone, and private is good, like a locked garden with walls. And who is to know, who would know, how wild that garden runs. Her lack of calculation she finds a relief. Who would want to live with a high maintenance girl? It'd be a fucking nightmare. Nic was bad enough when they were kids.

She wants her so much by now that she could tear her t-shirt off her, but instead she tugs it over her head very gently so as not to hurt her.

'Alright Rumpelstiltskin?' she says and puts her face against Gwen's and her hands on her shoulders and rubs her cheek on her cheek. Gwen's legs fold around hers, her arms rest on her back. Her breasts pressed against her are soft and hot, spreading into her armpits. She smells of bed and shampoo, lemony almost, grassy. Lawns, she makes her think of summer. Some imaginary Edwardian summer of heat and willow trees and the river.

'How are you?' Gwen says.

'It's been a hard day's night.'

'Have you been working like a dog?'

'Woof,' she says, and cracks a grin against her ear.

If she lies on her long enough, she can get properly warm again – the core of her warm, her heart back to beating. It's like when she goes out into the world her heart goes cold, it freezes up and ceases to figure in anything she does. It's all about her head, her body too, but mostly her head. Only head in the hedonism. Only by coming home and lying on Gwen can she warm herself up enough to feel it again. They are separate worlds, bisecting like a Venn diagram in the sojourn of their hot bed. She has closed the door behind her, and she makes love to her with her back to the door. That's what she has done to her. She has made her capable of having her back to a closed door.

She's hardly moving at all, just resting. She can actually feel the movement in her chest and the matching answer in Gwen's like a conversation, a dialogue. The rest of the time her heart taps a rhythm she doesn't really notice, unless she's shit scared, and she can't even remember when that last happened, unless she's so coked up that she's given herself tachycardia. But it doesn't feel the same. It's not the same kind of life. It's like being a shark or something and then turning back into a mammal. Reverse evolution.

'How are you?' she says.

'Happy to see you. Feel you. Happy. Do you want your word for the day?'

'Go on.'

'It's "wayzgoose." It means "a works outing made annually by a printing house." Eighteenth century. Unknown origin. Great word huh? Don't know how you're going to get that into a sentence but I'm sure you'll manage. Did you have a good night then? Or a bad one?'

'Not bad kid. Not bad at all.'

'I almost wrote you a poem,' Gwen says and lets out a sigh.

She leans over and opens the drawer of the bedside table and produces a packet of M&M's.

'Ta da!' she says.

'The big bag! And peanut ones. My favourite,' says Gwen.

'And Big Rob from the garage gave me a freebie.' She gives her a Crunchie. 'He said to say hello. Have you got something going on there?'

'We share a common interest in chocolate. Thank you very much for this. Is it a special occasion?'

'No.'

'Oh well then, don't look under the pillow in that case.'

'Who are you? The tooth fairy?'

She looks under the pillow and gets out a paper bag. It contains a notebook and a pen.

'To help you get over the agraphia,' Gwen says.

'Thank you.'

'You're welcome. I'm surprised you know what day it is.'

'I learnt to count days in the nick.'

'Oh yes, I suppose you did. Does six months get me into the hall of fame?'

'Six days would get you in there.'

She kisses her.

'You taste of Natalie Shaw,' Gwen says. 'Bushmills and Bensons. Sleeplessness and ashes.'

'You should write that down. I'd lend you my notebook but it's all pristine.'

'Yes.'

'Yes what?'

'Yes please.'

Emma Morgan

Nat's reading some Seamus Heaney, sat in Popper's armchair with her feet propped up on the window frame. She hasn't been round here for ages, she's either working or with Gwen and that's no good. Popper sits huddled up on his mattress chain-smoking, using a pint glass as an ashtray. He looks like a guttersnipe which is about right. At least it's not too bad in here for once, the kitchen doesn't look like a bomb hit it either, she even found a clean cup for her tea. No milk though. She swigs from it and grimaces. The mug has flowers on the side. She doubts Popper bought it, but you never know.

'Don't feel like it,' says Popper in a mutter.

'Aren't you writing?' she says and turns to look at him. Popper never looks good, he's not exactly what you could describe as healthy, although she's tried to feed him up over the years and failed, but today he looks even worse, a sort of sickly greeny-white, like he's a child in the workhouse who's never seen the light of day.

Popper doesn't answer her, he's too intent on picking at his duvet cover.

'What is it Pops?'

'Nothing.'

'And my name's Cilla Black. I'm going home to eat something. Do you want to come with?'

'No.'

'You know that girl Elle?'

'Yeah.'

'I saw her yesterday. Might be around later.'

'No.'

'She's your type.'

'What type?' Popper snaps.

'Moody. Too much make-up. That type.'

'Nah.'

'Right.' It's not worth the argument this. 'I'll be back round ten then. Grapes?'

Popper nods his head. She stands up to go and as she leaves the room, she tousles the top of Popper's head and then notices something sticking out of Popper's sleeve. Looks like loo paper, reminds her of the way their mum kept a tissue up her sleeve if she had a cold. She kneels down and takes hold of Popper's arm and rolls up the sleeve carefully and sees what is in fact a load of loo paper rolled round and round his arm just above the elbow. Shite. She starts to unwrap the paper as gently as she can.

'Don't,' says Popper, trying to wrestle his arm away.

'I'm looking at this. If you want me to knock you out first I will.' The last layers are bloody and when she peels them off there's a nasty cut underneath, about an inch long. Popper shows no pain and no interest in what she's doing. 'I thought you'd stopped with all this shite.' Popper is quiet and she wants to cuff him round the back of the head to get him to pay attention. 'Why does it look like this? This is only just short of septic.'

'Forgot to clean my knife,' Popper mumbles although he obviously begrudges the words.

'Have you got, by some remote chance, anything to clean this up with?'

'No.'

'For fuck's sake! Get up. You're coming home with me.'

'No.'

'Get up.'

She pulls him up, forces him into trainers and a top and has to manhandle him out of the flat and down the stairs into the car. When she reaches home, she sits him down at the kitchen table so she can clean up his arm with some Dettol and then put a bandage on it. Gwen is there, cooking Bolognese in her dreamy way.

'Iss it done yet?'

'Just about.'

'Ssee yousse later then.'

Popper slips out from under her grasp as though greased, stands up and starts to slink out of the room.

'Aren't you staying for supper?' says Gwen. She looks concerned, nice girl that she is.

'No,' says Popper, lurking by the door but not looking at her.

'There's loads. Please stay.'

'Going home.'

He leaves the room. They hear the flat door slam. She sighs quietly and starts to read the paper spread out on the table. She's seen it all before but still, the nastiness of it makes you world weary.

'He hates me,' says Gwen.

She looks up at her. She's still stirring her sauce.

'It's not really anything to do with you, you could be anyone.'

'He's so. Why is he so... difficult?'

'Never had what you could call a home, unless you count the care system which I don't.'

'What about his family?'

'His mum died, no dad as far as I'm aware, no siblings. He was feral more or less when I met him. And not much better now. And don't think I don't know he mouths off at you. I'm sorry about that.'

'I can handle it.'

'I know you can. I'm still sorry though. I have considered saying something but that will just make him worse. And I'm sorry Gwen but he's my mate and I can't just walk away from him.'

'I know that. It's OK. I know he's just trying to wind me up. What about the cutting?'

'Some sort of coping mechanism. I thought he'd stopped. And sometimes he used to hear stuff and it was his way of switching that off too.'

'What sort of stuff?'

'His mum's voice. He thinks it's a ghost.'
'And what do you think it is?'
'I dunno.'

She goes back to reading the paper. She knows Gwen's waiting, and she admires her patience.

'It's my fault, it's because he hates me.'

She looks at her. What's the point of denying what she knows to be true? But she can't walk away from Popper, they've been through too much together. She might not like to admit this to herself but although Popper is two years older than her, in some ways she treats him like she treats Petey – as something fragile to be watched over with care. Gwen is still waiting for her to say something but for once she doesn't know what to say.

'I don't expect you to dump him. I think you should know that,' Gwen says at last.

'He thinks 'cos you're around I'm gonna bail on him.'

'Maybe you should say that to him then,' Gwen says.

'What?'

'That you're not going to bail.'

Gwen turns back to the cooker and stirs the sauce again. She doesn't know if she wants to get up and go and kiss the back of her neck or walk out the room. She does neither, lights a fag instead, gets up and opens the window, stands next to it blowing the smoke out.

PART THREE

Nic

She's curled up on the settee in the dark, wearing jeans and Robbie's grey hoody, watching a programme on the telly. They are Yanks, surprise, surprise, eating burgers and drinking buckets of coke like the ones you get in the cinema that make you want to piss ten minutes into the film. There is this bloke sitting on the edge of a bed with his wife lying behind him. Whatever she's wearing looks like a grey and blue checked flannel blanket. Maybe it is a blanket. Maybe she lies around all day and sews blankets together. Maybe the man is kind or maybe he just likes keeping her where he can see her. Like chaining up your dog. Except if you did that to your dog them animal people would come and take it away, and you'd be in court and in the papers and on telly before you knew it. So how can people treat other people like that when they wouldn't even do that to a dog? Wouldn't be allowed to do that to a dog. She doesn't get it. It makes her gut heave.

And then, she thinks, all of a sudden, that that's what she's been doing with Robbie all this time. 'Cept with him it's the drugs, not the food. She isn't going out and buying them for him, but she might as well be. She's keeping him, isn't she? She's paying for them. And it's like their dad used to say, like the penny drops. She isn't thick though like they said at school. She just takes her time to think about stuff, she's never been one for snap decisions, except about people. She can make up her mind about them in two seconds flat which has probably served her well over the years.

She picks up her favourite memory now, the one she uses to comfort herself on the worst days. It's in her head, shiny pin sharp.

She's in a record shop, browsing around. She's never been in there before because she doesn't do vinyl herself. This is for Petey next time she goes to visit him. The air smells of incense, the place must be run by hippies. The record covers are pretty though. She's never thought about it before, bit like books then, you look at the cover, and then turn them over and read the back.

She's only been there a couple of minutes when some bloke approaches. He's younger than her, twenty-two maybe, and she doesn't normally have time for boys who are too cool for school and know it, but he's got a nice twinkle in his brown eyes and the way his long brown hair is held back by aviators looks good. She'd dress him differently mind, combats aren't doing him any favours.

'Can I help you?' he asks.

'I'm looking for something for my brother.'

'What's he normally listen to?'

'Crap. But it has to be on vinyl.'

'What sort of crap?'

'Foreign crap.'

'German? French? American?'

'Are you asking my prices?'

It's out of her mouth before she can stop it. Shit. Why did she say that? The bloke does a double take. She watches him as he goes and sifts through the racks and picks up a couple of records. He goes and pays for them at the counter and then brings them over to her.

'Sorry,' she says, 'I thought you worked here.'

'I do. Will you give me a discount now? Will you give me a taster?'

He's got a funny wonky smile and one gold tooth.

'I don't do tasters. I don't take coupons either. How much do I owe you?'

'Your knickers would do.'

'My knickers aren't for sale!'

'I wasn't asking to buy them, was I? I was thinking a swap.'

'For yours?'

'I was thinking the records.'

Is he messing? She has a proper think about it, just to amuse herself, as she sizes him up. He's got a pretty face, and a body that probably looks good under the baggies too.

'Fine,' she says, and she reaches up under her skirt and wiggles out of her tiny black silk knickers in the middle of the shop, and gives them to him, just to see what he'll do, just to teach him not to mess with her. And what he does is this: he puts them in his pocket, he takes her hands and opens them out, then takes both his earrings out, and puts them in her hands. Then he takes his watch off and puts that in her hands too. He gets his wallet out and gives her all his cash. He empties all the change out of his pockets into her hands, and he lays the records on top. She laughs.

'I don't wear boxies, but I'll go get my tooth pulled if you'll give me your number,' he says. 'I'm Robbie.'

'Nicola.'

'It must be my lucky lifetime.'

She goes on a date. She's never been on one before, well, not properly. No one ever asked her out; you just liked the look of someone, they liked the look of you and before you know it, you're shagging. Or that has been her experience. He takes her out to Chinatown, and they have those dumpling things, and laugh at each other trying to use chopsticks to grab the little buggers, and it's nice not to be switched on for once. He walks her up the hill to hers, and when they get to her front steps, she does that twiddling with keys thing, and he kisses her. It's nice, the kiss, and he holds the back of her head very gently, she always did like that.

'Thanks,' she says to him when they come up for air, 'I had a nice time.'

She opens her front door.

'Do you want to come up for a coffee?'

'No thanks,' he says. 'I'll give you a call.'

He pecks her on the cheek, and then walks away and she's insulted because no-one, no-one has ever done that before. She can't sleep properly after that, wondering if she did something that put him off or if he's just an arsehole or maybe he had second thoughts because of what she does. Then why ask her out then?

The next morning at 9 a.m. the doorbell rings and she answers it, half asleep.

'Come down,' a voice says.

'Who's this?'

'Robbie.

'Come down where?'

'Downstairs.'

'Why the fuck should I?'

'Come down.'

'No.'

'Please. It'll take fifteen seconds.'

She goes downstairs just to get rid of him, still wearing her silk kimono with the dragon on the back. He's there on the building's wide stone doorstep looking way chirpier than she feels. She's never been great of a morning and is irritated by people who are.

'Yeah? Fifteen. Fourteen. Thirteen...'

'Forgot to pay you. Sorry.'

'For what?'

'For the kiss.'

And he gives her a white plastic bag, and then goes over the road, and stands on the opposite pavement with his arms crossed.

'What's in here?'

'Look.'

And there is a signet ring, some bank cards, a couple of records in plastic sleeves, and a little gold nugget. She picks it out of the bag.

'What's this?'

He smiles at her with a gold-less smile, but she can see it's all put on this, that he doesn't know how she'll react at all. Maybe she'll just throw the bag at him, and that will be that. That's the moment, she remembers it now. That's the moment she could have stopped it all. All she had to do was close the door. That's all it would have taken. But she doesn't, instead she goes down the steps in her fluffy slippers and over the road to him and hands him the bag back, her stupid heart all over the place. It's not that people, men, haven't done nice things for her over the years, it's that all the things have been so ordinary, flowers and chocolates and jewellery, like they got them out of a manual.

She holds up the nugget, and says, 'For this you can get this, this, and this,' and she ticks off what she might do on her fingers one by one. And she pushes her hair back behind her ears where his gold hoops shine, and she says, 'and for these you can get this, and that's not a service I ever normally offer.'

And she can see he's still just a kid then, 'cos for all his cocky cheekiness and his know-it- all ways, he seems to lose his voice, and possibly the use of his legs. It makes her laugh, and her laughter is infectious and soon they're both leaning up against a house wall in hysterics. It's one of those moments when you couldn't explain to another person exactly why you're laughing. An old lady in sandals with tights underneath and breasts so enormous they probably need scaffolding, tuts at them as she goes past. But that only makes them laugh the more.

'You coming up then?' she says when she can speak. 'Or are you going to turn me down again?'

'I was just being a gentleman. Didn't want to push it.'

'I'm not into gentlemen.'

'What are you into then?'

But she just smiles at him and he's back to grinning. She takes him by the hand and leads him back over the road, the plastic bag swinging in her other hand.

In her flat she turns to him and takes off her kimono. He takes off his clothes, all of them, in a rush and when he's dressed in nothing at all, she gapes at him. The fact that he is ripped but not excessively so, not like a gym bunny who spends his whole day staring at himself in the mirror and the other half out of his brain on steroids is good. Wide shoulders, decent guns, long legs and arms, and that lovely muscle that men have if they're fit, just above both hip bones. It's not that that's knocked the breath out of her though. Because he's only naked if you don't count the fact that the whole surface of his pale skin, from collar bone to ankle and wrist, is an intricate mesh of tattoos.

'Bloody hell!' she says.

'That's a good response,' he says and puts his hands on his hips. She can see that he likes her reaction, that he wants to show himself off and she would normally be put off by that, but she's only intrigued. After all she's the same, isn't she? She likes to be looked at.

'Can I?' she says, holding her hand out towards him.

'Sure.'

She walks up to him and reaches forward and touches his shoulder and then starts to trace her way across his chest. There are pin-up girls and roses, stars and swallows, dragons and wagon wheels and skulls and all across his back a great big ship coming out of the mist.

'I imagine this is what pirates looked like once,' she says.

'Do you believe in love at first sight?' he says in a quiet voice.

'Dunno.'

'Feels like the whole world's been set on fire.'

'Does it now?'
'Only just found that out.'
'Sounds painful.'
'Yeah. But worth it I reckon. Hope so anyway.'
She tweaks his left nipple which is backgrounded by an hourglass.
'Ow,' he says.
'More of that to follow,' she says.

Now here they are, five years later and he's asleep on the couch next to her, like he is most of the time he isn't jittering around being fucking annoying and winding her up, or out scoring or in the bathroom hitting up 'cos she won't have him doing it anywhere else. But who knows what he does when she's out? And does she care that much anymore anyway about what he does and where he does it?

It's a waste of time trying to get him to watch anything on telly with her anymore, trying to get him to do anything much with her at all, expect put his hands around her neck and hold onto her, though it feels more like strangling most of the time, or follow her round the flat whining that he's run out of gear. They hardly ever go out anywhere, not even down the road to the pub for a quick one. They live two lives that don't gel. She is just like the bloke, the one who loves his blanket wife. It isn't love though, she can see that, though the husband seems to think it is. It's nasty what he's doing to his wife. He should be helping her instead. Or if he can't, he could have tried to get her some help. They must have Social Services or something like that in America. But sitting here on her couch, dirty now, she must have been stupid to think you could keep cream clean, and tatty because he drops stuff on it all the time, so she's given up trying to keep it nice, trying to keep anything nice, she thinks that the penny has dropped.

She sits there for a while longer looking down at his sleeping face in the blue light from the telly. He used to be so pretty once. Now his skin's gone to pot, and his teeth are pretty fucked and he's way too thin, and he looks old and wrecked, like he sleeps in the streets and not in her arms. She drags herself up and makes her way to their bedroom. She looks around the room. What's worth taking? He goes into her handbag but she's wise to that and takes stuff out of it when she gets home and hides it in the bottom of the Tampax box down by the side of the loo.

From the top of the wardrobe, she pulls down the old black Adidas bag he used to put his stuff in to go and play Saturday footie in the days when he loved doing that, she'd go up and watch him play, stand there in the cold warming her hands on hot tea from a polystyrene cup; now she uses it to put her clothes in, stuffs them in any old which way. A couple of pairs of shoes, she keeps meaning to go get them resoled. She keeps meaning to clean them like their dad used to do to keep them nice. She keeps meaning to do all sorts of things. She puts as much of it into the bag as she can. Her jewellery box. Nothing in there anymore worth anything, he's stolen most of it. Her make-up. Will just have to leave the rest. Pulls her grey suede boots on. She feels exhausted. She takes her handbag and the Adidas bag into the hall and dumps them there and goes to the bathroom, takes the Tampax box too, and some wash stuff.

On the way out she has a look at her face in the mirror over the sink. Her hair's scraped back into a pony, she's looks dead pale without any make up on, but it's a Shaw face, her sister and her brother are the same, it's still a beautiful face, she's seen them in black at funerals, and they still look fucking beautiful. It doesn't mean anything though. It means stuff to other people, but not to them. A beautiful face doesn't make you a good person, it's just a mask for her selfishness and for the fact that she's no fucking good at anything else except looking pretty.

Back in the hall she stuffs everything into the bag and stands there trying to think if there's anything else, but she's so tired now she's starting to lose it. She's got this far, now what should she do? Natalie. That's what she'll have to do. She kneels down on the carpet and fumbles around in her handbag for her mobile, but when she rings her, it goes straight to voicemail. Fuck. What's the landline? What's the landline? It won't come to her. Fuck it. She'll just get a taxi and if she's not there… well, then she'll think of something. She takes the chain off the door. Then she feels around in her handbag and finds her key ring. A metal dove swings off of it, Robbie gave it to her, she can't remember why.

The thing she hates the most about all of it, the worst thing of it for her is that … stupidly… that she misses being his best girl. It's not just the lying or the stealing or the way it's changed him, sucked all the person out of him, the person who she loved, so that there's not much left now but shell; it's not even that it's mucked up her life too, the effect it's had on her so that she just don't care that much about anything anymore, just like him, he doesn't care, so she doesn't either, you wouldn't have thought it would rub off so easy, the 'can't be bothered', 'nah, don't feel like it,' crap; it's the fact that he doesn't love her like he used to love her, he doesn't love her like she's his and he's hers, she's not his best girl anymore. All she is now is everybody's girl, and she never used to care about that, so what, it didn't upset her at all, other men on her, and it didn't upset him either 'cos he was sound enough to see that it didn't mean anything to her. But now that she doesn't mean anything to him, it's like she's his stingy mother or something, someone to beg from, whinge at, expect to look after you, lie to, let down. Someone who keeps on having to, again and again and again, come and bail you out, clean you up, get you sorted, thinking that if that's what it takes then that's what I'll do. It's not like her childhood didn't teach her to fucking well grit her teeth and get on with it. She did it because she thought that the old Robbie was under there somewhere and that if she kept digging down, she could get to him.

And it sounds like she blames everything on him. But she doesn't. It's not his fault, is it? Just bad luck maybe that he's like he is, not like they hadn't, Natalie and her, hadn't taken everything under the sun, it didn't make him a worse person or anything. But that's part of the problem, she's always making fucking excuses for him, but she can't help it, she feels sorry for him 'cos she remembers him as he used to be when he loved her best, and she remembers what that felt like, how good it felt, like warm sun falling on cold skin. So maybe it's just selfish, but who gives a fuck about that 'cos she misses it, she misses him, and the her she was with him, the her who was seen, and she wants that her back, she wants her back, and she wishes she could get him back too because the worse it gets the worse everything else gets and all she is now is everybody's girl and maybe she could, maybe they could, maybe it could get better after all somehow, there must be something she could do, could change. Maybe if she... no. No. No... no. Keep thinking about bloody blanket wives.

She throws the keys on the floor, and shuts the door of the flat, and goes down the stairs as fast as she can and slams the front door behind her, and marches down the street with her bags to look for a taxi. Except she can't find one. Why isn't there one? She'll have to go round the corner. She'll just have a rest first 'cos moving so fast has made her feel weird, like there's no blood left in her body, like there's air in her veins. She holds onto the railings that line her street with her free hand, she's always loved the fact that these big old houses all in a row have their own sets of railings, like their own sets of guard dogs. Her house, well not hers, it's only rented, but it's her flat, it's her home. She shouldn't do this. She should just kick him out like she's done before, but when she's done that, he's always come back, cleaned up and come back, and she's made the mistake of letting him in.

And he'll say sorry, she hates the way he says sorry because he looks like a little boy, which is so stupid 'cos a six-foot two bloke shouldn't look like that, I'm sorry he says, and goes to get his stuff, I'll just get this, and I'll be on my way. And then he gets his stuff and goes to the door, and she's standing by the door and something happens, like he touches her arm, like he goes to give her a hug, or she goes to him and hugs him, and she pretends that it's one last hug, a goodbye hug, but it never is, she should never touch him, it's the touching him that gets her in this mess. 'Cos there's no one else who has ever touched her that soft, held her in his arms so gently, and he'll say sorry Nic, I'm a twat, I know I'm a twat, I'm trying to get me shit together, I am, I don't want to… I don't want to lose you, life is shite without you, and he says, look, and he pulls up his sleeves, look at my arms. And she does and that's the worst thing she can do, because the insides of men's arms are the softest place about them, and that'll be that; they'll end up in bed, and it's not that he's the greatest in bed ever, though he's pretty damn good, it's that he knows her body so well, he knows what she likes and what she doesn't like, he knows what she wants. It's another thing about her that he knows more about than anybody else and that is nice, to be that known, and she don't want to have to start again, to have to start to explain everything all over again to someone else, not just the sex bit, but all of it. The truth is she doesn't want to be known at all, not by anybody else. It's private, her feelings and what she likes, it's private, she doesn't want anyone else to know except him, nobody knows much about her except him and her twin and Petey and their dad and that's enough. She's not got anything else left to give away.

She is so tired. She doesn't know if she can make it as far as the next street, why is there no frigging taxi, and now she is starting to have problems breathing. Shit. She reaches into her bag for her inhaler, but she can't find it; she scrabbles around in her bag and thinks, oh God, oh God, it's in the flat. Oh shit. I'll have to go back and there's no key now, and I'll have to ring the bell and… no, it must be in my bag, it must be, it must be, but she can't find it. She's going to have to ring the bell. And if she rings and he answers, and she goes back up. I'm not going back in there, I'm not. But she can't find her fucking inhaler and her breathing's getting worse, if it goes on much longer like this then things will get bad very quickly. She starts to drag herself back there, although she doesn't want to, or maybe she does, maybe she left it there on purpose because she doesn't want to leave because she loves him; she hates that she does, but she loves him with every bit of good that's still in her. She knows she needs to walk away, but she's so scared that if she lets go of his hand for good, then all she'll have is everybody else's hands on her, not hands that love her, not hands she loves.

She's standing on her top step now with her forehead pressed against the blue painted wood of the big, old splintery door, holding onto the brass door knocker that's shaped like a fish, but what fish, she thinks, what fish is this, and that's like that book Natalie used to read to her, she never did like reading to herself. And she's gasping for breath, but the fight in her, the fight, she's slid down the door onto the cold stone step, feels like there are splinters in her forehead but she won't… she… fucking… well… won't. And every bit of air that she can get into her now comes to her down a wire wool tube. And then she remembers, she remembers the landline. Answer it. Answer it. Please, please be there. But it's Gwen who picks up.

Gwen

'Natalie?' says a small voice.

'No, sorry Nicola but she's out,' she says, so surprised that she almost drops the phone, 'Have you tried her mobile?'

'Voicemail,' says a small child's voice, like the littlest children she teaches, the ones she feels for the most, the desperate, battered, bruised, hammered into the ground tiny ones, the ones that make her cry in the evenings when Nat isn't home. But maybe she's just imagining that this is what she's hearing because she's tired and it's been a long day.

'If she's really busy she sometimes doesn't pick up but if you leave it a while then she normally will, eventually. Or you could leave her a message. Or you could text her but she's unreliable with texts. Or I'll give her a message when she gets back but I don't know when that'll be. Or you could try Popper. Do you want me to go find his number? I wrote it down on a scrap of paper but I'm not sure where it is and I forgot to put it in my mobile, I'm useless with phone numbers, can never remember them, do you want me to go and look for it?'

And there's just silence. She was on her way to bed. There's just this silence, like the line's gone dead except somewhere in the background are cars and somewhere near the phone is something else.

'Nicola? What is it? Where are you?'

'House.'

And she hardly knows Nicola, she hardly knows her, she's scared of her to be honest, but something clicks in, and she has, never, ever, in her life, ever moved so fucking fast.

'Don't you move. Don't you move from there. I'm getting a taxi. I'm coming right now.'

There is no answer. She drops the phone, stuffs her feet into trainers, and runs out into the night, up to the main road, hopes for a taxi, there must be a taxi, and she sees one with the light on and hails it, waving frantically.

'Alright there, love? You shouldn't be jumping around in the road like that. Where to?'

She doesn't know the number, but she sees Nic anyway, slumped on a step, screams at the driver to stop, throws a tenner at him, and when he unlocks the door, jumps out of the cab and runs up the front steps to her; she is curled up against the front door, breathing in rasps. She looks barely conscious.

'What's the matter love?' the taxi driver is saying, he must have got out of the taxi behind her, 'Is she pissed?'

She kneels down next to Nic, and the taxi driver follows her up the steps. She has no idea what to do.

'I think it's the asthma. My grandson has that. Have you got your inhaler love? Where's your inhaler? Is it in your bag?'

She reaches into the bag that's on the step next to her, but there's too much stuff in it to paw through so she empties it out on the step. The taxi driver searches through it, finds the inhaler, and hands it to her. She is stroking Nic's head and trying to get her to come round.

'There you go love.'

'I don't know what to do,' she says.

'G'is it here.'

He takes it from her and puts it into Nic's mouth, pushes the end. Nic sucks in the air like she's never had air before.

'I told you it was the asthma, my grandson's the same,' the taxi driver is saying, 'Come on girl, let's get you into the cab then.'

In the back of the taxi, to calm herself down, she says a poem out loud to herself and to her great surprise, Nic giggles. A tiny, muffled giggle like a hiccup. Nic puts her arm round her and she holds her tighter. They ride home like that, wrapped around each other, Nic's head on her chest, her breath still ragged, that awful terrible wheeze still coming out of her lungs.

'I call that "Definition of love in Scouse",' she says but there's this enormous lump in her throat, like a gobstopper stuck there, even after she puts Nic to bed under their duvet, even after she strokes her hair and holds her hand and looks at her beautiful face.

'Do you wanna hear one of Nat's poems from way back? Can only remember a few lines though,' Nic whispers.

'I would love that. She's never told me any. She denies their existence.'

'I see the stigmata/On the soles of her feet/Where she has walked/All this way/Across glass'

'Is that about your mum?'

'Think so. The rest of my stuff's still there Gwen. Didn't even tell him I was going.'

'Nat can go and get the rest of your things for you.'

'You get used to things being shite. Wasn't like that before. He used to do nice things. Like he used to iron the sheets for me. Sometimes I'd get home late and get into bed and it would be all clean and soft.'

'What else was nice?'

'He brought me brekkie in bed, and he always remembered to tape me Enders if I was out. And he used to tickle me behind the knees. Things like that. Stupid things. And we used to go to this place in town he called "The Sex and Curry"'cos it had these booths with curtains, and we used to, you know, mess around. And you know he used to DJ? Well sometimes I used to turn up there in this big fake fur coat I had with nothing on underneath, and he'd completely lose it and fuck up the mix. My mum used to say that see, "All fur coat and no knickers."'

'I'll remember that one.'

'And he could have left me after I lost the baby, lots of men would have, but he didn't.'

'I'm so sorry. I didn't know about that.'

'No reason why you should.'

She lays her hand in Nic's hair and strokes it. Then she cuddles right into her, and Nic starts to cry onto her chest.

'I used to be his best girl.'

At three a.m., after Nat has finally come home, she sits next to her on the sofa, feeling like she's got ice in her bones.

'She thought she'd left her inhaler inside. But we found it in her bag. The taxi driver and me. Just as well he was there, I didn't know what to do. It was awful Nat, bloody awful. She was hardly breathing. I was so scared. I don't understand. Why would you almost die on your own front doorstep when all you had to do to save yourself was ring the bell? Why would you do that?'

'Because she didn't want to go back in.'

'I got that. I got that. But… I don't understand. Was he so bad the boyfriend?'

'That depends on what you describe as bad.'

'Did he hit her?'

'She wouldn't have taken that.'

'Are you sure?'

Nat considers it.

'There're things you don't get Gwen. That you're never going to get. And that's a good thing.'

She tries to get up, but Nat won't let her.

'I'm not dissing you. I'm just saying how it is.'

'Then why did she stay?'

'You ask her.'

'I did. She said something about how she used to be her best girl.'

Nat smiles, but it's a very sad smile.

'The thing is, you think her behaviour is an anomaly, don't you? You think it's what? Excessive? You seem to have forgotten that the world's best band got so fucking good by playing ten hours a night seven days a week in the red-light district of a run-down port city fuelled by alcohol and amphetamines. Stubborn as fuck? It's called a strike. Perseverant? I don't wanna mention the other thing because it's disrespectful like, but we still won't read the fucking Sun and we never will. I think the word you were probably looking for, while you were casting round in there, was proud. She's a Scouser Matt. No, she's worse than that. Because even Lola, even Pop wouldn't do that. I'm sorry and I'm so fucking grateful for you getting there that. Well. Thank you. Thank you. But she'd made her mind up, and I never, never mess with my sister once she's made her mind up, because I did it once and I won't do it again, and if it took her dying on her own front steps to not go back in there then that was her decision.'

'Did what once?'

'I don't want to talk about it.'

Nat gets up.

'It's dead simple when it comes right down to it,' Nat says. 'She's a Shaw. She's a fucking Shaw.'

'I know you are stubborn… I know it, but that was just… it was mad.'

'Leave it alone, come to bed.'

Nat

She comes to in the morning, in the spare room, not much more than a box room really, empty apart from a single bed and the inevitable bookshelf. She's never slept in here before, the light's different, must be why she's woken up after only a couple of hours kip. Gwen slept next to Nic, didn't want to leave her, or wake her up and she couldn't fit in this bed with her anyway. She stands up and goes to the toilet and then into the kitchen where Gwen is frying eggs and Nic is at the table eyeing up a full plate of food with a fag in her hand. Nic looks up at her as she comes in and gives her half a smile.

'Gwen came to get me. I called, and she came to get me.'

'How do you like your bacon Nicola?' says Gwen.

'Greasy.'

And there you go. Everyday banality, a bit of kitchen sink drama: two girls, her girlfriend plating up fry ups in his kitchen and her twin sister, the one who hardly ever bothers to eat, sitting at the table with a full plate in front of her that she has desecrated with brown sauce, stuffing down beans for Christ's sake and fried bread, wearing nasty trackies that she recognises as her own and one of Gwen's green t-shirts, a fork in one hand, and a fag in the other. She sits down, and Gwen passes her a mug of tea and a plate full of breakfast.

'Alright monster?' says Gwen. 'I never can understand why you drink your tea like that, it's orange, tea's not supposed to be orange, Nicola's isn't orange, see, it's brown, like tea, brown.'

Gwen takes the third out of the four chairs and Nic smiles at her and puts bacon into her mouth. She looks at Gwen. Our Gwen. She doesn't seem to find it odd no more, the fag and the food and the tea all in one go. She doesn't seem to find any of this odd, not that she doesn't notice idiosyncrasies, just she doesn't care? Or doesn't say? She leans over and kisses her, she snogs her full on, she tastes of bacon, if her sister wasn't here she'd... Well she can't for once. So she doesn't. Ah, a good thing that, having to curb your own enthusiasms. Or is it? Is it good having to change to fit? Gwen does it so easy, it makes it look effortless. It's all very well going with the flow when it's something you don't mind doing. It's the other bit she's always had the problems with.

'This is very, very good bacon,' Nic says with her mouth full. A song comes on the radio and Nic starts to hum tunelessly along with it and puts three sugars in her tea, then another one just for luck.

'What's this song Nat?' says Gwen. 'Oh venerated arbiter of perfect musical taste, what may I ask is this song?'

'You know what it is sweetheart. It's Van the Man. Let it all hang out. Is that what it's called? Don't look at me like that girl, I don't know everything. Yeah really. And what I'd most like to know is how you can criticise my tea when my sister thinks tea is some kind of minor adjunct to sugar? Pass us the sauce then Nic.'

'So can I stay?' Nic asks her.

'She could sleep in the spare room, couldn't she?' says Gwen.

Nic looks at her, waiting for her answer. It isn't really a decision though. She promised their dad she'd always look after her and look how much she's failed.

'It's not much of a room,' she says in apology, half expecting her to take it the wrong way.

'We can do it up though how you wanted it,' says Gwen. 'Take the bookshelf out. Put a wardrobe in. Even paint it a colour you would like.'

She's a kind girl is Gwen; she's always liked that about her. It comes easy it seems. She doesn't think she's kind herself.

'It doesn't matter,' says Nic, drawing on her fag.

'Nat,' says Gwen.

'Stay as long as you want,' she says.

'We'd love to have you,' says Gwen.

'I've got no stuff.'

'That's not a problem,' she says. 'I'll go get it later. Or…'

'No, I don't want to go back there. Not ever.'

'It was your flat.'

'It's alright Nicola. You don't have to. Nat will sort it out for you.'

'Would you Natalie?'

That surprises her, she never asks her for anything.

'I'll go after. Pick up whatever you need and then I'll get some paint and stuff. The skirting boards could do with going over and all.'

Nic, as it turns out, wants it "dusky pink", whatever the hell that is, she'll have to go to B&Q with her. But first she takes her keys off her and goes back to her flat. There's no sign of Robbie which might be no bad thing. She's going to have to get him sorted out one way or another though. Would have done it ages ago if she could have found a way of doing it without Nic going into orbit. The flat is more of a mess than she was expecting; Nic was always so particular, but there are scratches on the walls from something, did she have a cat? And the washing up is piled up in the sink in a way she finds disgusting. And as for the bathroom, it's worse than Popper's. She's given her a list of what to take but it's not a big list she now realises because there's not much to take. All Robbie's vinyl has gone; he must have flogged them. Nic doesn't even have that many clothes, and all her shoes are buggered up. She always cared a lot about her shoes, in fact, the whole flat and everything in it are just indications of what has happened to her sister. It makes her feel both sad and furious at the same time and she has an urge to trash what's left of the place, burn it down. That would teach that bastard a lesson. But it doesn't matter that much maybe. She's got her safe now at least. And Gwen will take care of her. That's the main thing. She'll ring their dad later too. And all the time there is this thing in her head saying, you shouldn't have let this happen, and worse still is the question of how far her sister had actually sunk. Was she still working for the escort agency as she said she was? Or had she slipped down into some other place that she didn't know about? She would have heard surely, that's what she says to herself, but now she looks back at it realises that she never delved into it like she should of in case she couldn't stand the answer. At least she wasn't shooting up herself. At least she was only paying for the brown for Robbie. And surely, she wasn't doing street stuff? She hadn't gone down that far, into that place where you'll take anyone for a score. Or had she? She pickaxes that thought from her head because it's not that she would despise her for it, it's how much she would despise herself.

Gwen

So now there is Nic in the spare room, with her sweet, bitter hardness and her fair Shaw skin and her nails that she's constantly repainting. Her pretty clothes and her shiny hair pulled back behind her pretty ears. No-one talks about how long she's going to be there; it should be the elephant in the room, or Robbie should be, but no-one talks about him either. When she asked Nat, she said that she'd got it sorted and she decided not to ask what that meant. That might have been cowardice on her part.

She watches the twins fit back easily together just like a well-made jigsaw would. Had Nat always been missing something then? She doesn't even complain when Nic takes an hour in the bath. She brings home not just Cadburys for her, but also the Haribo Nic likes from the all-night garage. She had thought that maybe it would be uncomfortable having Nic there, but this isn't the case. It's easy and Nic gives them space, goes out to have coffee on her own, spends time in her room. And it's good to have company of a night when Nat's out, they watch telly together, they like East Enders and crap films and shows with pathologists, which they watch from between their fingers. Nic sews sometimes because it was true what Nat said about her being amazing at it. She appliqués a cushion cover with tiny stars. They drink white wine and put their feet up, side by side, on the coffee table. Her fives in socks. Nic's eights in fluffy slippers. It reminds her of Rosa and makes her realise how much she has, since she left home, missed her. Except Nic is not Rosa, open and expansive, a large part of her is closed off like Nat is. All her history is a mystery. That's a terrible line. She's not going to tell it to Nat.

Nic

And at night, when she should miss him, when she should be lying awake missing him or pawing over all her many regrets, she sleeps deeply instead, tucked into the little bed in her sister's spare room under the pink cotton duvet cover that Gwen bought her to match the walls. She doesn't want a double bed, what would be the point of that? It's like her childhood has been recreated but in a much better way; there is no screaming in this house, no chaos, just her sister in the next room as she always was, dreaming whatever she dreams off, probably about books or something, next to this surprising girl who came to get her like she was the princess in the castle and the dragon was at the door. Her clothes are in the wardrobe, she has been mending them bit by bit, her shoes are in there too. Her jewellery box is on the windowsill and Robbie's earrings are still in it; she never puts them on anymore, but has decided to keep them anyway, just to remind herself that there is escape after all. You don't have to keep doing the same stupid thing again and again. She knows that now.

Gwen

'Do you want to come down to Chester at the weekend? I'm taking Nic to see Petey,' Nat asks.

She's so surprised that she nearly falls off her chair. She has her own chair now that Nic is here, and she is embarrassed by how pleased she is about this.

'Yes, yes please,' she says, and is slightly embarrassed too by her eagerness, because she's like a dog which has been suddenly given the bone it was longing for but then wants to pretend that it wasn't waiting at all.

The house is in a suburb, thirties red brick. There are hanging baskets with pink petunias in them by the front door. Petey opens the door and runs down the path and grabs hold of Nic and hangs round her neck. She accepts this for a moment, patting him on the back, and then says, 'You're too big for this now, you idiot. Try your other sister.'

Petey throws himself at Nat and they fall to the ground where they wrestle into a flowerbed, and then roll over and over on the manicured front lawn. It's lovely to see.

'How old are you, Natalie?' says Nic.

'Are you working hard? Promise me you're working hard!' Nat says.

'I am. I am. I am. Aren't I, Dad?'

Their dad is there standing in the doorway, tall like the twins, with a curly reddish beard; he comes and shakes her hand firmly.

'Nice to meet you Gwen, I've heard a lot about you. Show them you're A' level stuff then lad,' he says.

Nat lets go of Petey and Petey gets up and runs into the house.

'You're lying on my lawn Natalie. I think you'd better come inside before you confuse the neighbours. There's Neighbourhood Watch round here you know.'

'Cos you wouldn't want to do that, would you Natalie?' says Nic and then turns to their dad. He takes her by the hand and the look on his face is one of such happiness that she realises she is gawping and looks away. Nat gets up off the lawn and puts her arm around her which is good because it makes her feel included. She had got very nervous in the car, chattering on about this and that until Nic raised her eyebrows at her and she shut up.

'Neighbourhood Watch?' says Nat. 'They'll be onto me in no time,' and their dad frowns and then pulls the frown off his face like someone stretching out elastic.

'Come in the garden,' he says, 'Jill's made scones.'

They go inside, Nat's hand in hers, Nic's hand in their dad's and their dad ushers them out into the back garden where Jill is putting out a trayful of tea things on a table over in the corner underneath the tree. The lawn is manicured to within an inch of its life. She is a small plump woman, wearing a pink flowery apron like a mother in a story.

'Happy families. I like this game,' Nat says, and she is smiling her biggest smile, and she can see then how glad she is to get her family back together. She has no idea how long Nic was absent, but it must have been a while.

'Hi kids!' says Jill and Nic's mouth tightens but Nat steps towards Jill and she is pulled along with her.

She half expects there to be some kissing or hugging or something but there is none of that.

'And you must be Gwen,' says Jill. 'Natalie didn't tell us you were so pretty.'

She blushes.

Petey runs out with a large black folder which he shoves into Nat's hands.

'All my own work,' he says. 'The teacher didn't help me or anything.'

'Good lad,' says Nat.

'I've made scones and a cake,' says Jill. 'Chocolate. Didn't know what you would like.' She is a slightly anxious host at a surprise party. It must be strange to be a stepmother. She doesn't even know how long after their mum's death that their dad and Jill got together. She should have asked way more questions but who to ask? It might be best to go for Petey. But then again, maybe not. She wouldn't want to upset him. She is just grateful to be here, that's what she needs to concentrate on, the here and now.

'I love chocolate cake,' she says and is rewarded by Jill's hand on her arm.

'What would you like Nic?' says Jill.

There's a brief moment, a spike in the air, and then Nic says, 'I'll have a scone. Except I dunno if that's how you pronounce it. Gwen?'

'What am I? The scone expert?'

'There you go Nic. That answered your question,' says Nat.

'So Gwen, Natalie says you're a teacher. Terrible burden of administration this bloody government has put you under. Always chopping and changing,' says their dad, as he slices up the cake.

'Here we go,' says Nic, 'he's started.'

'Everything is political,' says their dad in time with the twins and Petey, and then Nat and Petey laugh and Nic moves towards the scones.

Nat

Nic has gone to see a friend or so she said. She is relieved that she's gone out. Not because she doesn't like having her here, it's much easier than she expected to be honest, but because her hardly ever leaving the flat was worrying her. She knew better to ask about what friend. As far as she knows she's never had many.

Gwen's sitting at the desk in their bedroom with her back to her, a pencil tucked behind her ear, a chewed pencil, she always chews her pencils, it's a disgusting habit. She's told her off, but she takes no notice, she bought her a retractable one and Gwen said thank you, how kind of you, but she's never used it; the flat is full of manky pencils and half chewed biros, Gwen gets ink on her hands, on her tops, her mouth full of splinters and pencil lead, mouth full of ink. And you know what? She likes her more for this grim habit, not less. Kiss a girl who tastes of words. Maybe she should write that down. She's started writing stuff down again, like she used to at school, she's started to carry her notebook and her pen around secretly, just writing down the odd word, the odd thought about something or other. She doesn't admit it to herself, but she, someday, one of these livelong days, has the intention of writing something for Gwen. Not a letter, something else, though she doesn't know what just yet. Well, yeah, she does. A poem maybe.

Living with Gwen is good, great really, but it's also paining her because she can't stop wanting her, thinking about her, she can't fucking concentrate. This is ridiculous. They should be out of this shit by now. She should be losing interest. She should be bored.

The worst thing? The absolute worst thing? It makes her want to leave. But she can't. Because she's in her home. She asked her into her house because she didn't want to be without her, and now she can't do without her. How fucking stupid is she.

'Like that?' she says.

Whispers fill her up her mouth, her lips pressed together to keep them in; a tiny sound escapes her, like air pressure. Anything Gwen asked for here, she would give her or try to give her. And what she delights in, is that this, for the first time ever in her life, and she hasn't told her this, she won't tell her this, it's hers, this thought, for her, is that this is completely reciprocal. She is a match for her brain, and she is a match for her lusts, and she fits around her, around what she wants so perfectly, it's like she was made for her. Because there are girls built for comfort and there are girls built for speed, there are girls like show ponies, wonderful to look at but no good to ride, and there are girls who love it and girls who don't, girls who want to and girls who pretend they want to. And she can do it for most of them. And they can do it for her by their mere presence, by trying to work out what makes them tick. But how many of them make a proper effort to try to make her tick, beyond the posturing they have learned from porn stars? And how many of those do it because they want to make her as happy as she has made them? Who will put in the time and the thought to do that.

And this sweet girl she comes home to becomes somebody else when she puts her mouth on her. She gets so lost in her that she forgets everything. This is what love on top of lust feels like, she has never had the two overlap and interlink like this before. And it is fucking terrifying. And. And. She's not sure she can deal with it. This. This creature in her bed that she can feel nuzzling her back before she has to get up to go to work, she can feel her happiness that she's there, she can feel the happiness in her own chest, to wake up next to her. She has to look down at her chest to make sure her heart's not glowing through. She doesn't want her to see how her hand on her back, her mouth on her skin makes her feel. Gwen whispers absolute filth in her ear, filth that makes it so she can't see straight so that even while she's saying, 'I've got to get up Gwen, I've got to go,' she has to be inside her anyway, and she's mumbling into her neck, 'just a quickie,' and she's panting, 'but you don't do quickies,' 'yeah I do,' she says, 'yeah I do,' and sees her mouth open.

When she's inside her body, pushing into her, deep inside the soft wet of her, and Gwen's under her, they've turned the lights off, it's like they are speaking another language, an older one, muscle, gland, blood; she feels like she's pushing her way into Gwen's heart and that she is letting her, out of her goodness and her generosity, and she, who has never wanted to be loved, has never needed it before from anyone outside her own family, not even from Evie, feels lost there, in the map of her, in the foreign country to which she has emigrated and in which she is absorbed. It's like tripping, that's what it's like, she is completely off her head with her and she feels almost as if she were forgiven for every wrong thing that she's ever done, the thousand stupidities she's committed, that somehow, through the miracle of Gwen's body, she is absolved of all her sins: original, venial, cardinal, even the mortal ones and she thanks God for it, although she doesn't believe in God; she thanks Gwen for it, over and over under her breath and all she can hear is her own name coming back to her as she says hers. Nat. Nat. Nat. Gwen makes her name sound like the best of words, the only word she can remember, the only word she wants to know.

Sometimes, especially when they are in bed at night, she just wants to get it all off her chest. Confess. Both of them nearly asleep, her arms wrapped around her, her mouth opens, and she tries to whisper her secrets into the back of her neck. But she doesn't. She wants to. But she can't. She can't. She doesn't. She can't be anything else than what she is. Instead, on the edge of sleep, she remembers bits of poems 'O the mind, mind has mountains; cliffs of fall/ Frightful, sheer, no-man fathomed. Hold them cheap/May who ne'er hung there'; instead, on the edge of sleep, she entertains the fantasy that Gwen, who would have been just one letter before her in the school register, is walking ahead of her down a corridor or across a playground as they file along in alphabetical order. Robertson. Shaw. Shaw. Scout. General. Rear guard. Although she can't imagine Nic actually agreeing to that. Perhaps with a small child called Samuels between them. A small child called Rutter. Rumble. Rude. She imagines herself leaning against the wall in a corridor and seeing Gwen walk by with a green ribboned ponytail swinging. She wouldn't have deigned to speak to her, would she? But would she have come back behind the bike sheds with her? She stops her mouth with these ideas. But when she is asleep, she wets her lips with her tongue and marks words on the back of Gwen's neck. Would you mind? Would you leave me if I told you all of it? Please leave. You need to leave me. One of these days, one of these livelong days, I'm going to have to make you go.

Gwen

'If what?' says Nicola, her giant fluffy slippers on, doing the washing up.

She twists her hands together, puts one foot on top of the other.

'Well, if, if you wanted to... later... perhaps... if you wanted to... Lola's coming round if that's alright and we're going to just... you know... finish up our marking... and then hang out and her friend Amy might come round, and then we're going to play Monopoly.'

'Monopoly?'

'Yeah, Lol and Amy love Monopoly. I hate Monopoly, but they can't play chess and draughts is boring and you have to be pissed to play Twister and you can't play Pictionary with just three people and Lola is brilliant at backgammon and I always end up depressed and hopscotch is just impractical and we're too old to skip... and Lola and me have to go to school tomorrow... yeah I know... we are five... so no booze... no drugs... just some TV and Lola building mansions on Mayfair, while I cry onto my cereal.'

'Cereal?'

'It's every other Tuesday. It's Cereal Night. We haven't done it for ages. So... if you want to...'

'No worries. I'm the Monopoly champion of No. 8 Hatton Drive. I used to make Natalie cry.'

'She never told me that!'

'Well, she wouldn't, would she?'

So here they are, playing Monopoly with Lola and her friend Amy, the one she's in her band Libellula in.

'Bloody hell!' says Lola. 'What are you like you? No-one's never beaten me before. Not even our Lee and he can count. How much did I just lose?'

'Five fifty,' says Amy. 'Gwen, you owe four. I owe eight. Shite.'

'What could you do me for seventeen fifty Amy?' asks Nic.

'Pretty much nothing. But if I was feeling especially generous one of those Chinese squiggles. Only wankers ask for them though. How'd they know I'm not writing "wanker" on their arm in Mandarin? Or something tiny. A daisy. Or a star. Amateur crap. I'll do you something way better than that.'

'Could you do me a name?'

'I do good lettering. What you want?'

'Mercy.'

'Are you calling for divine intervention?' asks Lola. 'You'd be better off with a few Hail Marys.'

'It was the name of my baby,' says Nic. 'But I didn't have her. Miscarriage. I could get it here, couldn't I?' She points to her heart. 'That'd be nice.'

'Oh shite Nic! I'm sorry,' says Lola and for the first time ever in Gwen's experience of her looks embarrassed.

'S'alright. You weren't to know.'

She puts her hand on Nic's shoulder, and then goes to the kitchen counter and demonstrates the long line of cereal boxes that she has bought with a sweep of her hand, like a game show host showing off prizes.

'What kind of cereal would you like for your supper Nic?' she asks.

'The dead posh expensive one.'

'The Dorset Organic?'

'Yeah, that's the one.'

'Christ, don't you be getting hooked on that stuff, it'll bankrupt you,' says Lola. 'But this isn't supper Matt, this is tea.'

'No, it's not. Tea is what you have at four o' clock,' she says.

'What like at the Ritz? With scones? And yes Lola, I am pronouncing scones right 'cos I asked Gwen,' says Nic.

'Good to know that sort of stuff,' says Lola. 'You never know when you might have to attend a royal garden party.'

'And you need one of those cake things,' says Amy. 'A stand. With those little sandwiches with the crusts cut off. Cucumber. I hate cucumber. I'll have to borrow something off you Nic to wear though. I don't have that kind of gear.'

'Course,' says Nic. 'I'll sort you out. To be honest you can't do any worse than what you've got on.'

'I like this. It's all vintage,' says Amy.

'It smells vintage too like.'

'Me cago en la madre que te parió!'

'What the fuck was that?'

'Lola taught it me for emergencies. She wouldn't tell me what it meant but I got the impression it's not very nice.'

'Oh I know that one!' she says. 'It means, "I shit on the mother who gave birth to you."'

'Useful,' says Nic. 'Say it again Amy.'

'Does it? I like it even more now.'

'And there's this other really good one about shitting in the milk? Lol?" she says.

'Would you lot shut it? I'm starving,' says Lola.

'What you having anyway Matt?' asks Nic.

'Cocoa Pops.'

'Dead common that,' says Lola.

'It'll be tea bags in the ashtray next,' says Amy.

'You wanna be careful. It's only a short slide into sovereign rings and a Staffie,' says Nic.

'Tea is what us common northerners have at six Gwen,' says Lola. 'Not supper at eight dressed up like our Lee at his Shirley Bassey best, and not tea at four dressed up like Nic on an off day. Six. Half past pushing it. How many times do I have to tell you this? This is the 'Pool girl, get with the program and hand me my frigging Weetabix.'

Nat

She comes out of a bar and looks at her watch. She lights a cigarette and walks off down the street.

'Where you going?' she hears Popper shout. 'I thought we wass going up Lennie'ss.'

'Home.'

'What? It's only half one. Going home to see your girlfriend, are you?'

She ignores him and keeps on walking.

'For fuck'ss sake. What's the fuck'ss wrong with you? I thought we were going to Lennie's!'

'I'll ring him, and we'll do it tomorrow.'

'For fuck'ss ssake Nat. Nat! Sshe tells you when you gotta be home now doess sshe? Got a curfew, have you? That bitch's got you wrapped round her little finger. Fuck that good doess sshe? Maybe I'll have a try out mysself!'

She runs back to him and, quick as, punches him in the stomach. He bends over in pain. She takes hold of his left ear very calmly.

'Don't you never, never, say anything about Gwen ever again. Do you hear me?' No answer comes. She pulls on his ear. 'Do you hear me?'

'Yeah.'

'I am not gonna bail on you. Just 'cos Gwen's here now I'm not gonna drop you unless you drive me to it on purpose. Which you seem to be trying your best to do. Stop it. And it was Gwen who told me to say that by the way. Stop being a jealous little twat.

Calm the fuck down. Got that? And if you cut yourself again apart from in a complete emergency, then I'm gonna fucking take your knife off of you and finish the bloody job.'

She lets go of him and walks away. He slumps down on the ground coughing. She starts to run.

They're barrelling down the M6 to meet Gwen's parents. Gwen has insisted that Nic come with them too, which is just asking for trouble, but that's Gwen for you, she doesn't want to leave Nic behind on her own. And then she co-opted Petey into it too, for fuck's sake. Nat has a strange feeling in her stomach which she realises halfway there is nerves. The last time she felt nerves was on her court date way back when and then even not that much. She feels uncomfortable and when she looks over into the rearview mirror, she can see Nic chewing her nails, the ones she's just painted and she grins at her in solidarity but it's a smile as in, we shouldn't have done this, should we? Nic raises her eyebrows, and she can see that she's even more freaked out than she is. And as for Petey? She glances at him in the passenger seat. But Petey is far away, as he so often is. She tries to remember sometimes if Petey was always like this, disconnected on bad days, drifty on good, but she can't. The lad was only four when their mum died, his personality wasn't even formed yet. But she does remember when their mum hit Petey once when in one of her rages and Petey told them solemnly that it was alright, at nursery he would tell them that he'd banged his head on a cupboard. Such an old head on such small shoulders. But thinking back she and Nic were the same. They'd stood and watched their mum set fire to the chip pan on purpose aged only three. It's her first memory.

'It feels weird going down south,' says Nic, staring out the car window.

'Ever been before?' asks Gwen.

'Been to London. Didn't like it though.'

'People not nice?'

'Nobody looks at you. Or they look at you funny when you open your mouth. 'Cos they hate us. They all hate us. Will they look at me here?'

'Don't you think that's paranoid, to think that everyone hates you because you're from Liverpool?'

'Tell her Natalie.'

'They all hate us Matt. The English. We're all scallies. "Eating rats in council flats." In tracksuits. Robbing old ladies.'

'Are they all posh down your way?' asks Nic.

'What? Posh like me? Am I posh?'

'A bit. Not very.'

'That's your social status sorted out then,' she says.

'I can rest easy knowing my place,' Gwen says.

'Looking down on us?'

'There's south Nic,' Gwen says, putting her hand on Nic's hand and squeezing it, 'and then there's Somerset. They'll think you're fab.'

For a moment Nic squeezes back and then she lets go.

Constance and Vervain, Emilia and Diggory, Claude and Maisie. Grown up to be teachers and vets and environmental protesters, workers for Amnesty International, organisers of festivals, organic farmers, TV researchers. Gwen chatters away about them. She's never asked them about their schoolmates. Perhaps she doesn't want to know.

Gwen's mother Veronica is a potter, a big lady, she's like an older Gwen, warm and messy and scatty, she keeps wandering about with her glasses pushed up onto her head, wondering where she's put things. Harry is a college lecturer in Sustainable Development; he's serious looking in glasses and a collarless shirt that's way too big for him. Rosa, who Gwen obviously adores and looks up to, she flirts with her but she likes it, yeah, she would, course she would, bit of padding on her, but nothing wrong with a good bit of padding, and she knows this but she's not the kind of woman who'd exploit that; she lives just up the road with her husband Marcus who's terribly tall and likes puns, you have to watch what you say around him; one of them managing independent housing for people with disabilities, the other one with a small business selling cider. Their two children, both at the same primary school down the road that Gwen and Rosa went to. Hector who's seven and obsessed with soldiers and Cassandra who's five, a twirly whirly girl who has fallen in love with Nic, follows her around, sits next to her at the table, stroking her nail varnish and asking for her nails to get painted too. All the stripped wood floors, all the organic veg you can eat, addictions not to speed or porn, but to composting and The New Scientist. Hens in the garden, no caffeine in the tea.

She loves it here, sits on the sofa in a room littered with books, with her feet in her grey socks because she was asked to take off her shoes when entering the house, a request which amused her no end, reading D.H. Lawrence and listening to Blood on the Tracks, looking out the window at the terraced garden with the scarecrow in the veg patch, talking to Harry about the pros and cons of solar panelling.

She understands now why Gwen just lies down on the pillow and is away. It's because of the smell of lavender in the oil burner and the china Buddha in the upstairs hallway, because of the flowers in the jam jar on the pine chest in Gwen's bedroom. Because of no fear in this house and no pain, no sound of sirens, because she always knew she'd go to uni, get a good job. She grew up with the expectation of happiness, and they say, don't they, that you get what you expect. She's glad Nic's here to see it too but something in her resents it. Yeah, you'd be like Gwen too, you'd be good and kind and sweet if you'd had it this easy. Is she supposed to feel grateful then that her world bred the fight into her, bred her strength and speed like some superior animal built to survive the slings and arrows? Because she doesn't. She feels invidious.

See Nic trying to be dead polite and proper and giving up after a day when she realises that it's not necessary, that whatever posh is it doesn't require her pains to keep her elbows off the table and her skirt down past her knees.

'It's great here,' Nic says after she's been out shopping with Veronica, 'we met some bloke called Charles and your mum talked to him about dowsing. What's that Gwen? And all the little kids riding round on their bikes with their dads. They're wearing helmets. Even the dads. And I bought some of this. What is it? What do you do with it?'

'It's arnica,' says Gwen, 'you put it on bruises.'

'We're not in the Pool no more Toto,' she says.

'Fucking right. Oh sorry!' says Nic.

'This is not Buckingham Palace. You are allowed to swear here,' says Rosa, 'shit, shit, buggery. There.'

'Shite. Shite. Buggery,' says Nic.

'Only not in front of the kids.'

'Oh shite. Oh sorry. Sorry.'

'Fear not, they're outside using Petey as a climbing frame. We sometimes use fish knives Nic but not on a regular basis, and Harry is in the process of building a windmill, and I seem to have married a man who thinks that Middlemarch is appropriate to read to the children at bedtime, but how was I to know that in advance, and Veronica, well you've seen, she's Veronica, but we are actually quite normal. Gwen and I went to a comprehensive.'

'Bet it was a posh comp though.'

'It was an interesting social mix. Estate kids on one side -Tanisha-Dawn - do you remember her Gwen? She's a lawyer now. And then there were the children like us, the children of the libertarian hippy left all called things like Verbena. The meeting of the parents on sports day was especially entertaining.'

'That's not a comp then Rosa,' she says, 'that's a utopian social science experiment.'

'You can call me Rosie.'

'Ignore her. She's a terrible flirt,' says Gwen.

'You can call me anything you like girl.'

They even manage to get Nic to go out for a walk in her pristine white city girl trainers and her tight, tight jeans. Nic is huffing and puffing, and they have to keep waiting for her, but Harry doesn't seem to mind. She likes him, although part of her was wanting not to. Part of her was also hoping he'd dislike her, but he doesn't seem to. Or perhaps his manners are just very good. That's the middle classes for you – good at dissembling, burying it all under a layer of politeness.

'You're not fit for nothing. Where's your stamina our kid? You're going down the gym when we get back. I'm gonna start running again. And you're coming with. You'd be a good runner. You've got the build,' she says.

'Yes, your sister is right,' says Harry, who is slight himself in his cagoule, 'it does help if you're naturally athletic, but anyone can train, I think. I used to run half marathons and it's mostly just about putting in the practice. I've got out of the habit now, but I keep telling myself I'll start again one of these days. I used to love it. I solved all my dilemmas when I was running. Always came home with a clear head.'

'Solvitur ambulando,' she says.

'What's that Natalie?'

'"It is solved by walking."'

'Yes, that's right. Say that again. Where's that from?'

'I don't know,' she says.

'I get my fitness shagging,' says Nic. 'Oh, I'm sorry.'

'Well why not?' says Harry. 'It's a wonderful form of exercise. It's how I hope to exit the earth when my time comes.'

'Me too,' she says.

'I don't like this walking lark. I'm getting all sweaty.'

'As compared to your other fitness regime that keeps you sweat free?' she says.

'But I haven't got any clothes on then to get ruined, have I?'

'Nicola, I think that is a most pertinent and interesting point,' says Harry. 'The Greeks you know exercised in the nude.'

'I used to know people who exercised in the nude. But they got filmed, so maybe that doesn't count,' Nic says.

Nic is huffing so much now she is hard put not to laugh at her but when she gets to the top, she puts her hands on her hips and looks at the view and Nic stands next to her. Hills and fields. Beautiful.

'Good here,' Nic says, when she can breathe straight.

'It is that,' she says, looking at Gwen who is trying to disentangle a kite string with Petey. And when they finally succeed and the wind catches and bears it away, a kite shaped like a phoenix, she breathes in the air deep and wishes that this had been her childhood.

Nic

Veronica has got Gwen's hair cut into a thick bob that's going grey and Gwen's green eyes ringed with lots of eyeliner, but she's more graceful somehow, although she's heavier. It's because she's a queen and Gwen's still only a princess. I wish you'd been my mum, she wants to say to her. I wish we'd grown up here, I wish you could have looked after Petey for us.

She sits down on the bench next to her, still out of breath, the others have moved away to look at the view.

'I'd hoped you could stay longer, but I suppose you all have to get back to work. Gwen says that Natalie works very long hours in her job,' says Veronica, smiling at her.

'I suppose she does, yes,' she says. Nat gave her the lowdown before they left.

'I have never understood quite what marketing is.'

'Me neither.'

'And you work in a shop, is that right?'

'Yes. A clothes shop.'

It seemed the easiest way to go – to give an answer that once was true. Her eyes are watering in the breeze. She hopes her mascara isn't running. She dabs at her eyes with her sleeve.

'Which is why you are always so elegantly dressed.'

'I didn't know what to wear to come down here. I thought you might, you know, dress for dinner or something.'

'Oh goodness! Well maybe we should start. I'm afraid we're much less aristocratic than that. You know I consider you very lucky to have such lovely siblings. Natalie is, well, don't tell her I said this, but quite dashing! Is that very silly of me? Can you say that about a woman? It's such a ridiculously old-fashioned word but it does seem to fit her.'

That makes her smile. She likes this woman, the warmth of her that's Gwen's warmth too. She wants to lie her head down in her lap.

'She hasn't got a horse though,' she says, 'You need a horse don't you to be dashing?'

'What a wonderful idea! She would look very imposing on a horse. And what about you Nicola? Have you got a nice someone in your life? I'm sure you must have plenty to pick from, being as you are so very beautiful. I'd have killed when I was young for cheek bones like yours.'

She hadn't prepared herself for this question. Yeah, I used to live with a junkie, but your daughter rescued me from him sounds way too honest.

'Used to live with someone but it didn't work out.'

'That's a shame.'

'I'm not very good at liking the ones who might be good for me, if you know what I mean. The nice ones. I just get bored. Stupid.'

'All of us women love some excitement. I found Harry exciting when I met him, and I still do. It was a look across a crowded room at a party. The French call it "un coup de foudre". A lightning bolt. Wonderful. And then I found that going to bed with him was so very atavistic. I still find him exciting, although he is a terribly nice man too. These things are not necessarily opposites. Do you know what I believe? That one of these days you'll find someone who will open your heart up like a box, and you won't have time to judge them, it will have already happened.'

Chance would be a fine thing. Petey appears with a camera slung round his neck. He sits down next to her.

'I saw a buzzard!'

'We should have brought the binoculars,' says Veronica.

'Doesn't matter, I got some good pictures. I like it here.'

'Well, you must come down whenever you like. And that invitation extends to you too, Nicola, of course. It's been such a pleasure. Shall we go home for tea and cake? I've liberated my best teapot for this very purpose.'

It reminds her of Jill, she's big on the cake too and it's gone right to her hips. She should be friendlier to her; it would please their dad. She didn't know people still used teapots. Mad place this. But nice.

Gwen

She stands with Nic and Rosa, watching Marcus and Nat dig in the garden, as though they were court ladies, and they are their travailing knights of the greenery. Petey, Cassie and Hector crawl merrily about the treehouse so that they are backgrounded by their shrieks. It's nice to be home, comforting and easy and familiar. And the Shaws seem to like it and are liked in their turn. Was she doubting they would fit in?

'I've got another couple of rows to do,' says Nat, leaning on her spade, 'and then I think we should be making a move.' She goes back to digging and she wants to go over and lick the sweat off the back of her neck.

'I think I'm in love with your girlfriend,' Rosa says. 'Why didn't you warn me about how gorgeous she is?'

'I did try,' she says with a shrug.

'I think I might also be in love with you too, Nic,' says Rosa.

'That's alright. I like girls like you.'

'Like me how?'

'When Fern Britten was bigger, I used to tape Good Morning, and then if I had a bad day, I could watch it and imagine lying down and just resting my head on her breasts.'

Rosa puts her arm around Nic who leans her head against Rosa's ample breasts.

'It's just so relaxing,' Nic says.

'What is this? A flirting convention?' she says.

'But she's so beautiful,' says Rosa.

'Yes, she is,' she says.

Nic kisses Rosa on the cheek, disentangles herself, takes off her shoes, and goes and does a cartwheel on the lawn so that she sees a brief flash of Nic's knickers. Nic lands in a heap and laughs.

'Good God almighty!' says Rosa.

'And those are the Shaws,' she says.

It's hard to say goodbye but then it always is. The nice thing is that everyone seemed to have a good time here. Nat drives them home.

'I like it in your house,' says Petey.

'Veronica said you could come whenever you like.'

'Next weekend?' Petey says.

'Maybe not next weekend,' she says. 'But we could go up the coast somewhere if it's windy enough and fly the kite.'

'Thank you for giving me the kite,' says Petey, holding it in both hands.

'You're welcome,' she says. Nic leans forward and puts her hands on Petey's shoulders and squeezes them.

She's in a cab. The taxi driver asks her if she's a cockney. She resists the urge to tell him to fuck off. She's sure Nic or Nat would but she's not capable of it. No, she says, I'm just confused, and he starts going on about bad drivers instead. This city will never be hers. She will never belong here. She will always be on the outside, looking in. She sees it in the way the mothers at the school look at her, even the nice ones. Some of them, the more in your face ones, actually tell her.

'You don't belong here girl. You should go back where you come from. Mind your own business. Sort your own kids out. Leave mine out of it.'

'Mrs Martin. I was just trying to tell you that Liam is struggling with his reading.'

'Are you saying that's my fault? I'm working fifty hours a week. I've got no time to sit with him.'

'No, of course I'm not saying it's your fault.'

'Well, it's not. It's yours. Yours. You're the teacher. You teach him to read.'

When she walks into her classroom some mornings and looks at the sea of little faces, she wonders what hope they have. What sort of jobs will they get? Will a single one of them make ever make it into higher education? What is the point of all this? Giving them hopes that rewards are just, that there is a system that is fair, that if you knuckle down, obey the rules and are good, then it will all turn out right. That crime doesn't pay and that working hard does. And then she goes home at night to her drug dealing girlfriend.

'Gotta nice fella, have you?'

She never talks about this here. She wonders if they know. Not that she hides it, just it's important to have a private life she knows now. Just like Nic. Just like Nat.

'Yes, I have,' she says and hears in her own ears just how posh she sounds.

'From round here?'

'Yes.'

'Oh aye. Well just make sure he treats you nice.'

Sometimes she thinks that they don't believe that she will stick it. None of them. They all think she'll crack and run back home. Teachers, parents, kids. Popper. Maybe even Nic. Lola. Maybe even Nat.

'Miss, Miss. What was it like where you were born?'

'Are there cows Miss?'

'Do you like it round here Miss?'

Does she? Is "like" the right word? Sometimes there's a wind off the Mersey that blows chip papers around her feet and bowls empty coke cans around corners, and she thinks of rolling down a hill, of chewing grass and making noises through it, of climbing through hedges, of boosting Rosie onto the back of the horse that lived in the field at the end of their road and jumping and scrabbling up behind her. She passes a KFC and a group of scrappy teenagers spitting and smoking skunk that stinks. And she's ungrateful, isn't she? There are nice bits of this city, there are parks and trees, it's not so bad. And home isn't perfect anyway. Every place has its bad and good bits. So why does she judge this place so harshly? Will it always fall short in some way? Will it never quite feel like a home? Which is wrong obviously, because her home is Nat, for however long that might last. And Nic too now. It's probably stupid to rely on that but she can't help it. She is addicted perhaps to Shaws.

In a week or so they will have been together nine months. She knows what Lola would say. I told you, she would say, I warned you about her. Yeah, she was warned. Yeah, she should have known better. A woman who is rarely there and she pretend she doesn't mind. A woman who deals drugs and she pretends it's all fine with her. A woman with a reputation. She spends more time with Nic than she does with Nat. Ascertain if she is in love with you. How is she supposed to know that if she won't ever say? It's not so hard to say, is it? She has never said she loves her since, knowing she will get nothing back but that look on her face. That gone away somewhere else look. She doesn't want to be the reason for that look, she wants to be part of the reason that look goes away. So she swallows it down. She swallows all of it down.

'Does it bother you?' says Lola.

'Does what bother me?'

She looks at Lola's face as she stands in a shop with her, watching her flick through racks. She hasn't the energy for this today. Lola has the small frame she got off her mum and is body dysmorphic in relation to her. She is always trying to get her into stuff that fits her own miniature hips. It makes shopping with her amusing but tiring. Lola is wearing a yellow blouse with her long hair swept back with a hairband and her jeans and her red jacket. She always looks so co-ordinated. There must be something I like, Gwen thinks, about skinny, pretty, beautifully dressed, Scouse street-smart girls. She feels shit today; she's not sleeping great. She wants to go into Waterstones and make herself an igloo out of books and sit in it.

'You know what I'm saying.'

'I have no idea what you're on about. Can we get some lunch? I'm getting a headache.'

She can hear herself starting to whine like a child would. Why do these places never have anywhere you can sit?

'What do you think I'm on about?'

Lola holds up a top against her and then puts it back on the rack.

'I just told you. I have no idea. I have an idea though about my need for something to eat. Soup? What I need is a muffin. Multiple muffins.'

If she was a child, it would be better, it would be permissible to slump down on the floor. She could even hide under the racks. It might be nice under there. The feel of the clothes on her face. Nat says that Popper has a wardrobe full of old coats that he sits in because he's into Narnia. She finds that hard to believe but maybe it's a good idea.

'Nat.'

'What about Nat?'

'She can't be easy to live with.'

'She's fine. Yellow suits you Lol. There aren't many people who can get away with yellow. You look like a miniature human sun.'

Lola stops flicking and fixes her with a hard look from her big brown eyes.

'That's how I know you're a real Scouser. That look. It's a little bit mob. Blueberry muffins.'

'Don't mess me around here. I'm asking you about Nat.'

'She's Nat. I can't change her. You can't change other people.'

'That's very mature.'

'I've got a headache.'

'I'm worried about you Gwen. Why is that wrong? I see you and you're not always you and I'm concerned.'

Lola starts flicking again, in an ever more manic fashion.

'What do you mean I'm not me?'

'More far away. I dunno. You're just different.'

'And this is a bad thing? What's wrong with changing?'

'You know what I mean.'

'No, I don't.'

'Or you don't want to. It's like you're growing armour or something. I'm not getting at you but you're not like us.'

'You mean I'm soft. And you warned me.'

'No, I don't think you're soft. When did I say that? You're just not like us. We grew up here, we're different from you. We should be different. It does something to you living here.'

They reach the end of the rack and she, relieved, turns to go but no, Lola is onto the next rail. How long can this process possibly go on for?

'Well big cities are different. Liverpool is different. It's the wild, wild west.'

'Really? Never would have thought of that on my own.'

Lola holds a skirt up against her and tuts.

'Take this.' She hands her the skirt. 'You're not listening.'

'Yes, I am. I just don't know why you're having a go, Lola.'

'I'm not having a go. I'm just trying to talk to you.'

Gwen looks at a display dummy in a pair of tight red fake snakeskin trousers.

'Those trousers are horrible,' she says. 'Even on you they'd look horrible. Why are we in this shop for pixies? Nothing's going to fit me and no, I don't know what you're trying to say to me Lola.'

She shoves the skirt back on the rack.

'Right then. If you're gonna be difficult.'

Lola stands in front of her with her arms crossed. They've

all of them got this thing. This don't mess with me thing. She should practice hers in front of the mirror, see if she can get that iron into her soul, knife blades into her eyes.

'Does it bother you? Where she is. Who she's with. Come on Gwen, do I have to spell it out?'

'I don't want to talk about it. That's how I deal with it Lola. It's called denial. It's a useful psychological defence mechanism.'

'Gwen.'

'Please. Can we just get some fucking food?'

She turns her back and walks away. She goes towards the escalator, checking her shoelaces as she does so. She has always been afraid of getting stuck in one. She doesn't look back for Lola but goes down to the ground floor and deliberately hides among the handbags, half thinking that Lola might just bypass her and leave the shop. Childish revenge tactics. Ridiculous. She sees Lola walk past and then double back.

'These prices are shite,' says Lola, fingering the nearest handbag. 'Let's go get some fucking food.'

Nat comes home early, and she can see that she's been drinking vodka, there's something about vodka that makes her different. She can see how hard she could be. How hard she must be sometimes when she's not with her. She lies down on the sofa and looks up at the ceiling.

Nat

'Hass sshe ponced up your flat?' Popper had said, and she could see that it was time to walk away, that if she stayed out, this could turn into one of those nights. There have been far too many nights like this when she has walked forwards not back, into the storm, not away from it. But not no more. This must be maturity. Girlfriend. Proper girlfriend. Living with her. Long term. There's a points system. When is she getting the star?

It's all good, isn't it? Nic's finally getting herself sorted. She's here where he can keep an eye on her. Gwen's her best girl. Nic and her are company for each other. Money coming in. Not too much stress. It's all good. So she comes home and lies on the couch and it's so early the pubs haven't even shut yet and she can't tell if this has been a good decision or not, the coming home, because Gwen's still up even though Nic isn't and she kinda wishes she wasn't. She wants to be on her own. In her own flat. And then she is pissed off with herself for thinking this. Her flat. Should be theirs. There is nowhere to be on her own anymore and mostly she likes that, but not tonight. She feels surrounded. By women who she cares about too much. Having one of them here was bad enough but she is so stupid that she hadn't accounted for what it would be like with Nic here too. The responsibility she feels, all over again. It's a familiar feeling though, she's had it since she was a kid. She grew up too quick. They all did. Watching their mum wailing in the street and then the bloody bizzies coming and arresting her. Watching them put her in the police car, handcuffs on. The Social coming round and talking about Care. Part of her, part of Nic too she knew, thinking please take us, this is too much for us. Their dad did the best he could, but he was out at work most of the time, trying to put bread on the table. They were left with the unpredictable. They lived with it. She remembers what Nic said after their mum died and she asked her if she missed her. 'No,' she said, 'I say thank you to God every fucking day.' She missed their mum more than Nic ever did, she still misses her, the mum from the nice days, the mum who fussed over them, made sure they were turned out nice, taught them to cook and sew. She wishes she had had a better life.

'Do you want a drink of anything?'

She comes out of her reverie.

'No ta.'

Gwen

Nat just lies there with her arm up behind her head, smoking a spliff. She is scared to ask her anything else. Is this why other people calm down around her, back off, go quiet? Because they don't want to mess with her? Because she is frightening? Maybe it's not that she doesn't get into fights. Maybe it's that nobody wants to get into fights with her. Fights they won't win. She always thought that her calm rubbed off on others. Now she's not so sure.

'Good night,' she says, 'I'm going to bed.'

She kisses her on the cheek. Nat doesn't even look at her. She goes into their bedroom and takes off her clothes and puts on Nat's t-shirt and gets into the bed and puts the duvet over her head and thinks about the not thinking that she does and how much it has become a habit. Sometimes she wonders how she has ended up here. It seemed such an easy decision to make to come and live with her, it seemed so right. But maybe that just meant she is stupid not to have thought things through properly. And what is mine here? What is mine? Too many books. My duvet. Some kitchen stuff. The curtains I bought and a couple of cushions. A picture or two. Your furniture. Your bed. Your flat. Your city. Your history. Your family. Back in the other room is an argument that will happen if she steps back into it, the first real argument, the big one, and possibly, therefore, the last. You will never leave, she thinks, and I have always known this, and I didn't care before so why now? And no, she thinks, no, no more thinking. And she curls herself up. And does not sleep for hours thinking about what her friends are doing. They are working in London.

They are teaching in nice village schools. They are moving home and starting families and buying flats and making plans. They have emigrated to Australia. They are lost in Thailand. They contact her and she sketches out a life for them, as she has sketched one out for everyone she has left behind. They have moved on and where has she moved to? Nat will not change. Why should she change? She used to be so insouciant about it all. But now she's not. But that's her secret. She thinks to herself that Nat is entitled to her secrets too. Except that Nat's secrets are her own and Nat is her secret. She is never going to be able to tell her mother or her father. They are never going to be able to live a normal life. Whatever that is. Is she ashamed of Nat? Is Nat ashamed of her? Oh bollocks.

In the morning, she goes into the other room, and sees her asleep on the sofa. Her clothes are on the floor in a neat pile. She stands over her. You are wonderful but this hurts and I don't know what to do. She puts her hand in her hair and strokes her head. She kneels next to her and puts her mouth onto the pulse on her neck and Nat stirs.

'Hi. Sorry. Didn't mean to wake you up.'

'Mmm. Come here.'

Nat turns towards her, and she lies down to face her on the sofa, and Nat puts her arms around her.

'You'll get dead arm.'

'Mmm.'

'Would you like a cup of tea?'

'Mmm. Lovely girl,' Nat says and kisses her. Kiss of absolution. Maybe she is becoming her religion. Her kisses absolve all. She stops her questions with her mouth. Nat's body is her off switch.

Later she goes down to the shops to buy some food. Nat has had to go out in a hurry. But where? She stands in a queue for the tills and thinks that most of all it's her curiosity about it that disturbs her. She wasn't about to tell Lola that. Or anyone for that matter. She wants to know but she's worried that if she asks and she tells her, her curiosity won't be sated, but will expand to fit the available space, she'll want to know details. She'll want to know it all, even if it hurts her and made her feel sick at the same time. And then what? How could you go forward if you knew everything? She would have to leave, and she can't imagine being without her now. And yet where is this going? World's stupidest question. She can even see this in Nic's face sometimes. And the undercurrent with Popper is as charged as ever. It's electric. The air is full of spikes. Sometimes all that comes out of his mouth is vitriol. Sometimes not. She wonders if Nat ever does belt him one. It must be tempting. He gives her a headache. She's started to get them.

'Getting any writing done Gwen?'

'Some.'

'Time on your handss yeah?'

'Some.'

'Don't wanna talk then. Alright.'

And then she will try to make the peace.

'Yeah Pop, doing some. How about you?'

'What'ss it to you?'

'You were talking to me remember?'

'Don't get narky. Wass only assking.'

'I'm not narky, I'm tired. I've got a lot on at work. I bring a lot home.'

'Yousse are working hard then?'

'Yes.'

'Proper job kidda. That musst be nice. Ssaving the world. Do them kids have nitss?'

'Sometimes.'

'Have you got them? Better check. Well, if you don't wanna talk to me…'

'I just have been.'

'Narky.'

'I'm not fucking narky.'

'Didn't know you ssweared Gwen.'

'Swore.'

'What you correcting my fucking Englissh now? What do you think I am? Thick? Bet you think I'm thick. Bet you do. Sstuck up bitch. Pissss off.'

'Piss off yourself.'

'Narky cow.'

And off he bounces, with his evil smile. Grrrr. So tiring, the little shithead. And saddening. She wishes she could talk to him, turn some key in him that will get him to settle down around her. She feels sad some of the time, but it's difficult to say why. She stands in the living room in the moonlight at 3 a.m. and pushes up the sash. She kneels down and rests her cheek on the sill. She would like to throw things out of the window. What could she throw? Probably Popper if he was here. He would be easy to throw. Little druggy bastard. Why does Nat put up with him? Why doesn't she ask her? Why doesn't she ask her anything? Is she scared of her too? Maybe. A little. Is there anybody who isn't apart from Nic? What could she throw? What have they going spare? She turns to looks at the room. Books. The shelves and shelves of them, the piles of them, no order at all, Nat's and hers all jumbled up together, but she can't bring herself to do that. She needs to do something with herself though. She feels so twitchy. She could go and wake Nic up but that doesn't seem fair, even though Nic probably wouldn't mind. She could watch a film. She could do some school stuff. Read a book. Eat something. She could ring her. She could ring her and ask her where he is. What you up to? But there are rules aren't there, even if you never say them out loud. And it's Saturday night. Not a good night to call. Never a good night to call. She finds some paper instead. And a pen. Always safe with a paper and a pen.

Nat

The distance between the door of the house and the door of the flat, she thinks, how do you measure that? What is the measurement of the anticipation of quietude? She takes her boots off in the hall, puts her coat on the peg, and looks into the bedroom. Where's she got to? She goes down the hall and into the front room. Gwen is asleep with her head on the table. There are books all over the floor, she has pulled them all off the bookshelves, they're all over the carpet. And she has started to put them back, arrange them according to colour. A rainbow span. The blue is especially beautiful. The green is a work in progress. The yellow is a small section. Finished. She's into the white now. And from the light fitting a few white paper snowflakes are hung from pink thread. She brushes them with her fingers. The table is piled with bits of crumpled paper. She picks one up and smooths it down. *A sharp undoing*, it says, and then:

> *I said*
> *Give me a reason not to care*
> *About you*
> *Give me one good reason*
> *But you shook your head*
> *And in your eyes I saw birds*
> *I saw starlings at dusk*
> *I saw a tern*
> *Rising and falling on the breeze*
> *I saw the long slow stall*

Beggars Would Ride

*Of a white owl
In the moonlight
And there was no reason
Not one
That could ever be good enough.*

She sits down to look at her. She gets the scissors and tries to cut out a paper chain of Christmas trees like she used to be able to do once, but she's lost the knack. She wonders what else she's lost the knack for. She wants to put her hand in her hair, but she doesn't want to wake her. She gets the paper, *A sharp undoing*, and writes, *the one with yesterdays, the one with futures*. She puts it her pocket. Fuck it, she thinks. She picks her up and carries her to bed, and yeah, she is too heavy to carry, but it's a comforting weight that she loves, and she takes her clothes off and gets in with her.

'Hi,' she says.

'Hi.'

Gwen turns over and goes back to sleep. She slides down and puts her hand on her belly. All the hot words she thinks, all of the prayers, and for the first time in many, many years she wants to pray. For aid. She wants to pray for aid.

Nic

She sometimes thinks about the ducklings that were on the mobile that she bought to put above the crib. Little yellow fluffy ducklings. She hadn't found out if it was a boy or a girl at that point, so yellow seemed like a safe bet. She was all sorted out – nappies, crib, the tiny clothes, some of which she'd made herself. And Robbie was into the idea, although he'd been shocked at first. She wasn't even going to have it, wasn't even going to tell him but she'd made the mistake of telling Natalie who'd gone off on one big style, all Catholic. She hadn't been expecting that. She was persuaded easily, well, not really persuaded because, secretly, she'd been in two minds anyway. Which was probably why she'd told her.

The Dr in the hozzy said that it wasn't her fault, it was just something that happened sometimes. Of course it was her fault. Of course it was something she did. Now and then she still goes and lights a candle for the baby and says an act of contrition. She's never talked to anyone about it. Maybe she should have seen a counsellor or somebody. The only way she could deal with it was to bin everything the moment she got back from the hospital. Pretend like it never happened. She got Robbie to chuck out the crib. She doesn't even know where he took it. The dump at Otterspool? Or did he flog it, along with everything else? It doesn't matter. But sometimes, just sometimes, she wishes she'd kept the ducklings.

Nat

She comes home to see a gaggle of girls dancing wildly, giggling stupidly, and she leans against the door jamb and watches them mess about until they fall over and become hysterical.

'That's hydroponics for you. I'd pay to watch this.'

She drags Gwen up.

'I'm borrowing your girl, if that's OK.'

She closes them into the bedroom.

'I think I must be very stoned because I've been hallucinating gerberas,' says Gwen.

'At least it's not gerbils.'

'You're home early.'

'Needs must.'

'When the devil drives.'

She bites her so hard by mistake that she makes Gwen's lip bleed, she can taste the blood.

'Oh fuck, I'm sorry. Sorry. Sorry.'

Gwen bites her back so hard she has a split lip for days. She wears it like a badge of honour.

She redresses Gwen and takes her back into the front room.

'What's happened to your mouth?' says Nic.

'None of your business,' she says, and Nic laughs at her.

'Each to their own,' Nic says.

'I don't think I can make it home,' says Amy.

'We could have a sleepover?' says Gwen.

'More like a pass out,' says Lola, who can no longer even stand up.

She makes little beds in the living room for Lola and Amy

and Nic out of cushions and pillows and duvets and blankets, sorts them out. Then she lies down with Gwen and puts the DVD of 'All about my Mother' on, Gwen passed out on her arm, Lola snoring, Amy sleeping on her face, Nic talking to herself in her sleep. How fucking lovely, room full of women, harem. Lola? Lola is a fine girl, and she can't remember now why she never did. Amy? Yeah, why not, although she's not that keen on tattoos. Anyway, she's seen the size of her boyfriend. Nicola? If she wasn't her sister? Too skinny still.

The taste of blood in her mouth, the pain in her lip, the lump in her throat, and the way the film goes up and then down and then up, like a roller-coaster, and she doesn't cry at the deaths, she cries with laughter at the life, and the tears bathe her mouth. Gwen? Yes.

And yes/And yes/My girl's eyes are nothing like the sun/They are
They are
The colour of
Oak, no, birch, no, but maybe her skin is the colour of the bark, but too papery?
Need more trees

'Nic, wanted to talk to you about something.'

She sits down in her chair, starts to skin up. Nic is reading a magazine. She likes her magazines does Nic. Never could understand why herself. Vacuous nonsense. She has argued that point before, it has to be said. The repetitive nature of conversation. Especially between siblings. Discuss.

'Worst words in the English language those are,' Nic says.

She clears her throat.

'Apart from when you go for a blood test and they say, "Do you normally have problems getting a vein?" Not keen on them either,' Nic says.

'It's about work,' she says. 'Your work.'

'Yeah?'

She can see her go immediately on to the defensive. Might as well be straight about it. There doesn't seem to be any better option.

'What you going to do about it?'

Nic stands up, quick as, crosses her arms.

'Do you want me out of here?'

'That's not what I'm saying.'

'Cos I can find somewhere else to stay thanks very much.'

'I know you could. It's just I had an idea. Sit down.'

'What?'

She remains standing.

'Sit down Nic.'

She sits but glowers at her, still with her arms crossed, looking like she might bolt at any moment. Or hit her. She sometimes wonders if she came to that with Robbie but hasn't asked. They never came to blows when they were kids, but she thinks it might have been better if they had, relieved the tension. All there was in that house was tension, the smell of bleach, sadness and words not said. At least until their mum died anyway.

'I know this woman. Ingrid, her name is. Runs a shop in town. You've probably been there. Glimmer. It's called Glimmer. Not too keen on that but there you go. Do you know it?'

'Yeah, I've been in there.'

'And what did you think of it?'

'It's not a bad shop,' Nic says, looking like she has to force the words out. 'Expensive like.'

'What's that thing you used to say to me when we were kids and you worked in that shite shop down the arcade?'

'Don't remember.'

'"Crap zips,"' you said, '"no decent buttons. Threads hanging off and all".'

'Cheap shite. And Fat Louise in Lycra that showed her rolls put me right off my food. She was nice though to me.'

'Well, I was wondering… if you wanted to…'

'For fuck's sake, out with it Natalie!'

'This Ingrid, she's got staff problems. One of her girls on maternity leave and another one's just gone off with glandular fever. She's basically running the shop on her own. Could do with some help.'

'And you want me to go and help her? What am I? A fairy fucking godmother?'

'Just thought you might not mind it. Would do for a while. So that you can have a think about things. What you reckon? She says the pay's not great, but you get a 30% discount. You can work the hours you want, more or less. And you'd like her, I think. She's an interesting person.'

'She a customer of yours, is she?'

'I just know her from around and about.'

'Oh aye.'

'You could go and meet her if you fancied it. Check her out. And you can stay here. As long as you want. We like having you. Save on rent and that.'

'Stop hassling me.'

She stands up and goes over to the sofa and sits down next to Nic, passes her the spliff, puts the ashtray on the coffee table, leans back. Nic comes off red alert, tucks her feet up on the sofa.

'Might be OK,' Nic says.

'Gotta be better than… .'

'Don't.'

'I haven't, have I?'

'Don't know what's got into you today. My legs need waxing. I like Gwen,' Nic says.

'Were any of those thoughts related to each other?'
'Just saying.'
'She likes you too.'
'You sure you don't mind me staying?'
'Course I'm sure.'
'You'll have to keep on muffling the shagging.'
'Nic!'
'You blushed there.'

Nic leans her head against her shoulder, and she nearly reaches up to stroke her hair as though she was Gwen. Her phone goes from the other side of the room. She gets up to answer it.

'Alright Dad?' she says.

'You'd better come down,' he says. 'Right away.'

Petey's bedroom is a complete tip. Well, it's never been what you'd call tidy. Nic used to have a sort out now and then when they were kids, try to get all the fossils and shells and bits of twig under control. But now. There's stuff on every available surface and stuff scribbled on the walls and a great chaos of art things and drawings and paintings all over the floor. In the middle of it all is Petey in his underpants feverishly drawing with charcoal on bits of paper. When Petey sees her, he seems overjoyed.

'Nat! Nat! What you doing here?'

But he doesn't get up and he doesn't look her in the eye, and he doesn't stop his manic drawing. Their dad's got an appointment for him but how she's going to break it to him she doesn't know.

She stands over him at a loss at what to say or do.

'I've got all this stuff to show you,' says Petey, not looking up from his drawing, 'I've been doing loads and loads. All the time. Drawing all the time.'

'Bit of a mess in here lad,' she says eventually.

'Yeah! I know! Been changing stuff round, haven't finished yet, it's gonna be brilliant, much better. See I'm gonna put the bed over there instead. Maybe you can help me!'

She kneels down next to him but doesn't touch him.

'Dad says you've been having a problem sleeping the last couple of nights. Is that right?'

'I don't want to sleep. I've got too much to do.'

'Have you been to school?'

'Yeah.'

'You haven't, have you?'

'Don't tell Dad. Don't tell Jill!'

Petey grabs her arm with his grubby hand. It reminds her of Popper. He needs a bath and all and she wishes he could do that, resolve things easily like she did when she and Petey and Nic were kids, and their mum was off on one. Make him take a bath, make him eat veg, walk him to school where he'd stand at the edge of the playground looking up at the sky with all the other kids running around him. Petey's still only a boy, things shouldn't be like this.

'What about food?' she says.

'You're just like them. They keep asking me this stuff too, just like I'm a little kid. I'm not a little kid you know. I haven't got time to go to school. Too much to do. Oh look, this one, this is great this one.'

He shows her a drawing of a horse rearing up.

'Great.'

He goes back to drawing. She watches him in silence, sitting there on the floor next to him, until Nic puts her hand on her shoulder, and she looks up at her. Can she see the desperation in her eyes? Probably. She recognises something similar in Nic's. Petey sees her.

'Nic! Nic! You came too!' he says but doesn't leap up to hug her like he normally would.

Nic clears a space and sits down on the bed. She pats it.

'Come sit down here with me,' she says.

Petey is reluctant but he does sit next to Nic. She grasps his hand between hers. She sits down on the other side of him and there Petey is sandwiched between them, just like he always was.

'Sweetheart, Dad gave us a call 'cos he's worried about you,' says Nic.

'I'm alright.'

'But you're not sleeping lad,' she says.

'I don't need to sleep. I've got too much to do.'

She can feel the energy radiating off him, the compulsion he has not to stop what he was doing.

'I know you've got lots to do, I know,' says Nic. 'But we think you just need to calm down. Sleep. Eat. We think maybe you need to go see the doctor just so he can give you something to help you sleep.'

Why didn't she think of that? For fuck's sake. She's useless.

'I don't wanna go!' and Petey tries to get up, but Nic holds him to her tight and she puts a hand on Petey's shoulder to keep him from bolting.

'Sweetheart, I know you don't wanna go but we think you need to,' says Nic. 'Will you go for us yeah? For me and Natalie? We'll go with you. Won't take long. And then we'll come straight back.'

'We'll help you sort it out in her and then it'll look really good. Get all your art stuff better organised so you can do more work,' she says.

'Better work?'

'Yeah,' she says. 'So will you come up the doctors with us then? I've got the car. We'll be quick.'

'And then we'll come straight back? 'Cos I'm dead busy.'

'Course,' says Nic. 'Shall we find some clothes for you then? You can't go out like that! You'll catch your death!'

'Alright,' says Petey to her surprise and gets off the bed and starts looking in the mess for clothes. Nicola takes hold of her hand, she hasn't held her hand for years, she's surprised at how soft it is.

She has a low tolerance for doctors' offices, and she can feel Nic stiffen beside her as they approach this one. It looks alright, but then you never can tell. They all get ushered into an office – her, Nic, Petey, their dad, and there aren't enough chairs to sit on and so they make Petey sit down in front of the doctor's desk and, as for the rest of them, they all choose to stand behind him, as though they are a guarding wall. She's not claustrophobic like Popper, she's never minded mean spaces, coped well with prison as a result, but there's something about this office that makes her want to go for the door and check that it hasn't locked behind them. She makes herself take a deep breath, realises that she's been holding it in. Next to him their dad is looking at his shoes, on the other side Nic is picking at his nails. Petey, she can see, is finding the whole sitting down thing a challenge. Their mum was the same, couldn't sit still when she was like this. She is glad the doctor is a woman but she's not sure why. It's impossible to see from this angle what she has written on the pad. You can never read their writing anyway. Maybe they learn it in medical school.

'You're gonna stick my son on a psych ward aren't you?' says their dad and she admires him for getting to the bloody crunch of it all.

'There are a number of options that we might decide on.'

'Then I'd like you to pay us the courtesy of enumerating them in language which we can actually decipher without the aid of the DSM,' she says. 'No, strike that, I'll suggest them to you. Either you'll do nothing which I judge unlikely in the current circumstances. Or you'll whack him full of anti-psychotics and tranquilizers and then you'll send Petey home with us to see if that will knock him into the middle of next week. Also unlikely.

Or you'll do the same thing on a psych ward on a voluntary basis. Or you'll section two him and keep him there for "his own safety". Right?'

'Er, yes,' says the doctor and looks at her for the first time, 'that is a rough idea.'

She's always preferred women but this one she can see is hard as nails. She knows that next to her Nic wants to take her stiletto off and stick it in this woman's eye. She'll help her. Their dad's hands are shaking. She puts her hand on one of them and Nic puts her hand on their dad's arm. There was something like this in his past somewhere? Oh yeah, that's it. Day of their mum's funeral. After she'd chucked greasy Father Doyle out the house for refusing to offer special dispensation to suicides, since Petey had been worrying that his mum's eyeballs were melting in a fiery furnace for all eternity. And then they had sat at the table altogether and fed Petey what was left of the fruitcake. It reminds her of that.

'Well get on with it and make a decision then. Otherwise, I'm walking out with him right now and you will have to answer for the consequences. Presuming you're competent. You are competent right?'

'I can...'

'You can call the police? You can enforce something? I know the police. I know all sorts of people. Get on with the job that you're paid to do and stop pissing us around.'

The doctor hesitates a moment too long and then she picks up the phone. Nobody relaxes.

'Dad?' says Nic, as their dad and her come back into the room where Nic and Petey are waiting, sitting on the floor. Petey is drawing rapidly in a sketchbook that Nic has brought along with them. She should have thought of that. Petey's hair needs cutting. Brushing. Washing too.

'They'll keep it voluntary for now,' says their dad.

'OK,' says Nic.

She sits down on the floor across from Petey. So does their dad and she can hear his knees crunch.

'This room is safer for you now yeah?' she says to Petey.

'Yeah,' says Petey, still drawing, even though she doubts he means it. She doesn't want to think this way, but the lad needs to get some meds in fast.

'But what if you have to go to the toilet?' she says.

'I can't. Don't know what's in there. At home I went in the garden. Sorry Dad.'

'Don't you worry about that,' says their dad.

'The doctor that just came, he seemed OK, didn't he?' she says.

'Sort of,' says Petey.

'He thinks that for a couple of days, that he would like you to go into the hospital and stay there.'

'No! No! No!' shouts Petey, and he tries to crawl away into a corner. She catches him and holds him tight. His long thin arms, his long thin legs. No meat on him at all. Gwen would feed him up, what has Jill and their dad been up to? Why haven't they caught this before? They should have. But that's just her trying to wriggle out of the guilt that's building in her shoulders, stiffening up like she's overdone it in the gym. Petey wriggles, trying to escape her grip but she hangs on.

'I would never let anything bad happen to you,' she says. 'Not never. Would I?'

'We all love you more than anything,' says Nic, which has always been the case.

'We do,' says their dad with force, like he's taking an oath.

'Petey,' she says, as his brother calms slightly, 'I'm gonna explain all about what's gonna happen. Right now we're gonna go get into my car, all of us, and we're gonna drive up the hospital. It's not far. There will be some nurses there, really nice nurses, and they will give you a room and show you where everything is.'

'You can take your new pencils,' says Nic. 'And we put some things in this bag for you that are yours in case you had to go. There are t-shirts and jeans and pants and socks. Your best hoody. And 'jamas. And shampoo and toothpaste. And lots of paper. Everything. Just in case.'

'It'll be like being in a sort of hotel,' she says, 'And every day we'll come and visit you.'

'This is just to make sure you're safe, lad,' says their dad. 'You'll be completely safe.'

'It won't be for long,' says Nic, 'they'll give you some meds. Good meds.'

'Which colour pills?' says Petey, just like their mum used to. She feels something on her arms and realises they are goosebumps.

'When we get up there, I'll ask,' she says. 'I'll check. Are you ready to go? I know you don't want to. But we promise you that this will help you and very soon you'll feel better and be able to come home again.'

'We'll sort out your room all nice for when you come back,' says Nic.

'There is another option though,' she says into Petey's ear. 'We could take you and put you in the car right now and run away and nobody would never find us. But I can't promise you that the things in your head will not get worse. I can't promise you that. What if we're on top of some mountain and they get worse, and I can't stop them? What will we do then?'

'But we can promise you that in the hospital they will go,' says Nic.
'I promise son,' says their dad. 'I promise they'll help you there.'
'We all promise,' says Nic. 'Will you come with us?'
'I'm scared,' says Petey.

'Look at me' says Nic. 'Look at me Petey. It's all gonna be fine. Nothing bad's gonna happen. I know you're scared but you also dead brave. You're very, very brave. And you're gonna have to be brave now. You are safe. We won't let nothing bad get you. Do you reckon anything bad would be able to get past this great big sister of yours? 'Cos I don't.'

'Am I gonna be? Am I gonna be like me mum?'

'No, you won't love,' says Nic quick as. 'You won't have to be like that. We'll make sure you get the right things to make you better.'

'Am I gonna die?'

'No,' she and Nic say simultaneously.

'Promise,' says Petey.

'Promise,' they all say back.

'I'm gonna get you up now lad and I'm not gonna let you go 'til we get there. Alright? Can you drive Dad?'

'Course.'

'You can do this Petey, I know you can,' says their dad who is almost crying.

She stands up, pulling Petey up with her. She hugs him tight to her, not so much for fear of Petey escaping, but for her own good, needing to hold it all together, and together they all walk out of the room.

Nic

Psychiatric hospitals. She fucking hates them. Sometimes their dad used to take them to visit their mum. Things weren't so good back then in terms of décor so that's an improvement at least. The walls here are painted a pale cream and it doesn't stink of boiled food and the room they're in while the psych talks to Petey is a calm empty one with pictures on the walls of flowers and soft sofas. But what flowers? She should ask their dad, he knows about that stuff, except their dad looks broken. She should be angry for not getting this in hand earlier but she's not because she gets how much he didn't want to see it. She doesn't want to see it either, she'd have been the same. Maybe she looks broken too, but she doesn't feel like that inside. Inside a part of her has turned cold as razor blades and the other part wants to run screaming out the place. She knows that Natalie doesn't like locked wards either. She looks at her. Her tough sister has no expression on her face at all. Would Gwen know her well enough by now to know that she's really upset? She wishes in a way that they had brought Gwen with them because she'd like to hold hands with her. But that's a stupid thought, they need to keep her out of this as much as possible. And she's only a soft girl after all, she doubts she's ever been in a place like this. She hopes not at least. The psych seems alright as psychs go. Natalie used to say that psych was short for psychopath. When he hitches up his trousers, he has socks with yellow and black bumble bee stripes on and it makes her want to laugh. But that could well become hysterics. His shoes are black brogues and look expensive. He must earn a fair bit off the back of other's misery. If she tells their dad that, he'll take it and run with it. So maybe not. That last thing she wants to do is leave Petey behind, but they have no choice. A nurse comes to get him now and tells him that, if he wants, she's got some sandwiches he can have.

'What kind?' says Petey and she thinks then that things might be OK after all.

'Ham or tuna,' says the big nurse who needs her roots touching up.

'What kind of bread?'

'White or brown.'

'I like the crusts cut off.'

'No problem. I'll do it for you. Would you like to come with me? I'll get you something to drink too and show you where you're going to sleep.'

She knows that, once they get some food down him, they'll dose him up with something so strong that it'll probably knock him out. Some bloody anti-psychotic. Hopefully some diazepam in there for good measure. She and Natalie, they used to know the names of all the drugs and all the doses too. She's glad to have forgotten them. She bets that Natalie hasn't. See, being brainy isn't all that.

Nat

She and Nic stand at the back of their dad's garden in Chester, under a tree sharing a spliff. They've had their tea. Jill makes good chips. But then again, so did their mum. She looks up at the tree. It's a sycamore. Well, they say it's their dad's garden but really the house belongs to Jill. Their dad moved down here while she was in prison, out of their suburban council house. It's not a bad house this and their dad seems happy now. Well, apart from having a son who's locked up in a mental hospital. Must be hereditary then, at the back of her mind she's always wondered if she was going to get it. Sounds likes it's measles, something you can catch. Her poor brother, she felt so bad for him when they were driving away but she knows he's in the best place. She hopes Petey doesn't feel betrayed. She wonders if she might, were that to happen to her. No good to think about that.

She passes the spliff to Nic, takes her shoes and socks off, and hauls herself up into the tree, climbing up as far as the branches' weight will take her. The sway of it, the feeling of being enveloped by the leaves. She's always liked trees, taught Petey to climb too. Has Petey hidden in this tree in the past? Pretty likely. She climbs back down, remembering herself instructing Petey about this being the more difficult part, and at the fork between the first two branches, puts her hand out for Nic.

'For fuck's sake! I can't.'

'You can.'

'Never was no good at climbing.'

'I remember.'

She watches her thinking about it, which is a surprise in itself. She has often assumed over the years that their thought processes were similar in some ways, because of their childhoods, but that's bollocks because Nic is one of the few people with the capacity to surprise her.

Nic takes off her heels, because only her sister would wear heels in these circumstances and stubs out the spliff on the trunk and puts it in her pocket. Then she reaches out to her, and she hauls her a short way up the tree, and they sit there together on a low branch that's thick and steady. She feels more relaxed than she has in a while, Nic is wobbly and hanging on. She weighed next to nothing, always has done, but at least she seems to be eating now which is Gwen's doing. She thinks of Gwen and feels guilty for a second. She didn't even ring her. But that's because she wants her well out of this mess. Hopefully she'll get that and if she doesn't, she doesn't. Who matters most in all of this? Petey of course. Fuck. She hopes they help him. She holds out her hand to Nic for the spliff.

'You get it. I'm not letting go.'

She gets the spliff out of her pocket and lights it. She takes a drag and passes it back to Nic who refuses to take it because she's too busy hanging on for dear life and so she puts it in her mouth, and she inhales.

'How am I gonna get down?'

'The same way you got up.'

Nic clings on. She waits for her to get used to it. She smokes the spliff. The green leaves are waving about her face. She gets zen then – she's in the tree and she is the tree, she's in the tree and she is the tree.

'Sing us something,' says Nic.

Her voice wakes her out of her trance. Her movement shakes the branch.

'Fuck's sake. Don't be doing that!' says Nic.
'Sing what?'
'Ave Maria.'
'I haven't sung that since whenever.'
'You've phoned Gwen to tell her what's happening?'
'Texted.'
'You should have phoned.'
'I'll phone tomorrow. We got him in the hozzy Nic, we'll be able to get him out.'
'Fucking hope so.'

She looks at her, then back up at the leaves, starts to sing.
'"Ave maria, gratia plena"'
It comes out wrong, but replete with memories. All the cold stone.
'See, it's shite.'
'I always liked church. Not all the mumbling on about how bad you are and how many sins you've committed this week, I mean being in church, the smell and the singing and that.'
'They have got the odd good tune, that I will admit.'

Nic nudges her. She looks at her and Nic raises her eyebrows.
'Maria, gratia plena/ Maria, gratia plena/ Ave, Ave dominus/ dominus tecum,' she sings.
'Yeah, you're right. You sounded shite,' Nic says.
They sit there smoking and swinging their feet.

Gwen

She's down the pub with Lola, sitting in the back in the beer garden, well, not so much as garden as a beer yard. Lola goes to get a round in, and she considers asking the man next to her for a cigarette, except she doesn't smoke. It would be better if there was a beer mat to wedge under the table leg but there aren't any. She wishes Nat would phone but she doesn't want to phone her, in case... in case what? When she looks back towards the door, she sees Popper, who sidles up towards her. She wants to push him away but doesn't. He's the last thing she needs right now. He looks as unwashed as ever, the shadows under his eyes as big. Does he ever shower? Is this the time to ask him? She thinks not.

'Nat rung you?' he says. His accent is as Scouse as they come. Nat might say "scally" but she can't. Some things are just not done. She would seem a snob. Is she a snob?

'Yesterday,' she says.

'She rang us this morning.'

"She rang uz dis mornin." She wonders what his spelling's like. She presumes it isn't great. She is a snob.

'Great.'

'That's about right though, isn't it?'

'I have no idea what you're on about.'

'That's how much you matter to her. You're yesterday's news.'

He smiles his lopsided smile and goes back across the yard, all skin and bone. It would be good if she had a bow, then she could shoot him in the back. She thinks, for the umpteenth time about whether Nat has a gun. Lola passes him with the new round, slams the glasses down on the table, and goes back after Popper. The drinks almost spill.

'Lola!'

Lola turns round at the door and comes back with great reluctance. She sits down, breathes out. When Lola is angry, she screws up her eyes. Lola would shoot him in the back, no question about it.

'I heard that,' Lola says. 'Does Nat know he goes on like that?'

'Don't say anything to him now please. He's got enough on his plate.'

'If I bite my tongue any further about your life circumstances, I'll have chewed the whole frigging thing off.'

'I know that. I appreciate your restraint.'

'I just dunno how you take it.'

'I take it because this is real life. This is what things are like. Complicated.'

'This isn't real life; this is Natalie bloody Shaw. I did warn you.'

'So you did. More than once. But I choose to be here. I want to be here. And it's not her fault that Petey is ill, is it?'

'I wasn't talking about that as you well know. Let me do something about Popper. Or Lee will.'

'Lee dressed in sequins?'

'Don't underestimate him.'

'I never would. Or you either. Don't think the offer's not tempting.'

'When are Nic and Nat back?'

'Soon, I hope. Pass me that drink. Tell me about something light and happy.'

Lola sips her prosecco; she gulps hers and almost coughs. Lola pats her on the back gently but more to comfort than anything else, she can feel that. It makes her want to cry.

'Well, Bobby Ferguson got his head pushed down the bogs by

someone who'd mistaken him for Bobby Matthews so Bobby's big brother Damian, all six five of him, came into school and hung the poor kid who did it up on the basketball hoop and pulled down his trousers, filmed it, and put it on YouTube. Although they removed it for obscenity reasons. Will that do you?'

She hangs her arm around Lola's neck, even though Lola is not particularly given to shows of affection.

'And that Lola Jones Garcia is the very reason why I love you.'

But in bed that night, all on her own, she cries into the duvet cover. She feels excluded, shut out. A stupid feeling but you can't help your feelings, can you? The truth of the matter is that she needs Nat, but Nat doesn't need her at all.

Nat

It takes three weeks to sort Petey out, which isn't bad. Could have been a lot worse. They put him on Quetiapine, and it seems to suit him better than it ever did their mum. And the nurses seem pretty good, they do what they call 'activities' with him at least – art and craft and that. He comes out with a whole sheaf of new drawings. They drive him home, Nic sitting in the back with her arm around Petey. She sees her relief in the rear-view mirror.

'Wait 'til you see it. It looks great,' Nic says.

'Are you staying?' asks Petey.

'For a day or two yeah, get you settled back in,' she says. 'Are you dizzy or anything?'

'Just tired.'

'Well, when you get home, you can have a little nap. And there's a surprise,' says Nic.

'What is it?'

'That there's a surprise,' she says.

They've sorted out his room between them, it looks all nice. Jill and their dad got him some more shelves and some frames for the best pictures. The rest of the frantic drawings well they threw them out, hoping he won't ask for them, and they repainted. The room smells of fresh paint as a result. Petey doesn't seem to notice any of it but is over the moon with his new hamster, which comes complete with a complicated cage with tubes in and a wheel on which it will be able to make noise all night long except they doubt that Petey will care. Their dad stands with his back to the door.

'And that son, is how much I care about you, that I am willing to have filthy vermin in my house. But if that thing gets loose anywhere, I'm afraid I'm gonna have to exterminate it.'

'Can I get it out the cage?'

'After I leave the room and only if you barricade the door after me. What you gonna call the little beast?'

'Can I have a dog too?'

'No.'

'Or a ferret?'

'No. And before you ask, no. No elephants.'

'But we could fit a llama in the garden. Or two llamas.'

'We could not. No.'

'I'm gonna get him out now. His name is David.'

'Then I am vacating the vicinity.'

'David Attenborough?' she asks.

'Yes,' says Petey.

'Not Gerald Durrell?'

'That's the mice's names.'

'What mice?'

'You know. The mice Nic used to give me to play with when I was little. I buried them in the garden back where we used to live.'

'He means Tampax Natalie. He calls them mice.'

'Somebody's gonna have a surprise when they dig,' she says.

'At least they weren't used,' says Nic.

'Nic!' she says.

Nic cackles and looks at her and she breathes out properly for the first time since this happened.

Nic

She likes the way Ingrid's dressed - understated, sophisticated - she's half Norwegian or something, although what the fuck that has to do with anything she doesn't know, she's just different is all. She probably was a plain girl when she was younger, but you don't even notice 'cos of her expensive clothes, and the way she walks like Lola walks, like a dancer, and her chunky black jet bracelets, her long twenties ropes of black pearls.

'I'm a prostitute. Has Natalie told you that?' She thinks it's better to get that out of the way straight off. She'd rather that than Ingrid fire her later when she finds out.

'No, she hasn't. Did you expect to shock me? I used to live in Soho when I went to art school. Nothing very much shocks me. Do you have any shop experience?'

'Yeah, from way back, but it wasn't this sort of shop.'

She looks around. It's immaculate in here, everything clean and in its place, like how she likes it. The air smells of roses from the ones on the counter, yellow ones. It's beautiful and she feels calm in here just like she always does in good shops. The smell of new clothes, the gleam of glass shelves.

'I'm sure you'll pick it up very quickly. It's not complicated.'

'How do you know my sister by the way? No, don't answer that, I never ask women that.'

Ingrid smiles and it breaks up her face and she looks prettier. Must be fifty if she's a day but she's wearing it well.

'I have some medical problems that are too tedious to go into. Marijuana helps me. She's a good woman. That's all I will say.

And I'm sure you're a good woman too, as well as a stunning one. So, what do you think? Sally is now on maternity. Alys is off sick. I'm run off my feet. I've had to have a temp in and she's not terribly efficient, although I'll keep her on to help until Alys comes back. The pay's not wonderful I know but there's a thirty percent discount and a sales bonus. You can work full time or part time; we can discuss your hours. Weekends would be very helpful though. What do you think? Perhaps you would like to think it over and ring me later.'

But she's already made up her mind. She doesn't want to go back to her old job, in fact she thinks she can't. Apart from anything it would remind her of Robbie and how good it was to know he was there waiting for her when she got home. Just the thought of all those hands, right now it disgusts her. She's not going to make any money working here that's for sure, but it will do for now. Ingrid seems nice. The shop looks good. Why the fuck not?

'No need like. I'd like to work here.'

'Oh, I'm so pleased! And when could you start?'

'Now?'

'Oh my goodness! That's wonderful! I can tell that you and I are going to be great friends! Now please tell me where you got those beautiful shoes.'

She walks home from work every day in the autumn cold; she's got the money for a taxi, but she likes the chill on her face and the feel of the scarf around her neck. She sways along in her black patent high heels, her hair down her back, her black leather gloves on her hands, the ones that go up to the elbow with rows of tiny pearl buttons. Her hands are safe in the pockets of her good coat, the ankle length military black one with the astrakhan collar that she sewed on herself; she loves the feel of it, the swish of the coat on her body, the sound it makes when it rubs against her tights and the soft fur framing her face, black and ribbed and silky. She loves winter clothes the best, the thickness of the material, the heaviness of them. Oh yeah yeah yeah. The Heft of them. That was one of Gwen's words of the day from last week. Gwen writes them down and sticks them on the wall in the hall like Natalie used to do for Petey when they were kids, so that when you go in there, there are words all over the place, like they're the wallpaper. And she didn't realise 'til she saw them that she knew some words too. So now she writes them down when she remembers them and sticks them up there too. You should have seen Gwen's face, first time she saw them, she was so excited she was almost jumping up and down, and she felt great, she reckoned that must be what it's like to be one of the little kids when you get an answer right, when you learn something tricky, you get that.

It would take her ten minutes max to get to her flat. His flat. The old flat. But she doesn't turn round. 'Cos she doesn't live there no more. She lives with her twin sister and her girl, her nice girl. Nice. Bollocks. She'll think of a better word. Words. Words. Words. Perhaps she should move out. Her excuse is her lack of money but that's not the real reason, is it?

She likes the way the air smells in autumn, the smell of rain and earth and trees and cold and things going buried and forgotten. She likes the way that the wind that she can hear in the trees now is the wind that sometimes makes her laugh out loud when she comes round corners into it and it almost knocks her over, whirls her skirt up round her knees, makes her do a Marilyn, knocks the breath out of her. It's a cold, clean wind, this Mersey wind, a wind that takes your troubles away. A wind like an old friend.

She thinks of Gwen who will be home now, she thinks of the bedspread she made her, a sea-green, Chinese silk and velvet bedspread with magenta and gold appliqué of peacocks. Natalie said that it was a marvel, she should make them and flog them, she'd find her an outlet no problem. Gwen says that if the flat burns, it's what she's dragging out the door with her, that and her poems. And that made her happier than anything in a long, long time. She's ten minutes away now from where she lives. Nic smiles. Daft. She's daft. Oh yeah. Metamorphosis. She is metamorphosing? What a stupid fucking word that one. Words. Words. Words. When she gets in, she's going to make herself a nice cup of tea. Nearly home. She kicks on through the puddles.

   Metamorphosis
   MUSLIN
   CHIFFON
   WATERED SILK
   FRENCH LACE
   BRODERIE ANGLAISE
   Antidisestablishmentarianism
   TAFFETA
   Contumely
   Logorrhoea
   SUEDE

Nat

She isn't surprised, not really. No, when she considers it, she isn't surprised at all. She's always been waiting for some reprisal that's never come. Until now.

Jack Sands walks over to a wall in the graveyard and switches on a torch he gets from his pocket. The light shines on the gravestone that lists the names of the deceased girl children from the Liverpool Orphanage.

'Saddest thing,' Jack says. 'All of them tiny bones. Know what I've done a time or two? Brought them flowers. Freesias mostly, I like the smell. Maybe it's because my dad was cremated, and we scattered the ashes and so I've not got anywhere to go.'

'Did you go for the Mersey?'

'Not even the Kop. Went full out. London. Highgate. Marx's grave. Where's your ma?'

'The urn's on the mantelpiece at Dad's. One of these days he's gonna take her to Rome he says. Or maybe Lourdes. Don't know if he ever will though.'

Jack looks at the lit-up Anglican Cathedral above them.

'Me, I'm not leaving. Gonna stay down here in the dark where I belong.'

'Yeah, reckon so.'

Jack switches off the torch.

'You got a Maglite? You should. Never know when you might need one.'

They wander over towards the nearest bench and sit on it. Jack lights a spliff.

'Never heard of no Saint Natalie.'

'My second name's Mary. Do you go?'
'High days and holidays. And I make donations in my dad's name.'
'To the Catholic church Jack? Like they need the money.'
'No girl! Liberation Theologians down in South America.'
'Thank God,' she says.
'I'd rather not,' says Jack, and laughs.
'Pops!' she calls.

There is no-one else around. Not surprising; it's two a.m. She has always been curious about graveyards, about the names on the graves and the lives of the people who once owned them, good or bad. She thinks about the bodies underground. She gets a chill, but she likes this place, St James Gardens, down in the abyss under the Anglican. She likes the way you have to come down a dark gravestone-lined tunnel to get here. She thinks that is apposite, that descent, though it surprised her that Jack suggested it. She thought she was the only one who ever came here at night. Well, apart from Popper and the odd hooker and her client. But then that's not so surprising, is it? To be down in the graveyard after midnight with the Prince of Darkness himself. Popper slides out from behind a tomb, a slight ghost with a white face.

'You do them open mics, don't you? says Jack. 'Gi's a recital then.'
'Nah,' says Popper.
'Go on then Pop,' she says, 'it's only us. He pukes you see. I normally have to bribe him.'
'With what?'
'A big bag of Doritos and a bottle blonde who sleeps in her eyeliner normally does the trick.'
'Step up then, let's hear you say your piece,' says Jack. 'No need to be shy.'
'Like what Nat?'
'Whatever you fancy.'
Popper stands precariously on top of a grave slab.
'Never tell the truth at night/Cos/Vampire reversal/It'll bite you/In the morning.'

'Currently on the short form tic as you can hear,' she says.

Jack passes her the spliff.

'Liked that lad, liked that. Simple but straight. I sensed a moment of Roger McGough in there. I like the poetry myself. Pleasure over. Down to business then. I presume you've heard.'

'Yeah,' she says.

Popper is sitting on the grave slab now, head in his hands, watching on like a bad sprite.

'And what are your thoughts?'

He's a big man Jack, grizzled, bear-like, and she has always found his physical presence, let alone the power he wields, comforting. She ought to be scared of him, but she never has been. She ought to be scared of a lot of things but she's not. Only losing her family, only them getting hurt, not her. And Gwen. Truth be told, she's scared of Gwen. They sit in silence for while, smoking quietly in the dark.

'Gonna have to take the offer,' she says at last.

'There's no 'gonna have to' about it. You don't have to do anything you don't want to do. I'll make sure of that.'

'You know what I mean Jack. It's about honour, isn't it?'

'You're coming over all Godfather with me of all people?'

She smiles and starts to roll another spliff.

'I just want it sorted. For the sake of my family, apart from anything else. I don't want a risk to them. Any more than they already are at risk.'

'I can understand that.'

'I've done worse.'

'Haven't we all?'

They are quiet then again. She likes that about Jack, he can hold a silence. She thinks of her ex-boss, the one who got her sent down. She hasn't thought about him for years. And the blood on her hands afterwards. Popper handed her a wet wipe as she remembers it. She found the gesture both surprising and thoughtful. She had thought only mothers with babies bought them.

'Does he look like Stan his lad then?' she says.
'Never met the boy. Why?'
'Just wondering.'
'You think too much.'
'That's not the first time that's been said to me.'
'I expect not. So, what you gonna do Nat?'
'Sort it. Can you set it up then?'
'For when?'
'Soon as.'
'Might as well get it over with?'
'Before I think about it too much? Yeah, probably.'
'If anything happens Nat, not that I'm saying it will, not that I think it will, I'll see your family is taken care of. And your girl. You've got a girl now, haven't you?'
'Yeah.'
'What's she do?'
'Primary school teacher.'
Jack laughs.
'That's the best one I've heard in a while.'
'What about your kids Jack? You've never said.'
'One lawyer. Obviously. One actor, of all things. Theatre in London mostly. Bit of a luvvie and all that crap.'
'I think that one ups primary school.'
'We'll call it a draw.'
He puts his hand on her shoulder.
'I've got respect for you girl. You always do what you say you're going to do, no fuss about it. So, I'll respect you on this too. Your blood, your choice.'
'Thank you.'
'Proper old school like. No guns, no knives. They used to call this 'a straightener' back in the day.'
'And what do they call it now?'
'For a man? Rash. For a woman? Insane.'

Nic

She's delighted that nothing is acrylic or has bows on. Nothing is made of red nylon mesh. The zips are smooth, the buttonholes well sewn, everything's properly lined. She gets to steam and fold and arrange and dress the window and find the right things for the clueless and have a chat with the clued up. She gets paid to have an opinion when she always had an opinion anyway. She likes all that stuff. She likes this job so much she even tells Jamie she wants to give the other thing a rest for a while, and while he's not very happy about that, he knows enough about her now to know better than to try and persuade her. It's all going dead well. Ingrid seems to have taken a shine to her. And then there's Alys.

She swaggers into the shop first day back, doesn't even smile at her, just says 'Hiya' to Ingrid and dumps her huge sack of a silver handbag on the counter, like she's been away and now she's back again, queen of the fucking castle, and everyone better get used to it. Her face is arranged into a bored sulk. She inventories her: hair bleached white-blonde, corn rowed up the sides, big quiff on top, ripped black mini dress, laddered black tights, dirty, sleeveless denim jacket, thick gold chain bracelets, knuckle dusters, a skeleton hand hanging round her neck on a long chain, black studded boots, and black eyeliner so thick round her slitty blue eyes it's like felt pen. When you look at her close up, she's not even that good looking, in fact, she's near enough ugly; her legs and arms are all gangly, she's pudgy round the middle, she's got thin lips and the remains of acne, and her eyes are too small for her face, her ears too large, but there's something about her that would make you look round in the street. It's cool, that's what it is, she's cool, but she knows cool, it's just boring disguised as interesting, it's shite. And she's posh. You can tell she's posh though she's tried to disguise it, private school but she talks like she's not, styles herself up like she's some ghetto superstar, listens to 'beats'. But she knows 'beats' from Robbie and her taste's for shite. She thinks a lot of herself, you can tell that much for sure.

'Need some music in here,' is the first thing that comes out of her mouth once Ingrid's left them to it.

'Like what?'

'You won't have heard of them. They're dead cutting.'

'Name?'

'Starving Masses. The P2P crew. Mighty Hands of Destruction. Patience Rush.'

'Like hip hop?' she says, just to amuse herself.

Alys doesn't even bother to reply.

Bitch.

Nat

Petey and her are climbing the tree in their dad's back garden.

'Sleeping?' she says.

'Yes.'

'Eating?'

'Yes.'

'Taking your meds every day?'

'Course.'

'Studying?'

'Yes.'

She stops and sits down on a branch.

'Not going round the bloody twist.'

'Yes. I mean no. This is what it's like when I go and see my psychiatrist,' says Petey, settling next to her.

'And he's alright?'

'Yeah'

'What about that psych nurse who comes to visit?'

'Judy. She's nice. She asks the same sort of questions though.'

'There's a downloadable sheet.'

'I speak to them now,' says Petey, looking out through the bare branches.

'To?'

'To the bits inside my head that went mental. I speak to them. See what they want.'

'And what do they want?'

'They like things. Small stuff. Sharpies. Charcoal. Pencil sharpeners. They like me going to art shops. Or they like them lollies, Soleros. Or I say are you feeling alright, and they say no, and then I go and listen to music 'til they feel better.'

'What music they like then?'

'Quiet, soft things. Old stuff like you used to play me. They like Nick Drake best. Or I come up here. They like it up here.'

'And your mental health professionals they know all about this right?'

Petey shrugs.

'I'd advise you not to tell them.'

'Wasn't going to.'

'And these voices, they don't tell you to do stuff that hurts you?'

'Those ones are different. I don't speak to them. They shout. These ones, they're really small. They don't wanna hurt me. They just get scared.'

'Will they like these then?'

She reaches into her pocket and hands Petey some green plastic toy soldiers with parachutes attached. Who'd have thought such things still existed. Petey is delighted and takes them and puts them in his lap and starts to untangle the lines with his long fingers.

'Brilliant! Nat?'

'Yeah?'

'When I leave school can I help you?'

'With what?'

'Your business.'

'Who told you about that?'

'I asked Nicola.'

'The answer to that question is no you definitely can't. And if I ever hear of you even so much as toking, I'll do for you.'

'I wouldn't wanna.'

'Good. You're not having nothing to do with it, not ever. You're going to art school or butterfly school or avocet school if I have to drag you there by the hair. Got it?'

'Yes.'

'Good. Don't mention it again.'

'Are you cross with me?'

'I am never cross with you. I'm cross with Nic. Gonna have to tape her mouth up. Or sew it shut. We better get on with this then. Are the lines untangled?'

'Yes.'

'Parachutes checked?'

'Yes.'

'High calorie snacks packed?'

'Yes. Is your GPS on?'

'I forgot. Hang on. There. Ready. If yours makes it first, I'll buy you whatever you fancy with my ill-gotten gains.'

'A better phone?'

'If you must. Give us one then.' Petey hands her a soldier and they each raise the one they have in the air. 'On three. One. Two. Three. Chocs away!'

They drop the men out of the tree. They don't hit any branches and Petey's reaches the ground first.

'I should have asked for an iPad, shouldn't I?' Petey says.

'You should have yeah.'

Nic

She goes on a crappy date, someone who came up to her in a café. She said yes because she liked his hands, he could do something with those hands, make stuff, either that or it was just to get him out of her hair. Or she was curious, just to see what it was like to go out with someone.

He lays bricks, which she supposes is a start, but he's fucked in the head to be honest. He's sitting on his couch, droning on about his life story, and he's having a right moan about the job and the boss and the pay and all that bollocks. And yeah, he's divorced and doesn't often see the kids, and the ex-wife sounds mental, and she got the house but… but… she can't even get a word in edgeways. Which is pissing her off. In fact, the whole evening has pissed her off. He took her down some restaurant in town, but it was only pizza, and she sat there eating it and it made her think of Robbie and how he used to make them because he'd learnt how to off one of his aunties who was Italian, and she didn't even want to go on with it after that. In fact, she wanted to cry onto the parmesan. 'Cos she knew that it might be hard to like someone else, but it shouldn't be this hard, should it? And he has a nice body yeah, which is probably why she said yes as well, she likes decent guns, but it's made her feel worse to be honest. Oh shut the fuck up. Want me to make a list of my pain, do you? I'd blow you out the fucking water. But then she doesn't, she remembers, not now she's given up the day job, the night job, she doesn't have to do this crap anymore. She's fucking slow sometimes.

'I have to go,' she says, 'I've got work in the morning.'

To just walk out the door, no consequences, no afterthoughts, how nice is that?

Gwen pulls the door open before she's even got her key in the lock.

'I heard you on the stairs. How was your date?'

'No.'

'No?'

'No. What you up to?'

'I'm going to bed. I was doing school stuff but I'm so tired now I've lost the plot. Nat's just gone out.'

'OK. I'll go to bed too then.'

'No, I want to know what happened. Just I might fall asleep on you. Tell you what, come get into bed with me, that way if I pass out you can just leave. Or stay. Sleep here if you want. Go get your pjs.'

'I haven't got any pjs.'

'What do you wear to bed then?'

'Chanel No. 19.'

'Well then wear that then.'

'Can't wear nothing. I'll just take my jeans off or something.'

Gwen goes into the bedroom and rummages around in a drawer.

'You can wear these,' she says, and she gives her some red tartan pyjamas made of that warm flannelly stuff. 'No, Nic, you can have these. I honourably convey on you the gift of the tartan pyjama for use in situations of sleepovers and emergency exits from buildings during the hours of darkness. Fires etc. But not police raids. I'd get dressed if I was you for them. Would they? Raid? Do they?'

'She doesn't keep her stuff here.'

'No, she doesn't. Where does she keep it?'

'You know if you wanna know that kind of shite then you're

asking the wrong twin, right?'

'She won't tell me. It seems very multi-disciplinary from what little I do know though. Maybe we should teach it in schools. Did you ever do it?'

'When we were kids yeah, just messing round. I liked the money, but I was never much interested in the cool, hard dealer shite. Natalie, she was always interested in the machinations. You impressed with my vocabulary? Does it bother you what she does?'

'She's so clever she could be doing anything. It just seems a shame.'

'Our dad says it's "a waste". And it is. And does anything else bother you about my sister Gwen?'

Gwen doesn't say anything for a while.

'What does it feel like to be so good looking?' Gwen asks suddenly. 'Is it a pain that people look at you all the time? For all of you I mean.'

'Petey hates it, 'cos he's so shy. Natalie. I don't think she even notices, she takes it for granted. And I use it. But don't think I like myself any better for doing that.'

'Did it bother Robbie what you did?'

Gwen's never mentioned any of this before so why now? She thinks before she answers. For once.

'At the beginning I think he found it a turn on – I'm so good I get it for free kind of thing. Good for his ego. But he never seemed to care after that. Realised it was just a job, 'cos it was just a job. It's not the same though, is it?'

'What isn't?'

'Sex with someone you don't care about means nothing. Not to me anyway. Not to Natalie neither. Never did. Sex with someone you care about is different. Really different. And sex with someone you love, Jesus. Takes the top off your head.'

'It hurts.'

'It does yeah.'

She starts to take her clothes off. Gwen looks at the floor.

'You're shy, aren't you?'

'No.'

'I've forgotten what that's like. To be shy.'

Gwen looks at her in the much too big pj bottoms and starts to laugh. She looks down at herself and starts laughing too.

'I look like a fucking Scottish clown.'

'Nic?'

'Yeah?'

'What you just said before. Is that why you did… you know. Because the sex didn't matter to you?'

'Are you trying to ask me why I was a prostitute?'

'Yes.'

'Because I left school and I was working in a crap shop, making peanuts and I was used to having some money. I helped Natalie sometimes but then she went to prison, and I went home with this bloke one night and in the morning when I got up, he'd gone to work and left some money on the bedside table. Dunno why. I was fucking furious at first. But I had a think about it and then I decided… yeah, why not? Give it a go. Natalie wasn't there to kick off. I was still living at home then, but my dad was so wound up about Natalie he didn't even seem to notice all the times I didn't come home. I joined an escort agency. And there you go.'

'That simple?'

'Pretty much.'

'Did you like it?'

'I didn't mind it. I made good money. That's all most people can expect from work, isn't it? It wasn't like I was some skanky junkie on the streets doing it with anyone Gwen, if that's what you think.'

'I didn't think that.'

'Then what did you think?'

'I… this is going to sound patronising.'

'Go 'ead.'

'I just thought you could be doing something much more interesting. Anything you wanted really.'

'Do you know what Natalie would say to that?'

'No.'

'My dad the same actually. That you're posh and so you don't know what it's like to be poor. I mean properly poor. And you don't know what it's like not to have choices neither. I was just using what I've got the best I could.'

'I'm sorry. I'm being intrusive.'

'I'll forgive you if you make me a cup of tea.'

She doesn't wake up until she feels her sister slide in between them. She is only wearing a t-shirt and is shivering. Gwen is fast asleep. Natalie kisses Gwen's cheek with the softest of kisses and strokes the stray hairs out of her eyes with her cold fingers. Then she tries to put her feet on her feet.

'Fuck off Natalie,' she whispers.

'Alright girl. I hate January. It's a miserable fucking month.'

'Alright. Gwen and me were chatting. She said to stay. So I stayed. See, she gave me her pjs.'

'Nice. Tartan army. Wanna smoke?'

'Go on then.'

Natalie puts his arm round her and lays her cheek on her hair and rubs her hands together, tries to skin up, but can't. She takes the box off her, pulls the duvet up to their chins, rolls a spliff under the covers. Gwen has her back to them, Natalie warms one of her hands on her skin.

'Got myself a good girl here.'

'Got yourself a fucking miracle is what you've got.'
'Don't think I don't know that Nicola.'
'Don't fuck this up.'
'I'm trying.'
'I know. Just don't. Please try not to.'
'I'm doing the best I can, alright? Has Gwen said something to you?'
'No.'

After they've smoked, she slips his other arm under Gwen and pulls them both to her. Two hot water bottles. Natalie can go to sleep like that. Crucified. She's not so good at sleeping. She'd go get some warm milk or something if it wasn't so cold, or a biscuit, or both. She is not used to feeling hungry yet, it still feels weird. She never could sleep on her back, she curls away from Natalie and looks at the wall, closes her eyes. Then she's sleeping. She dreams of midnight blue silk.

She can't stand it much longer. It's the scrolling and texting that's constant. It's the sighing, the sulking, the pout. It's the gum and the drawl. It's the being late and the leaving early. It's the walk like she hasn't got anywhere interesting to go. It's the hangover, the vomit not even properly cleaned off the toilet bowl. It's the two-hour lunch breaks. It's the fact that her clothes are so deliberately distressed, that her make up is meant to look like she had it on from the night before. It's her filthy nails. It's that when she's cleaned up or tidied or folded or been given stuff to dress the window with, she has to go round behind her and do it all over again, and yeah, she knows her standards are high, but Christ, so are Ingrid's. That the point of this place, isn't it? That's why this is a good shop. It's the crap that comes out of her mouth to her friends on the phone. On and on and on. It's how fucking useless she is with the customers, just looks at them like they're ugly or stupid or both, 'yeah,' she says, 'nah,' like it would cost her so much to speak a sentence to them, help them out. Like she's above all of them, she certainly thinks she's above her.

She goes and stands outside now and smokes a cigarette, looks at herself in the window, thinks she needs a facial, picks at her nails, tries to do deep breathing, weighs the pros and cons, thinks about ringing her sister, but she can't keep ringing her sister to get help, thinks about ringing Gwen but she'll be at work. She rubs at some smears on the glass. Then Lola turns up.

'How you doing sweetheart? I'm going to buy my mum a birthday pressie. Are you alright? Que pasa?'

'It's her.'

'Who?'

'Alice. Or whatever she's called.'

'That one in there?'

'Yeah.'

'Christ on a bike. She's a witch. She yours?'

'No. She's not mine. It. Not she. It. It's the girl I'm having to work with. Do us a favour Lola. Go in and ask to try something.'

Lola goes in. A couple of minutes later she follows her. Alys is half lying across the counter. Texting.

'Yo.'

'Have you asked the customer if she wants any help?'

'She doesn't look like she's got any rent.'

'Rent?'

'Yeah, you know. Moolah. Dosh. M.O.N.E.Y.'

Lola has heard her from the other side of the shop and has to be calmed down and escorted out.

'For fuck's sake!' says Lola as they stand outside.

'Exactly.'

'You're gonna have to do something about that Nic.'

'I know. I will.'

Nat

She's gonna have to tell someone in case anything goes down. She considers Gwen for about two seconds but there's no way that's going to happen. She wouldn't get it; she'd just be freaked out and try to stop her. Is she underestimating her? But how could she be any different, the world she's come from. There's only one option. All their childhood they were a united front, right up until she went to prison, and even after that, before Nic had her miscarriage, and she was so stupid about it. She puts that out of her mind.

'Come for a walk with us then Nic.'

'What do you mean walk?'

'Go down the Mersey, walk along to Otterspool. What do you say?'

'Listen to the wind out there! I'll ruin my hair.'

'Wear a hat.'

'Haven't got a hat!'

'Gwen has. Borrow one of hers.'

'I wouldn't be seen dead in some of the stuff she wears.'

'Well, have a word then. Come 'ead.'

They walk down past the station, cross the Festival Gardens, down to the grey river. The wind is up, she was right, but she likes it, it's a familiar wet salt wind specific to this city; it feels like home. They walk along but it's hard going to get anywhere, they are being pushed back the other way along the prom. It's difficult to even hear what the other one is saying which is for the best. It's why she wanted to do it down here – private, contained in the rush of the wind and the pull of the river running alongside them. Nic is wearing a black beret she got off Gwen. With her mac on she looks like a spy but it kinda suits her. She doesn't tell her that. They walk close. She considers putting her arm through Nic's but rejects the idea. It would make her feel a hundred years old. Nic is holding onto the beret with one hand.

'Bloody hell!' Nic says. 'Why are we here? What's all this about then?'

'Got an issue.'

'That doesn't sound too good.'

'I'll just go ahead and tell you then.'

'If you don't, I'm gonna thump you for dragging me down here and messing up my mazzy.'

'Remember Stan?'

'Of course I remember Stan! Practically slept with the bloke to get you out of nick. How could I forget?'

'Well, apparently he has a son.'

'As ugly as him?'

'Don't know yet.'

'And?'

'The son holds a grudge, as well he might. Wants us to meet up.'

'To do what? Go for a nice Chinese? Compare cake recipes?'

'Fight.'

'You're fucking joking, aren't you?'

'No.'

'What like one of them things they used to have in the old days? With swords and that?'

'A duel.'

'Yeah, that's the one. That's fucking ridiculous.'

'It's old fashioned it has to be said but I can see the lad's point of view. Revenge, done straight out, no messing around. Done that myself once upon a time.'

'What? Are you serious? Like fighting fighting?'

'Yeah. Straight fight. If I win, then that's the end of it.'

'And if he wins then what?'

'Things might get messy.'

'Can't that Jack Sands put a stop to this?'

'It's my decision.'

'You're serious about this? Jesus. Have you seen him? He might be a heavyweight for all you know. And, in case you've forgotten you're a woman. Had you forgotten that?'

'Nah. I could get someone to deputise me, that's allowed but I dunno. I'd feel bad if they had to take one for me.'

'And what if he whips out a knife, then what?'

'No knives. There are rules.'

They go and stand down by the railing. The water is a sludgy greyish brown. She wonders how cold it would be if you fell in.

'You're doing this then?'

'Yes, I am.'

'Why?'

''Cos otherwise I've got this loose cannon wandering around swearing vengeance and I can't afford that in my life.'

'What are you going to tell Gwen?'

'I'm not going to tell Gwen, and neither are you.'

'You think she's not going to notice when you end up in the hozzy?'

'If it comes to that I'll tell her I had an accident.'

'You've got it all figured out I see. And what if you? What if you kill him or he kills you? 'Cos that's possible in this messed up crap you've got yourself into, right?'

'Yeah.'

They consider the river.

'Well, if it's the first option I think that's survivable. If it's the second one, then that's then. Jack will sort you out.'

Nic turns to her, and the wind takes her beret and whisks it off and it falls into the river and gets swept away.

'Oh shite!' says Nic, the wind whipping her hair about her face. 'Oh well, it looked stupid anyway. It's not fair on Gwen, you doing this.'

'It's not fair not to Nic. It's the only thing I can do.'

Nic leans her arms on the railing and puts her chin on her raised fists, looking out at the water.

'I'm... I'm better now. The shop's doing me good.'

'I know it is.'

'I like her. Ingrid. Posh like but funny and she looks good for her age.'

'I always thought so.'

'I don't wanna know. So, what I'm saying is, if anything happens, I'll take care of us. I mean Gwen. I'll make sure she's alright. And Petey and Dad too. That goes without saying. Even Jill.'

'Jill's a good woman.'

'Yeah, I know. Some make-up would help though.'

'Thank you Nic. That means a lot to me.'

'Yeah, if you pretend hard enough that it'll put your mind at rest, maybe it will come true.'

'Maybe.'

'I'd prefer it if you didn't get yourself killed though.'

'Me too. Is that a deal then?'

She puts her elbows on the railing next to Nic's.

'Don't think I have an option Nic.'

'You wanker.'

The lad does look like his dad, an ugly bugger just like him. Short, acne pock-marked, no neck, but, unlike Stan, looks like he works out, possibly even steroids. She feels calmer than she had expected to be. Like the calm she gets on very good coke when everyone else is jumping about all over the place, mouthing off non-stop, she goes all Buddhist monk. Must be a blood chemistry thing. Nic's the same.

She wonders what Nic will say to Gwen if she says anything at all. Gwen never asks where she's going anyway, when she's getting home, what she's doing. She's good like that and she's always been grateful for it, anything else might make her feel strangled. There are not many women who would put up with her and there are not many women she could put up with. Must be a good match then.

She watches this bloke strip down to the waist. He's got a lot of definition. She's not bloody stripping. She empties her pockets. She wore her toughest boots. Jack Sands is here and about twenty other blokes. A few wagers going on. How good are the odds on her? Probably very bad. This is insane, as Jack said, a woman going up against a man who looks like that. She should have got deputised. Too late now though.

The other side's top bloke, a man she's never liked, is whispering in the lad's ear. She thinks about how much Stan said he disliked her and how much that dislike was only a pretence for longings he was too scared to articulate. How she used those longings against him. Manipulative. But Stan only got what he deserved. Is she supposed to try and rile this lad up with talk of his dad? Tell him that it took him a while to die, he did a lot of writhing, how the carpet ate up the blood like a thirsty creature. The carpet on the top of the stairs was red but he remembers that was about her mum. Her feet were wet. And she'd been thinking about Wilfred Owen while she was going up the stairs, she'd been memorising a poem for the A' levels she never took, thinking about the larks and the wire and the poppies the colour of blood. He was a genius the boy Owen. Such a shame. It's always such a shame. Why the fuck is she doing this?

She looks at the lad, sees a combination of hatred and fear in his eyes and part of her wants to step forward, put out her hand, say sorry, he had it coming your dad did, he was a bastard, but anyway, sorry. It's no good to grow up without a parent. But then is it any better to grow up with one who's fucked in the head? Maybe this lad was better off without him. Not possible to tell him that though. And any thought of reconciliation would look like backing down. And she's a Shaw, they just don't do that. No, there's no choice.

'Everyone clear on this?' says Jack.

'Yeah,' says the lad.

'Yes,' she says.

'I'm not gonna check your pockets,' says Jack, 'but if anyone pulls anything then there's hell to pay. And no eye gouging. That's about it. We'll stop when I say stop. Alright Eric?'

'Alright,' says their top bloke.

She fought at school. It's what they did, for fun, for showing off, to settle scores, to prove who was top, to defend their family's reputation. The times kids made fun of their mum got fewer and fewer until there was no-one left to fight. Last time she did fight was in prison. Some woman with 'Tiffany' tattooed on her neck was thumping some poor girl. She sees Popper standing next to Jack. Popper, in this situation, would have a knife down his sock. She smiles at that. She wonders if Popper has put a bet on.

'What you smiling at?' says the lad. His voice is croaky.

'Nothing,' she says. And steps forward. Everything after that is a blur, too fast to analyse. There's punching, there's kicking, the lad tried to bite her ear, she kicked him to prevent him doing that, his kneecap crunched, she felt the lad's nose crack as she socked him one. She's bleeding from her mouth now; something has happened to her side but she's not sure what. The lad goes for her ribs again and she grabs hold of his arm, wheels him around so it's behind his back and forces him down to the ground. Anyone sensible would kick him when he's down, go for his head. Jack said there are no rules to these things, but she has rules himself, even if they're not Queensbury. She concentrates on the arm. She finds herself sitting on the ground and waits to be pounded but when she manages to look up sees the lad still lying down five feet away. She's supposed to finish him off now. You're allowed to, it is permitted in these bizarre sessions to kill if you can. She decides against it. More fool her, she'll just have to live with the consequences of her actions, has lost all taste for death years ago. It is hard for her to breathe. Fuck. She passes out.

When she wakes, she wakes in her own bed. She tries to move but she can't. Everything hurts. Everything. She manages to lift the covers. Her ribs are bandaged. Cracked then? It hurts to breathe even. She tries to wiggle her toes, just to be sure, and they work, just about. She lies back, can't even move her arm enough to adjust the pillow to how she needs it. But she's here. She's alive. She's at home and not in the hozzy. She would sigh if breathing didn't hurt so much. 'Thank you,' she says to the air, and then wonders if she's having some religious moment, if she's had a blow to the head that has catapulted her back to Catholicism. No, she's not thanking God. Who is it then? What does she actually believe in? She hasn't got the headspace for any theology right now.

She yawns and feels the corners of her mouth crack out of their dryness. How long has she been here? What painkillers has she had? Whatever they were they weren't enough. Popper will have to get her something. That's the last thing she remembers, Popper leaning down to her when she was sitting on the floor. And what about the other bloke then? Shite. She's forgotten about him momentarily. 'Hello,' she says, but it comes out as a whisper. She lifts the cover again, tries to move her legs out of the bed but they feel too sore. She gives up and soon sleep overtakes her again.

Gwen

She sits in a chair next to Nat, playing cat's cradle with a rubber band. Her sister taught her this, but she can't remember how to do it properly. She doesn't know what she is going to say to her. She is so angry. She can't remember when she last felt so angry. She feels a tap on her shoulder. It's Nic, who points past her to the bed. Nat's got her eyes open.

'Hello,' Nat says, but there's something in her voice, a catch. She should stand up and go to her. She doesn't. Instead Nic goes round the other side of the bed. She's got a glass of something.

'Can you sit up?' Nic says, putting the glass on the bedside table.

'Don't think so,' Nat says.

'Here,' Nic says, and raising her head with one hand, pushes another pillow under it. Then she hands her the glass. She raises it to her mouth, wincing. Meanwhile, all she wants to do is thump her on a bruise. How could she not have told her? How could she have trusted her so very little?

'Gwen,' Nat says.

'Yes.'

'Come here.'

She considers walking out of the room. Instead, she stands up and approaches Nat but stays far enough back so that Nat can't reach her.

'I'm sorry,' Nat says.

'I doubt that,' she says.

Nat considers her.

'You should have told me,' she says.

'I couldn't.'
'Why not?'
'Cos it wouldn't have been right.'
'And this is right?'
'There's nothing more I can say apart from sorry.'
'Well, sorry's not bloody good enough,' she says and leaves the room, slamming the door behind her, although she regrets this immediately and wants to go back and hug her, ribs or no ribs.

Nat

She feels dead rough.

'She'll come round,' Nic says, sitting on the end of the bed, 'she's just freaked out is all.'

'Did I have to go to the hozzy? I don't remember.'

'You refused so Popper brought you back here, well, with help, was no way he was going to carry you on his own, and Jack Sands sorted out a doctor.'

'No questions asked?'

'That's the one.'

'No police?'

'No.'

'Good. So what's the damage?'

'A rib. Bruises. That's all. You were extremely bloody lucky.'

'And the other bloke?'

'Also extremely bloody lucky, by all accounts. Bit of concussion. Broken nose. Broken arm. And now you'll be wanting to know who won this stupid thing?'

'Yes.'

'You did. It was supposed to go 'to the bone' or something, whatever that is doesn't sound good to me, but, as it was, once you busted the bloke's arm, he gave it up. And I hope that's the fucking end to it and all.'

She closes her eyes.

'Thanks Nic,' she says.

'Bloody right.'

'What does Gwen know?'

'Said you got into a fight. And then she asked and asked, and I said something about you having a point to prove. Leave her alone for a bit. Let her get her head around it.'

'I need something stronger.'

'I bet you do.'

'Ring Popper for us?'

'You gonna start on the brown?'

She opens her eyes and looks at Nic.

'Was that a joke Nic?'

'Not a funny one.'

'Not at all. Did you ever?' she says.

'Only once.'

'Smoked?'

'Yeah. Can't stand needles as you well know. You?' says Nic.

'Nah.'

'Aren't you the boss girl then?'

'It was more fear than anything like bravery. I've seen what it does to people.'

'And I haven't?'

'Maybe we shouldn't discuss this.'

'Have you heard anything… about Robbie?' says Nic but she's looking away from her out of the window.

She can hear it costs her to ask this.

'Same old, same old, as far as anyone's saying.'

'Oh.'

'You did the right thing Nic.'

'I was watching something on the telly. Some Yank thing and there was this bloke with a big wife, and he said he had to get her the food, or she'd be mad at him. And I was thinking, yeah right, she's not exactly gonna go for you is she lad? There's not much kicking off going on there. And then I realised, I got it… all I was doing was exactly the same thing as him.'

'I think it's called enabling,' she says.

'Thanks. Never would have got that myself Natalie.'

'Sorry. Bit lightheaded.'

'So I got my handbag and I left.'

'I'm proud of you. I haven't told you but I am.'

'Do you mind me staying? Aren't I cramping your style? I could get a place. Round here maybe.'

'It's better for Gwen, I think. Having someone here when I'm not.'

'I'll talk to her.'

'Thanks Nic.'

'And I'll get Popper. Diazepam?'

'Please. You're a good girl.'

'Yeah, I know.'

They hear the front door click shut. Nic goes out into the hall, comes back with a note and passes it to her. 'Gone to Lola's,' the note says. Succinct. Should she put it in the shoebox with the others? This note looks like it was scribbled fast in biro. Gwen doesn't like biro. This fact almost upsets her more than the note. What else has she reduced her to?

Gwen

She hasn't gone to Lola's at all though. She has gone to sit in the park by the little lake. There are anglers trying to catch whatever lives in the murky waters. She saw what looked like a koi carp in there once. She has always believed that the anglers come here more to get away from their home lives than to catch any fish. They have a lot of equipment though, as if they were going on some epic trip to some wild place. Some even have small tents. They are always men. Maybe they come here to get away from the wives, away from the kids. It seems a sexist thought but yet an obvious conclusion. She has come here to get away from something too.

Behind her are rhododendrons. They like acidic soil she thinks, her dad told her that once.

She wants to run away home. She wants to go back to the house, pack up as much of her stuff that she can get into a bag, and just go home, back to a life that, she knows now, was privileged and safe and unthreatening. Because now she lives in a different world, one with edges she never knew existed. A hard cold world full of biting winds. She had no idea. She thought she had but she didn't. She could have been killed. She only sees the sweet side of her, but she's like Janus, she has a whole other face.

She knew this in some way but never properly took it on board before. Anyone she told from her other life, the normal life she lives to all apparent purposes, would ask her what the fuck she was doing here? And it's true. What the fuck is she doing here? She could be anywhere she wanted, get a job wherever she wanted. She could go to the other side of the country and stay there. She could go to the other side of the planet. But no, she lives here with

Natalie Shaw, they could have been dead. It's not real and too real at the same time. She can't bear to tell Lola, but Lola will hear anyway. She bets if she had brought her mobile out with her, she'd have missed calls. But she came out with nothing but her keys. Can't go forward. Can't go back. Perhaps this is a thing called shock? What has truly shocked her before? Back in her safe little life. Lola was right. Lola is always right. But what to do about it? She would miss her. That is an understatement. And she would, she realises now, miss Nic too. A lot. She has got used to living with the both of them, doesn't mind so much now how often Nat is out, always has somebody to talk to. She must have been lonely then; she hadn't realised it. And Nic is different from Nat, Nic speaks, she knows more about them now. Not about everything, just about some of it. After their mum died Petey didn't speak for six months, Nic said. Nat would never have told her that. She is such a private woman, at least in relation to her. Maybe that was a good thing. Yeah, maybe it was.

It's cold. She hasn't got a coat, pulls her sleeves down to cover her hands. She can't stay on this bench much longer. There is nothing for it but to go back and think it through there. All that is happening is that her brain is going round and round in circles. And anyway, she wants to touch her, make sure she's solid, makes sure she really is living and breathing. Natalie Shaw She loves her. What is she going to do about that?

She walks slowly home. When she opens the door of the flat, she can hear Popper, who is the last person she wants to see right now. She takes off her Converse and goes into the kitchen. Nic is boiling the kettle but turns round to look at her. Neither of them says anything until she walks straight into Nic's arms.

'There, there, girl,' says Nic, holding her tight, 'there, there.'

After she has cried into Nic's neck, she wipes her eyes dry on a piece of kitchen paper and blows her nose. Nic hands her a cup of tea.

'Get that down you,' she says.

She sips it.

'Yuk, it's got sugar in it!'

'Sugar for shock.'

'Is that what this is then?'

'I expect so. Sit down there.'

She sits at the table and drinks the disgusting tea. Nic throws a coaster onto the table.

'And you can put that under that and all. It's a nice table this, you'll get rings. And yes, I don't like rings. I'm quite particular.'

'I've noticed.'

'It was our mum. She was like that too. Coasters. Place mats. Tablecloths. No smoking inside.'

'What was it like? Living with her?'

'It was a fucking nightmare Gwen, and I don't like talking about it.'

'Yes, sorry.'

'S'alright. You're just trying to distract yourself.'

'It's not working.'

'No. Didn't expect you to come back from Lola's anytime soon to be honest.'

'I didn't got to Lola's. I went to the park. I hoped to see them catch a fish.'

'Any fish that'll come out of there will have been eating body parts.'

'Is it going to be OK? I mean, this thing. Is it going to be OK now?'

'Yeah. End of.'

'I'm scared. That's what this is really. I'm scared.'

'Not fucking surprised.'

Nic reaches her hand out and grasps her arm.

'I don't know what I'd do if you weren't here,' she says.

'Well, I am. Maybe you should go and see Natalie now.'

'I don't think I can cope with Popper.'

'Hang on then. I'll get rid.'

Nic gets up and leaves the kitchen. She throws the remains of the tea down the sink and rinses the cup, puts it on the side. It has crept up on her slowly, the order, so slowly she didn't know it was happening. Everything is washed up immediately and then dried and put away. She gets the tea towel which is always clean now too and dries the cup and puts it in the cupboard next to the other clean ones. She looks around the kitchen. Everything in its place. Even her piles of papers are neatly placed on a corner of the table with a book on top of them to weigh them down. She goes to look at the book. It is Sharon Olds. She tries to see if she can remember any off the top of her head. Nic comes back.

'He's gone.'

'What did you say to him?'

'Fuck off.'

'Did you?'

'More or less. Come on.'

Nic gets her by the hand and leads her back to the bedroom. The door is closed, and Nic opens it, pushes her gently inside, and then leaves, shuts the door behind her. Nat is sitting up. She goes and sits on the edge of the bed and reaches out her hand for hers. Nat's fingers curl around hers, she has always liked her big hands. They don't seem to know what to say to each other.

'Thought you were gone for good there,' Nat says eventually.

'I don't want to talk about it anymore. I'm just glad you're OK.'

'And I'm glad you came home. Would you read to me?'

'That's a strange thing to ask.'

'I'm a strange woman.'

'Maybe.'

'Maybe you'll read or maybe I'm a strange woman?'

'I'll get a book. Any requests?'

'Whatever you fancy girl.'

She goes to the bookshelf, scans it, rejects everything on it and goes out of the room.

Nat

She could do with a drink. The diazepam just isn't cutting it. She wonders if Gwen would get her a whiskey if asked but she doubts it. She used to keep whiskey in the garden shed at home, for emergencies like. When the house got too chaotic. She should start keeping a bottle under the bed and all. Nic will go out and get her something if she wants. Bushmills. That's what she fancies. In a good glass.

Gwen comes back, gets onto the bed next to her, sits close but not touching.

'What have you got?'
'Sharon Olds.'
'I like her. Go on then.'

Gwen

And that's that then, she thinks. Easily mended, best forgotten. But not mended, not really, and not forgotten, not forgotten at all.

Nic

How long does it take her to say something? About two weeks. For her, that's dead good.

'I'm in a real dilemma then,' says Ingrid. 'I love having you here, you're doing so brilliantly, you're like an angel fallen out of the sky into my lap. But her mother's a very good friend of mine and I promised her that Alys could work here you see.'

'That's me gone then.'

'Oh no Nicola, don't go. Shall I have a word with her? Would that help? Or you could? She might find it easier to speak to someone nearer her own age.'

'I've had a word. I've had lots of words. Soon they're gonna be the kind you couldn't say on the telly. She doesn't exactly go with the shop, does she?'

'That's part of the reason her mother wanted her to come here, to see if we could brush her up a smidgeon.'

'Brush her up? It'd take more than a brush Ingrid; it'd take a fucking hoover if you pardon my French.'

'She's very young darling.'

'And very stupid.'

'Oh no, not stupid. Not at all. She's doing very well at school by all accounts. I'm sure she'll do very well, just she's still only a teenager darling, you can't expect her to have any je ne sais quoi just yet. Please don't leave us. You're so good with the customers; you've got a real knack. What can I say to make you stay?'

She stands looking at Ingrid, tapping her foot.

'This blouse right?' she says.

'A lovely cut.'

'Vintage. But I altered it to fit see. Darted it. And I changed the neckline. Changed the buttons.'

'Let me have a proper look.'

Ingrid puts on her glasses and peers at the blouse.

'What beautiful stitching.'

'Hand that. Got that off our mum. She taught us. She mostly made stuff for the house, curtains, tablecloths, cushions. She could quilt though, smock, appliqué, embroider, anything. When we were little, she made all our clothes. You should have seen me and Natalie at our Communion. Works of art we were. So I had this idea. How about if I did a service in the shop? Tailor to fit kinda thing, or alterations. Like for example, this dress you've got on yeah, it could do with an inch off the bottom if you're gonna wear it with those shoes. But you've gotta do that sort of thing properly or it just looks a mess. And mostly people don't know what needs doing, but I do.'

'You do have a great eye. That might work. And how would you be paid?'

'Well, I was gonna suggest you bump Alys, but that isn't gonna happen, is it? So how about eighty-twenty. To me.'

'Alys stays, and I agree to forty-sixty on a trial basis.'

'I said eighty-twenty. And don't you be batting your eyelashes at me Ingrid 'cos you're not my type.'

'Fifty-fifty. On a trial basis.'

'I'll try and get on better with Alys. And if you give me sixty-forty I'll take up your dress for free.'

'You looked just like your sister then. Fine. Done.'

They shake hands.

It wasn't a word she gives Alys though. Well, not exactly. It was more like a get her by the throat in the stock cupboard kind of thing.

'I like this job. I like Ingrid. I don't like you. Stop talking about fucking beats, 'cos what you know about beats wouldn't fit on the back of a sequin. Now these love. These are tights. These are Wolfords. They cost twenty-five quid a pop. Put them on, wipe off half that slap, and start talking in your own fucking voice. Where'd you go to school?'

'Merchant Taylors.'

Nic lets her go and laughs, puts her hands on her hips.

'Well, that fucking figures. Couldn't get any bloody posher if you tried, could you? What you up to in that get up? Pretending like you're slumming it? The very least thing you can do is wear clean clothes to work. Put the gum in the bin. Put the t-shirt I saw you swipe back on the rack and go clean the toilet you threw up in this morning after your heavy night last night. And switch off your fucking phone while you're at work. Yeah, you heard me, Little Miss Sunshine.'

'You can't make me. You can't make me do anything. I'll tell Ingrid.'

'Go right ahead. What you gonna say? Nic tried to strangle me? She's mean to me? She made me cry? I hate her. She's horrid.'

Alys starts crying.

'You're faking.'

'No, I'm not.'

'Yeah, you are.'

'I'm not.'

And when she looks at her, Nic sees, that she is indeed red faced and snotty. Spotty. Young. Doesn't know anything. But what would you expect? Merchant Taylors for fuck's sake.

There is banging on the door out front.

'Oh for fuck's sake! What now?'

She goes out front. It's Popper. She unlocks the door. Could you find anyone who would look more out of place in here?

You could put him in Armani, and he'd still look like a fucking cockroach.

'What you doing here?' she says.

He walks around, touching things.

'It's nice in here. I like it. It'ss ssmart. Sssuits you Nic. You go with thiss sshop.'

Which is sweet, but he still could do with a wash and a shave and a decent haircut and a kick up the arse.

'Get your grubby hands off the goods,' she says, and he raises his hands in the air like he's waiting to get shot.

She goes to the till.

Alys comes in, still snotty, having rubbed off most of the make up so badly that she looks like a clown getting ready for bed. It's going to be a tissue and spit job, she can see. At least she's wearing the tights.

'Well, that looks better for a start. Popper, this is Alys who works with me. Alys, this is Popper who works with my sister.'

'What do you do?' asks Alys.

'What do we do?' says Popper, looking a bit confused.

'Yes, what do you work as?'

'You mean our professssion?'

'Yeah. I mean yes. Yeah. Yes. Sorry.'

'We're entrepreneurss. Jusst thought I'd you know, pop in to ssee you Nic sseeing how I wass in town like. Pop. Hah. Me and Nat gotta go ssee a man about a dog. Thiss is nice sstuff. Nice quality.'

'Keep your thieving little hands off of it.'

'I'm retired.'

Popper is eyeing Alys who is pawing around in her handbag.

'Got ssome good weed coming in end of week if you're interessted.'

Alys looks up at him. Nic can see the cogs turning in her head.

She's a bit fucking slow for someone who goes to that school.
  'Yes please. Yes,' says Alys.
  'Whass your name again?'
  'Alys. But not like you know, "Alice In Wonderland." A.L.Y.S.'
  '"Through The Looking Glasss" iss better.'
  'Do you think so? He was a very weird man.'
  'Yeah, right perv. Nic'll give you my number. Bye Nic. Bye Alysss.'
  He scuttles off out the door.
  'Well, my little posh friend, that's you on board then. And Alys?'
  'Yes?'
  'You be a good girl from now on. Alright?'

Nat

She sits in her car. Herds of kids come out the school. Then one, a very small boy, comes running out of the school yard and then races off down the road. Gwen comes running out after him.

'Jason! Jason!' Gwen is yelling. She doesn't run down the road though but turns to go back into school then sees her and comes over. No smile on her face. No greeting. She buzzes the window down.

'It's POETS Day,' she says. 'Thought you might like a lift home.'

'I like the bus.'

Gwen goes back inside. She waits. Smokes a cigarette. After about ten minutes, Gwen comes back out dressed to go home and gets in the car. Ice picks in her eyes but her eyes are red too.

'Why was that little lad so upset?' she says.

'"Repeated instances of extremely challenging behaviour. Difficulties in interacting with other children. Difficulties, challenging, borderline, remedial, authority issues, extra support, complex home structure. The Child Protection Register." That sort of thing. But do you know what's the worst thing for me? I can see him in there, the little kid that wants to learn, but I can only get to him about ten percent of the time.'

'That's not all your kids.'

'Not all, no. But enough. Fucking enough. I am so impotent, and we are all so impotent and sometimes I think we are doing nothing for these children. Nothing. We might as well just be crowd control.' Gwen pauses. 'What's Poet's day? Is that like Bloomsday?'

'Piss Off Early Tomorrow's Saturday.'

'Oh. I get frustrated with them. And I get angry. And I get exhausted. But mostly I just get sad. They make me so sad.'

'The interesting thing about the At Risk Register is that when they've red flagged your case file you get the higher-up grade social workers. The SS, not the rank and file. We always thought it was quite stupid that because the ones you gotta watch out for are the fresh off the boat rookies because they're genuine and warm and they might trick you into letting your guard down. Ten percent is pretty bloody good. Because if he isn't giving it up at all then his privacy and fragile sense of autonomy have already been so violated that clinging on to the vestiges of them is the only thing that's he's got left. You've got a chink there. Use it. And so it's hard? So? You like that it's hard or you wouldn't be here. Can Jason read?'

'Some.'

'Can he write?'

'A little bit.'

'Then he's like an upscaled version of Popper girl except Popper never got lucky enough to have a teacher like you who could actually get past the aggressive chaos enough to care. If he had had someone like you he might be Poet Laureate by now. Or at least a little less trouble. Jason knows that you think that he can learn to do stuff. That may well be like a fucking miracle for him. So don't you tell me this defeatist "it's only a drop in the ocean of the untermenschen" Tory shite. Anything, and I mean anything, that someone of your calibre can do is a fuck of a lot better than nothing. And you can come with me right now and we'll go do something you like. Anything you like.'

She puts his hand in her coat pocket and takes a packet of pencils out and holds it out to her.

'I was gonna try and get a packet of chocolate éclairs in there, but I thought it might get nasty. Is that what a proper day's work looks like then? A proper hard day's work?'

'As opposed to soiling your hands with the used notes of the Friday night partiers? Then yes.'

She withdraws her hand.

'Could you please just take me home?'

They are silent on the drive, a charged silence, a bitter one. She regrets coming to get her.

'I'm sorry for saying that,' says Gwen eventually. 'It was a mean thing to say. Thank you for coming to get me. It was really kind of you.'

'True though. But this is who I am Gwen, this is what I do. You've never said it was a problem for you before.'

'Do you ever wish you had gone to university?'

'So, are we alright or not?'

'Yes, Miss Bennett we are.'

'What would you like to do now then?'

'Could we run away to sea?'

'We could run away to West Kirby. That do you?'

'Will there be candy floss?'

'It's not Blackpool.'

'I've never been to Blackpool.'

'What a sheltered life you've led. Kiss me.'

'Only if you take me to Blackpool.'

'That's blackmail.'

'Yep.'

Gwen

Her make-up done, which took all of a minute, she sits on the bathroom floor and watches Nic doing hers, which is a precise activity that takes some time. Nic smells of Chanel No 19, which she uses on herself reverently, as though it was holy water.

'It's a private thing, isn't it? Putting on make-up,' she says.

'I know what you mean. Shit. Ow. I nearly stuck the wand in my eye. No, I don't. I don't care who sees me, what I don't like is anyone seeing me with it off. Apart from you. And Nat. And Petey.'

'Why not?'

'Dunno. Our mum was the same. Never went out the house without her face on.'

'Protection? Disguise?'

'Just makes you feel better, doesn't it? Gives you a lift.'

'Survival mechanism.'

'Something like that yeah.'

She is pointing her toes, stretching her legs out in her baggy jeans. She's got her best pair of Converse on, which is not saying much, and a green top.

'Gwen love, you can't wear that.'

'This? I like this. Do you think she's bothered? That I'm not like. Well, I'm not like any of the girls who are always dancing round her. You know. Proper girls. In girls' clothes.'

'Ha. Shouldn't think so love. If their clothes were any tighter, they'd be inhaling them. I think she likes you as you are. But you could do better than that. You're a pretty girl. Why you wearing a sack? Did you make that?'

'No. I bought it. In a shop.'

'You were robbed. Come on,' she says.

In Nic's pink bedroom the radio is on. An old song comes on, "Janie's got a gun".

'Nothing you've got is going to fit me.'

'It's called stretch.'

She looks at the photos on the chest of drawers. The twins on the day of their first communion in their matching white satin dresses. The cleanest children you ever did see. Their parents on their wedding day, their mum, small and skinny and beautiful, with her brown hair up, with a long cream lace dress that Nic said she made herself. Petey, chubby and laughing, in his highchair, banging a spoon. A skinny teenage Nat on the beach with Petey on her shoulders. Nic is the keeper of things that she didn't even know she was missing until she saw them. The before bit of their life.

She leans over and strokes Nic's bedspread, all silk and satin. She looks at the small skirt that Nic is holding up and laughs. It's the sort of thing that Lola has tried to get her into before.

'That'll never fit.'

'Don't count on it.'

'I've got fat legs.'

'Try. It.'

She takes her jeans off. Stands there in her black knickers and her ugly top.

'Your legs are nice.'

'They're going to look like sausages in that skirt.'

'Skinny legs aren't all that.'

'Says the owner of the world's best legs.'

'You think I've got the world's best legs?'

'Pretty much yes. In my next life I'm going to have legs like yours. Only if I'm very good obviously. And especially nice to old ladies and kittens.'

She pulls the skirt on. Nic tugs at it. It feels snug round her bum, too tight and her knees are exposed. She hates her knees.

'Good,' says Nic, 'put this on.'

'It feels too tight.'

'Shut it.'

'I hate my knees.'

'What did I say?'

Nic hands her a grey top with a high neck but with a long split down the cleavage. It's the colour of gunmetal, silky.

'It'll look good. You've got the tits.'

'Breasts.'

'Why?'

'Don't like the word "tits."'

'Put the fucking top on.'

'I like this,' she says holding it up. She takes her own top off and puts the other one on. Nic inspects her.

'Thanks Nic.'

'Sexy.'

'Really?'

'Classy. Gorgeous.'

Nic reaches under the collar and pulls up the bra strap.

'I don't think you're going to lend me a bra.'

'No,' laughs Nic, 'don't think so. But I am gonna change these straps. Take it off again.'

She takes the top off. Nic goes behind her and adjusts the straps of the bra.

'Now come in the bathroom and I'll sort your make-up. We'll fuck with our kid's head a bit. Make a bloody change.'

'It's like being in "Pretty Woman".'

'Yeah. Right.'

Her mouth hangs open.

'Oh shit. Sorry Nic. I didn't mean, oh bollocks. Sorry.'

'S'alright.'

'It's not. Sorry. I'm stupid,' and she hugs her, 'thank you,' she says.

Nic takes her chin in her hand. Puts her mouth on her mouth. She breaks the hold, moves back.

'Sorry,' says Nic, 'can we just forget that? Sorry Gwen.'

She looks at her.

'Have you ever heard of that American bumper sticker: WHAT WOULD JESUS DO?'

'Nah.'

'I'm going to print up a new set. WHAT WOULD NAT DO?'

'Great.'

'So Nic? What would Nat do?'

'Now?'

'Yeah. If I was your girlfriend not Nat's and Nat was you right now what would Nat do?'

'Let's go out.'

'No. I'm not going until you say.'

'We're nuts. We've always been nuts.'

'No, you're not.'

'Yeah, we are. It's a mess in our heads Gwen, it's a fucking bundle of wires up there to be honest. Crossed wires. You should… you should leave.'

'Leave Nat?'

'Yeah.'

'Why?'

'This isn't gonna end well. Things don't for us. You're not seeing us straight 'cos you're head over heels but it's not gonna be good for much longer 'cos it never is. It's fucked. We're fucked.'

'And now you're kissing me.'

'See?'

'Do you like women? Have sex with women?'

'Sometimes. Have done.'

'Work?'

'Yeah. And play. But it's just sex. Only seem to fall for bastard men.'

'Do you want to have sex with me?'
'Yeah.'
'Why?'
'Because I fancy you. And I think you're great. And I'm jealous. I'm jealous I think. And I don't like being jealous of her. And I'm not used to…'
'What?'
'To not doing whatever fucking stupid thing I feel like doing. Just like her. But it's about time we stopped.'
'And if I said I fancied you?'
'You don't.'
'I do. Actually. Worryingly. I find it difficult sometimes being around you sometimes. When you sleep in my bed, I want to touch you. Messy eh?'
'You've got that right.'
'I don't know if it's because you remind me of her. Would she mind?'
'Probably not.'
'So shall we?'
'No. I like it as it is. I like you being a friend. A proper friend. Never had a real friend like you before. Don't wanna fuck this up.'

Nic is grasping her hands together. She goes and picks up her hands.

'You're lovely. Whatever you may think about yourself Nicola Shaw, I think you're lovely. I am biased, being a big fan of Shaw genetic material, but I think you're beautiful and sexy and funny and smart and great fun. And I love being your friend. When this all goes down, will you still be friends with me? Somehow. Although it will take me a lot of time to get over this. When your sister goes. I know she will. So. But. Be my friend. Always. Promise?'
'Promise.'
'On what?'
'On our Petey.'

She puts her mouth on Nic's, just to seal the deal. Well, in her head that's what she's doing but really she wants to feel it again. What she just felt. She takes her mouth off Nic's who is looking at her in the way Nat would be looking at her, neutral, watching, head slightly cocked, the wicked smile twitching in the corners of her mouth, the control in the corners of her eyes. Ah, what she would do, how far she would go, for that smile. She watches it bloom in Nic's eyes: the decision to let lust have its way.

'Oh fuck Nic. Don't look at me like that.'

'Is she good?'

'What do you think?'

'Course.'

'She makes good look like a tea cake Nicola. She makes sex with anyone else look like a complete waste of time. Do you want to know why?'

'Yeah.'

'She's there, completely there. I've never met anyone else, not that I have that much to compare it with, who is. Well, that's how she is with me. And presumably Nicola, with everyone else too. Because I do, despite what Popper says, have some fucking clue.'

'I know you do love. Never said you didn't.'

'Are you good?'

'Try me.'

'What is that? A challenge?'

'Yeah. Try me. 'Cos yeah, you are my best mate but now I've started I can't stop. I can't walk away. Never was no good at walking away.'

'You are so like your sister.'

That wonderful, loveable, full-on smile.

'Wanna see if I kiss like my sister?'

Nic's tongue in her hot mouth. Nic's hands on her back, then one hand under her bra strap, the other one up to the nape of her neck. They kiss and kiss and kiss, Nic leaning against her but it gets worse not better, Nic undoes her bra, she takes her top off and undoes her own bra, and somehow they are up against the wall, Nic is pushing her up against the wall, she has her hands on her breasts, she is biting them, she has one nipple in her mouth but then Nic moves her mouth away, holds her so tight, grips her. She is shaking and Nic moves her hands down her back to touch the top of her bum under the skirt she lent her. Nic kisses the sides of her neck, her ears and puts her mouth back on her mouth and holds her hard against the wall, presses her pubic bone up against hers. Nic takes her mouth away. When her voice comes, it comes out deeper, just like Nat's does when she's gripped with need, but her face is a blank.

'Sex for me Gwen and sex for our kid, it isn't what it is for you. It's something we can use. And I know you know, but you know what, just for once, I've got one over on my sister, 'cos she doesn't. It's something she just doesn't wanna see. She's hanging on by the skin of her teeth here with you and I feel sorry for her 'cos she wants this so much and she's fighting so hard for it, you haven't got any idea love of the way she's having to fight for you 'cos you must think that she's always like this. But she's not. Not never. With no one.'

And Nic presses herself so hard against her, it's like Nic's skin is her skin.

'You wanna know what would Natalie do? Or do you wanna know what could Natalie do? 'Cos it's anything, it's anything, and I hate that about us and you know what, Natalie hates it too but that's what we're like. I can do sex standing on my fucking head and so can she, and it doesn't mean fuck all to us and the thing is I like you more than that. She likes you more than that. And you're in the next-door room and it fucking kills me sometimes to be honest but I know this is the best she's ever had and I know you're the best person we know and I don't want to. And no, I don't think she'd mind. But I do. I mind. I need some help here Gwen. Please. I don't ask for much 'cos I've never got much. But please. Please.'

She brings her hands down from the wall, holds onto Nic's wrists so hard it must hurt but Nic doesn't move. She takes Nic's arms and wraps them around her own back, wraps her arms around Nic. She holds onto Nic as tight as she can. It is the strangest of things. It is as near as she will ever get to being with Nat by being with someone else. She puts her hand up to Nic's ear, traces it with her finger.

'The first time I met you, you put your hand in my hair. I couldn't work you out. It felt like you were flirting with me and giving me a warning at the same time. What were you doing, do you remember?'

'I was messing with you.'

She pushes herself away from Nic by using her arms as levers. Then she puts her hands up and takes Nic's chin in them and kisses her with the softest of kisses on her mouth, on her eyelids, then back to her mouth. Then she lets go of her and moves away, her back to Nic, she takes the skirt off and puts her jeans back on, finds her bra and puts that on, fastens the back. She finds her flowery socks. She stands there facing away.

'I won't forget that Nicola. Thank you.'

She turns round and looks at Nic, the other loveliest woman she knows, naked from the waist up, who is standing with her hands on her hips, looking down at the floor. They throw her for a loop. Both of them. How strange is the world. She thinks then that they will always, the two of them, have this effect on her and how wonderful that is. And how terrifying.

'You are so beautiful, and you deserve so much better than this,' she says.

Nic looks up. She picks up Nic's lacy push up bra.

'I'm presuming you have the matching thong but please don't show me.'

She goes to Nic and slides the straps back up her arms, fits her breasts into the cups and reaches around her to do up the back.

She is trembling but determined. Then she passes Nic her top, picks up the one she had on from the bed.

'Can I wear this with my jeans?'

'Have it,' says Nic, 'it looks better on you anyway. It looks better. With breasts.'

Nic's eyes are wet, her tongue is in the corner of her cheek. She puts the top on and Nic slides her own top back over her head.

'Gwen.'

'Yeah?'

'Thank you for stopping.'

'You may not realise it, but you were the one who stopped.'

'Did I?'

'Yeah. I didn't have a hope in hell there. But you've already stopped, haven't you? You said you didn't want to do it anymore. And then you stopped. Do you know how much I admire you? How much I am always admiring you?'

She holds out her hand.

'Nicola Shaw. Let's go out and get totally fucking wasted.'

Popper's wearing a t-shirt that reads - GAS TAP FEVER.

'Yousse are late.'

'Didn't know you had time frames Popper,' she says.

'Didn't even know you had a watch,' says Nic.

Which he has, she notices now for the first time. What else hasn't she noticed?

'Coursse I've got a fucking watch.'

You never know with him, what he'll pick up on and what he'll miss. He has an ability to know when you're off colour without you saying a thing. He can work out when you're vulnerable, when you're sad, tired, lonely, confused, just come on, longing for a quiet time. And he'll go for you. It's not a nice characteristic. It is, she has thought in the past, a killer instinct, something primeval, like the way predators can smell the wounds of dying animals from miles away across the tundra. But it depends on his extremely volatile mood and his particular narcotic mix. What Would Nat Do? She looks at him head on, stares him down calmly but her fists tighten. Luckily Nic is next to her. She can feel Nic's thigh on her thigh. She remembers to breathe in. Presses back. Nic leans into her.

'I'm trying not to think about your breasts,' whispers Nic.

'Tits,' says Gwen, putting her mouth right up to Nic's ear, touching her ear, her arm snaking around her back, tucking itself up under her top. She feels the prickle of the skin on Nic's back in the tips of her fingers, she feels her goose bumps. She giggles. Nic giggles.

'What you two mingersss laughing about?'

'Mingers? Very nice. Got a mouth on you tonight lad. What? The coke's off? No screw?'

'I wouldn't ssscrew you if you begged me for it,' he hisses at Nic.

'What's "Gas Tap Fever"?' she says.

He ignores her. But she can't be bothered to be ignored. Not tonight. She can't be bothered with all this back down, soft girl rubbish she's always doing. How come she has to play nice and everybody else gets to play dirty, just because it's what's expected of her? Why does she have to always be such a fucking good girl?

'Gone deaf Popper? Or just ignoring me? What's "Gas Tap Fever"?'

He doesn't look at her. He looks at the crowd around him. He rubs his eyes.

'Popper. I'm talking to you. When someone talks to you it's generally considered polite to answer. If one can speak that is. If one can string words together into a coherent sentence. If one isn't too out of it to understand what's going on.'

'It's a band you twat. Yousse wouldn't have heard of them.' Cos you know fuck all.'

'Don't talk to me like that.'

'I'll talk to you however the fuck I like.'

'What? Are you going to start with your spiel now? I know

fuck all. I've seen fuck all. The standard crap you come out with every fucking time.'

Nic puts her hand on her arm.

'But it'ss true,' he says, pushing his face up to hers, 'you do know fuck all. You're a sstupid little ssoft as sshite fat girl who don't know nothing. So fuck off.'

'It's not me who knows nothing, it's you. You twat.'

Eyes on the both of them now like the keep out warnings on disused quarries. Like the skull and crossbones on the backs of chemical trucks.

'Fuck off.'

'You ever, and I mean ever, come on to me again, make me an offer behind Nat's back again...'

'Fuck off.'

'That's an extensive vocabulary you've got yourself there. You nasty little selfish bastard. Why are you like this to me? I haven't taken her away from you. Why do you hate me so much?'

'Where's the boss?' says Nic, getting between them.

'Fuck off. Fuck off. Fuck off,' he is spitting at her. She can see his hands in fists. She tries to get past Nic who holds her off with one arm.

'Where's my sister Popper? Try to concentrate. Where the fuck is my sister? Tell us that and we'll leave you alone.'

'There'ss Nat.'

They look. She's at the bottom of some stairs. She hasn't seen them. A girl is leaning into her whispering something. Nat laughs. Passes her something and then kisses her. On the mouth. Nat puts her hand into her hair.

She feels like the metres between them are a hundred miles, like she's seeing this happen in front of her but very, very far away. Nat puts her hand on the girl's arse. She's talking into her ear now. She is near enough to see that smile. She knows that smile. It was always going to come to this, wasn't it? It's just been slow getting here that's all, slower than you would have thought.

She gets round Nic, who seems to have forgotten where she is. She feels like she's very drunk or very high. She stands right up in Popper's face.

'It's interesting.'

'What?'

'That you always wear things with writing on. With names. Just think of the mistakes you must have made over the years. Did Nat help you? Make sure you didn't buy a Westlife t-shirt by mistake? Considering the fact that up to very recently you were illiterate. Illiterate Iggy. It's the name of a band. A very fucking awful crappy band. All the 'i' words. Illiterate. Ignorant. Impotent maybe? Shall I spell that for you? They start with 'i', do you know 'i', it comes after 'h', 'h for house, h for home,' not that you would probably know either of those words either, would you? Wouldn't know what a home was like would you Popper? Unless the Children's Home qualifies.'

His eyes. He says what he says so slowly and quietly she has to lean in to hear him.

'She's been fucking her. For the last half an hour. She's been upstairss fucking her. You don't know nothing. Nothing. That girl could get her off in wayss you never could. 'Cos you're fucking ugly. Fat. Ugly. Cunt. Cunt. You're a cunt. And you, you're a bag of fucking boness,' his volume rising as he spits at Nic as she moves towards him, 'it'd be like fucking a xylophone, I wouldn't have fucking paid you for it if you were the last hooker on Hope Street. It's a wonder you ever made a fucking penny.'

She hits him with all the force she can muster. She has aimed for his mouth, and she hits his cheek but the blow glances off and he is on her before she can even lower her arm. He has his hand on her throat, has her down to the floor, before she can make a sound. Nic is tearing at him. Nic is screaming.

'Natalie!' She is screaming. 'Natalie! Natalie!'

Nat

In the taxi, she hangs on to Gwen, holding her in her arms, cradling her, she has her head on her chest, retching.

'Don't want that girl throwing up in my cab. If she's gonna puke, you're all out,' says the driver.

Before she can say anything, before she can think of anything to say, make her brain work in any way whatsoever, Nic leans forward and hisses.

'We are driving to fucking A & E. Where do you think we were going? Butlins? You fucking wanker. Put your fucking foot down. You aren't there in four minutes it won't be puke you'll be stressing about; it'll be the fucking knife in the back of your fat fucking neck. Now get a fucking shift on.'

PART FOUR

Nat

She's sitting in her chair with her legs stretched out in front of her, feet up on another chair because her feet seem to be aching. She's still dressed in the clothes from the club, still wearing her coat even, hasn't even managed to get her boots off, can't seem to get her boots off. Nic is in bed. She made her go to bed although she bets that she isn't sleeping. She was sitting on the floor next to Gwen lying on the couch and she wouldn't go but she insisted.

'One of us needs to be with it tomorrow. You go to bed girl. I can watch her from here, can't I? You go to bed and when you wake up, I can have a kip. Alright?'

'Doctor says she's fine. She's fine. I dunno how but she is. Otherwise, they wouldn't have let her out, would they? She'll be alright Natalie. She will. She'll be fine.'

'I'm so fucking stupid.'

'It was gonna happen sooner or later, wasn't it? It was just bad luck. Tonight. All of it. She'll be OK. No head injuries. Fucking miracle. She was just sick 'cos of the shock like.'

'I will kill him.'

'You won't do nothing. You hear me? Nothing right now. We'll see about it in the morning.'

She sits in her chair. She stares at the wall. Drinks tea that has gone so cold there's a skin on it. Smokes cigarettes. She looks at Gwen lying there. She has lit all of their candles, and their books are illuminated. It looks like a medieval library in here. Gwen looks as beautiful as she has ever seen her. Like a short haired Ophelia floating downstream.

Behind her is a wall full of pictures, ones the kids at Gwen's school made for her. She found them on Gwen's desk one day and went out and bought a load of those clip-on frames and trimmed the paintings and drawings to fit and put them up there. She was thinking of the Lady Lever where there are so many paintings that they look like they've been hung any place they'll fit so that you can turn a corner and come across a Rosetti casually placed up above a door frame, as though to say, oh this old thing. She liked that exuberance, that abundance, and wanted to recreate something like that but she realised after she'd done it and was sitting there waiting for Gwen to come home, that it wasn't just to please her, wasn't just to show off some of the stuff that's lovely, but because it was a record of what she'd done, what she is doing. My girl, say the pictures to her, my girl does this. She helps little kids make this. It's like happiness framed. And so yeah, it was worth it for the joy it brought Gwen to see it, a kid's joy, she doesn't know any other adult that has the capacity for that level of excited joy, maybe the kids rub off on her.

On the wall are dogs and cats and houses and stars and cars and lorries and people and fields full of flowers. Red flowers and blue flowers, yellow and orange and purple rampaging through slats of bright green grass. Pale blue impressionist splodgy skies. Butterflies made of pipe cleaners. Who knew they still made pipe cleaners? Thank you, Miss Robertson, that's the one she put in the middle for her, words obviously laboured long over. And now she lies under all of this, her supine sweetheart, under a blanket that spent years in the airing cupboard of the house she grew up in, and she can't see the marks on her neck that are her fault, but she knows they are there.

'What would you give me if I asked you?' says a small voice.

She held her on the way to the hospital she remembers but she hasn't touched her since. It was Nic who held her hand on the way home, Nic who put a t-shirt and trackies on her,

'I'm alright. I'm fine,' Gwen said to Nic then. 'Look at me. I'm fine. It's only these marks. Nothing else. Look. I'll have some lovely bruises tomorrow. Today.'

And Nic came close and touched them softly, but she looked away.

She looks at her now.

'What do you want then? Ask.'

'What's the point of asking for what I won't get?'

'Gwen.'

'Am I a liability to you?'

'Yes,' she says.

'How many? Are there lots?'

'Yes.'

'How many?'

'I don't count.'

'You do count. You count everything. You calculate all the time.'

'Not that.'

'Why?'

'Because it's not important enough to me. They don't matter.'

Gwen sits up. She puts her hand up to her throat. She is looking straight at her now, angry. She is waiting to see if she will hit her like she once threatened to do. She wishes she would.

'You would have been a good lawyer,' Gwen says, and she didn't know she could sound so bitter.

'Maybe.'

'Then why aren't you? Why aren't you doing that? Why didn't you go to uni? You would have loved it. Why not? I know your mum. But later. You could have gone later. Why didn't you pull your finger out?'

'Because I'm lazy.'

'That's not true. That's so not true. That's a lazy answer, yes.

That's a cop out but it won't wash with me. It's bullshit. Don't bullshit me just because you can get away with it with everybody else.'

'I'm not a lawyer because I don't believe in other people's rules.'

'What the "Scousers as Anarchists" speech again?'

'Listen to me. Calm down alright. You brought this up. I'll tell you whatever you like. But you need to stay still.'

'What are you going to do? Walk away? Go on then. Off you go. Out into the night again like a bloody vampire, back to your floozies.'

'That's a good word.'

'If you tell me its morphology, I will thump you one.'

'You've had enough fighting for one night. You've had a big shock. Please don't do this.'

She's so tired that her ears ring. There's a pain in the back of her neck that just won't shift. She rubs the bridge of her nose between thumb and forefinger.

'Why are you doing what you're doing?' says Gwen. 'Still. Helping the coke barons install more marble in their bathrooms? Diamond encrust their platinum taps?'

'I work for myself. Private fucking enterprise. On my bicycle.'

'Mephistopheles got you anyway then. What about the thousands of deaths every year in Colombia? Would you like to present me with a justification for Colombia? Drug mules? Gang wars? Civil war near enough in Mexico. The living dead out there on the streets? How does your inner anarchist deal with that?'

'Why you starting with this stuff now?'

'Because I fucking well feel like it. So what's your answer? Go on, justify yourself. Why are you a drug dealer? Why are you doing something that you could do with one arm tied behind your back when you could be absolutely anything you wanted to be by now? Anything at all. You are so brilliant, and you are using ten percent of what you have, running around in the night selling drugs. What the fuck are you doing?'

'Everything's tainted.'

'That's such a good answer. Let me write it down.'

'Tell me something that you can buy that's pure. That doesn't involve corruption and greed and shit wages and God-awful working conditions somewhere along the line. That doesn't involve slavery, and I don't use that word lightly Gwen because this city, this house you're in right now probably, was built off the back of that. That top you're wearing. Know where that comes from do you? Can justify its path from a field to your back and swear to me that it didn't cost, along the line somewhere, some poor bugger's exploitation? Some child labouring over the making of that zip? And don't get me started on the Catholic Church please or the shampoo you use that puts out rabbits' eyes. So you tell me one thing what doesn't involve the death of innocents or the exploitation of the impoverished and I'll give you a gold fucking star.'

'You got angry,' Gwen says.

She says nothing.

'I knew Nat. Of course I knew. I just didn't think about it, and I hardly ever talked about it. Nic didn't talk about it. Even Lola was remarkably restrained. Even Popper for God's sake managed not to shove it directly into my face most of the time.'

'Popper. He started this.'

'No, he didn't. Tonight? I started. But it's always been here. Right from the get-go. "I don't do more than one-night stands." You told me straight.'

'Yeah, I did tell you.'

She leans her arms on her knees and looks at the floor.

'Do you know what I wanted?' she says. 'I wanted you safe. I wanted you innocent and tucked up in bed and safe. And I'm not dissing the fact you're innocent, I'm not, it's a good thing and for your own good. I wanted you safe and I've been trying not to think, Jesus, not to think that I've been the one who's been damaging you. And I can't breathe when I think that; I can't breathe. And I've got to be breathing kid, I've got to be here breathing, on my toes, all the fucking time. There is no let up. It's fucking survival. It's the game.'

'Then stop playing the game.'

'You have no idea,' and she says this with some kind of hopefulness.

'That's what Popper says. Except he makes it sound like a threat.'

'When I saw you on the floor Gwen with him on you. Jesus.'

'Where is Popper?'

'I'll get it sorted.'

'All he did was put his hands on my throat because I hit him. It's not that bad.'

'It is that bad.'

Gwen's crying now.

'You expect so much of people. You expect so much of me. And I can't or won't live up to your expectations. I can't. And I won't. What do you want from me Gwen? I don't think I can give you anything you want. It's not that I don't wanna try. I've been trying. This last year. Every day. But look at how big I've fucked up. I just. It's impossible.' She crosses her arms over her chest and one leg over the other. 'I know none of this will make any sense to you. The person I am out there is so different from the person I am with you. This is it Gwen. This is fucking it.'

Gwen's sitting on the carpet now with her head on her arms and she can't see her face.

'If you wanna go now I'll help you any way I can. I'll help you with your stuff, I'll find you a flat. Money? I'll give you whatever you need to sort yourself out. Or I'll get Nic to help you if you'd rather. I'm not justifying what I do and I'm sorry if that's what it sounded like. It wouldn't stand up in court and that's why I wouldn't cut it, I wouldn't cut it. I can do this though and so this is what I do. I'm good at it and I must like the craic or something. Gwen? Are you listening to me? This is your choice. And this is the line. This is the line right here.'

For a while there is silence. Gwen sits curled up with her face on her knees. She lights a cigarette. Then she says, as though speaking to herself,

'It was easy to slide into if the truth be told and not so easy to slide out of. I was making money hand over fist when you were still doodling on your schoolbooks, and I got used to it. And I like some myself and it was just easy. Truth is it entertains me, the subterfuge. And it's about being part of a community. That lovely, debased term. And yeah, it's a ridiculous way to link people, the taking of mind-altering substances, but that's how it works. Freaks like us. Why am I telling you this stuff now?'

Gwen turns her face towards her.

'I'm so sorry. I know it means fuck all but I'm so very sorry.'

Gwen blows her nose on her t-shirt. She looks so young to her then, like a girl, like the girl in her parents' photographs back in Somerset but she's not a girl is she, that's just the way she treats her half the time. She's got a brain that outdoes hers, and yet she treats her like a kid.

'I ragged Popper about the Children's Home Nat. I said that he wouldn't know what home was. Nice eh? Then before that, even earlier yesterday evening, and if the past is another country, yes, well then yesterday evening was Australia as far as I am concerned, it feels so far away now, I snogged your sister. Is that better? Have I evened things up now? Do I get to compete in the 'I'm not a very nice person' competition?

'She's had a thing about you for ages. I didn't know if you'd noticed. Was it nice the kiss?'

'Yes. Yes, it was. Not just the kiss. All of it was nice. But she stopped.'

'That's a first. Why?'

'Because she didn't think it was right. Which it isn't. Obviously.'

'Is that why you stopped too?'

'Because I'm the good one? I couldn't see how to make it all pan out. I couldn't see how sleeping with your twin sister would improve the quality of our lives. Mine, yours or hers.'

'The concept of logic as applied to desire. I've always wondered about that. I'm sorry Gwen. I should never have asked you to live with me. It was such a selfish thing to do. You shouldn't be living like this. I've got blood all over my hands and you've got poster paint. It's gotta stop. Do you want me to take you to Lola's?'

'I'd like to be on my own for a while. But I'd like to stay here. I mean, I know Nic's here but right now I can't cope well with you being here as well.'

'OK.'

She gets up.

'Are you sure you're alright?' she says.

'Yes. Will you come home tomorrow, and we can talk more?'

'If that's OK with you?'

'Yes. I'm going to bed now then,' Gwen says and goes out of the room.

She leaves the flat.

She couldn't study anymore after their mum died so, much to their dad's anger and disgust, she left school. For a year or so she hardly even read anything, would open a book sometimes, as she had always done, looking for something new, and then close it again. Even the soft sucking pull of the poets didn't do it for her anymore. She could hardly even skim the paper; the headlines would rise up at her in a sickly grey fuzz. All she wanted to do was go out and get wrecked, get wrecked, stay out, make cash, fuck women, go to clubs, get stoned, drink anything she could get his hands on, sleep on a sofa in a club, waking up with the cleaners looking at her, in the bed of some girl she couldn't remember the name of. Classic really. Oblivion.

She was only nineteen when she went down. In a way, in a funny way, it helped her. Being confined calmed her, being caged stopped her being so wild. She started to read again and then got into it, re-addicted, read and read and worked out and smoked her weed and watched and listened but kept to the fringes. And then one day they gave her a new cell mate. And there was Evie. She made her feel better, Evie did, maybe just because she could talk to her and hold her. Her air of absence, that daydreamer's eye, that reminded her of Petey. A girl with good hands, tidy little boxer she was. She'd chosen her own text and the Icarus wings, because she wasn't a girl anymore, but a woman, a woman burnt by death, fallen down from the face of the sun. Perhaps she has never stopped falling.

She traces her fingers in the grooves of their names.

Eliza Parry. 26th March 1882. 14 years.
Emily Williams. 30th March 1882. 9 months.

Jack was right, she should have a Maglite. Her lighter goes out. She looks up at the cathedral. She loves that building, it's her landmark. Her side's one is at the other end of the street, she has always thought that they looked like duellists facing each other in a stand-off. A duel Nic said. She thinks about that lad lying on the ground. Up above her on Gambier Terrace, John Lennon and Stu Sutcliffe once lived for a while. Liverpool is a funny place, a place of pain and poetry, sea shanties and sousing. She thinks of the people on the Kop rising up to cheer a goal. That surge. The red.

Evie was what, twenty? She'd got out three months before she was due to and she was chewed up by a pair of Rottweilers that her ex-boss had sent to frighten her, back alley, she'd fucked up a forgery, perhaps deliberately, she had a funny sense of humour did Evie, was capable of that, or maybe just drifted off, too stoned. She remembers being in her cell when she was told. She remembers sitting on her bed and looking at the pictures on her wall that Petey and Evie had drawn him. Evie had a thing about fake heraldic insignia, Petey was going through an imaginary animal phase, so that her wall looked like the wall of some great castle, all red and gold griffins and blue and silver crests. She remembers that she didn't feel anything, not the way she felt after her mum died, when it was as if her emotional system had been butchered, no she felt blank, spacey even. Maybe, she had thought at the time, I just can't fit any more pain in. What a stupid thing to think. She's a coward when it comes down to it, an avoider. And after she got out, she did what had to be done. But the blood didn't stick. Not no Macbeth then. She's not haunted. Well, not by them. It does help, here's the thing, not to care that much.

Why doesn't she want more? She's been asked that before by Jack Sands, the first time they met.

'What you doing? You're too bright for this. I could use a bright girl like you. I like the way you did what you needed to do, no fuss. I like everything I know about you. You're old school like me. I like that.'

'No thank you,' she said, 'I appreciate the offer but no.'

And it could have gone either way for her then. The man could have really taken offence or just decided to get rid of her anyway for the sake of convenience. That was crunch time. It was her Rubicon. She sat there and looked at the man in front of her, and thought, in a couple of years' time, I could be you if that's who I wanted to be.

'What do you want then?' said Jack.

'I'm very grateful for you offer but I want to live without fucking bodyguards outside my own fucking door. I want to deal only to people I actually like. Small scale. Freelance. Give me some leeway Jack. You be Amazon, I just want to be Hay on Wye.'

And Jack just looked at her and laughed and said, 'Do you want BUPA?'

Turns out that honesty was the best policy. Honour amongst thieves. It is who you know and not what.

And there is no going back now, and it doesn't make no never mind anyway. What is she supposed to do now? She looks around at the graves. All the dead underneath her. Is that all there is for her? Hanging on to this past, stuck, never moving forward. What is the way out of this mess? Mess, she thinks. I love you because you make an awful mess Gwen. I forgot to tell you that. She rolls a spliff and then she gets out her notebook and pen. She writes a list in the cold, foggy light of a graveyard grey Liverpool night.

Because I don't like the way you don't rinse the plates after you wash them up.
Because you leave origami cranes next to my toothbrush.
Because you make book rainbows.
Because your socks are funny.
Because you have fat knees, and I love fat knees.
Because of cereal night.
Because you broke the hoover and tried to mend it with ga☒*er tape and made it worse.*
Because of your pencil kisses.
Because you have bedhead in the morning.

Because when you sit on my lap you have been known to fall asleep there and leave drool on my jumper.
Because you saved my sister's life.
Because you bought my brother a Christmas present of a huge box of pastels and a book about the sea birds of America.
Because the first time I took you to Anfield you were converted and your smile was like lighthouses.
Because you make good tagliatelle.
Because you once wrote a poem about tagliatelle: Potatoes never make me think of sex/ they're far too lumpy/ But tagliatelle is something/ you can really get your tongue around.

She thinks about what size Mercy Shaw's fingernails would have been when she died. She thinks about their mum watching telly with her head leaning on her shoulder. She thinks about Evie laughing at one of those comic books she liked so much. She has no fucking clue what to do. She's supposed to be the strongest one, the one who holds it all together, and she is by far, far the weakest. The biggest kid of them all. She's still fucking it up every day, because she is the dragon. And she has fallen in love with Andromeda, like the picture in the Walker. She always thought that Andromeda was getting off on the dragon and Perseus was coming down to rescue her, but she wasn't that interested. But what would she know? She is a study in arrested development. She put her hand on that girl's arse. It was alright as arses go. She fucked her on automatic. She could do that in her sleep. She put her hand in her hair and what she thought was, my girl, she's not got hair like you, gummed up with hairspray or whatever that shite is, my girl's got silky hair, and I want to go home to her right now and get into bed next to her warm back and put my hand in it.

One bloody girl comes home with you, and it all falls apart.

Emma Morgan

Mistakes are so tiny. She should never have gone to see Popper read. She should have stayed home and read Yeats and made herself a nice omelette.

Mary Belly. 18th October 1868. 3 years.

'Mercy Shaw,' she says into the night, 'Minus 3 months. Linda Shaw. 43 years. Evie McNair. 20. "The unnamed dead that go unheard of/The unquiet dead that go unmourned".'

All the lost children. All of those little girls in the ground down there, piled on top of each other. And all those little boys too. All of those tiny bones. Next time she comes down here she's going to bring flowers for them. See if there are still some daffodils around. Narcissi. Hyacinth. Freesias. She likes the ones that smell nice. Nice. Nicest. Best. Because you smell the best. Dunno why. You just do. Maybe she can't help it then. Maybe it's just chemical, pheromones. Magnets. Unseen forces. Impossible to stop.

The fact is that Gwen is not made up of metaphors or of similes. There is no need to compare her with anything else because she is not like anything else, anybody else. Her voice sounds of her voice; her body feels of her body; she smells of her. Gwen. Although she sometimes tastes of Cocoa Pops.

She stands up to go, although she's not sure where. There is a shape in the shadows. A ghost? Here, in this place of shades that would make sense. But then it solidifies, moves towards her. Nobody in their right mind would come down here at this time. It's what? So late it's early. It's not someone in their right mind though. He's standing in front of her, like a very unwanted hallucination. Like the ghost of Banquo. But he's no ghost yet.

'Anne Dempsssssey. 24 yearss. It's not true Nat.'

'What isn't?'

'About my name.'

'I thought it was Iggy. Or amyl nitrite. Is it not?'
'No.'
'Is it not? Didn't know that.'
'It'ss not.'
'What then?'
'My mum. Sshe turned trickss. Brought them home. And I loved her, sshe wass my mum. But sshe wass a junkie and sshe didn't have no veinss left, she wass a fucking messs and sso she ussed to assk me to help her, sso I'd help her.'
'Did you inject her?'
'Yeah. In her leg mosstly or in her neck. Not into the vein like 'cos there wassn't none.'
'Into the muscle?'
'Yeah. Jusst had to get it in her 'cos sshe was dessperate like. I wass only five or ssix. Sseven. Eight when I sstopped. Eight. Sskin popping we called it. I wass the Popper. Would you tell me a poem? I can't remember any. One of yours.'
'There aren't any.'
'Don't believe you. S'alright. It's only me like. You won't puke.'
There is a silence that is as silent as you can find in this city. Up above on Hope Street there is some traffic, but it sounds very far off. It is almost peaceful, down here in the dark.
'There's only a bit of it.' She coughs. 'It's only rough.'
'Go on then Nat. Don't be embarrasssed.
'We're the most un-English of all English cities, perched here on the edge/a defiant city made up of eloquent protesters and professional extroverts/a city proud of its lyrical ways/a sea shanty of a city - rough and roiling - rollicking and ravaged/a city of jokes and songs and nous/a kingdom of melancholy and wishful thinking, similes and sousing'
She stops.
'That's as far as I've got,' she says.

'Not bad. What'ss it called?'

'Fabulate.'

'What doess that mean then?'

'Something like – to invent a story,' she says. 'Or to tell a story full of fantasy. We're a city of fabulators.'

'Better than real life, making sstuff up like.'

'Not always.'

'You need to finissh it. And then you can do an open mike.'

'No way.'

'You could Nat. I'm ssorry you know.'

'About what?'

'About tonight. I sshouldn't have hurt Gwen. I losst it.'

'Yeah, you could say that.'

'Are you gonna kill me?'

'I've been considering it.'

'It'ss alright. You can if you want.'

Popper turns his white throat up to the night. He's a dog, barking at the moon.

She doesn't move. She's never done it cold. You have to warm up to it but now she's here she just feels exhausted. This has been the longest of nights. Must be dawn soon. She likes dawn, the passing of the dead hours, a sliver of optimism about the new day.

'Before you do though, would you come back to mine?' says Popper. 'If you want like. I want to sshow you ssomething.'

'OK.'

She doesn't have it in her now and Popper knows that. It will have to be delayed. Might as well go with him. They go back up the grave lined path, Popper in front, slightly out of breath, and she feels like she's come out of something that had nearly claimed her for its own, but not quite. She shivers. At least she's got her decent coat on.

They trudge up the hill together, the sky the faintest of pink, up into Toxteth, neither of them saying anything. Just like any other long night with the hope of a cup of tea and a bacon butty.

In his bedroom, Popper pulls out a key from under the mattress. She lights a cigarette. Popper goes to his wardrobe and unlocks it. Popper turns to her and gives a big gasping breath.

'What? Have you made Narnia in there again?'

'Not exactly.'

Popper opens the doors and kneels down front of it as though it was some sort of altar.

'I don't ssleep,' Popper says. 'I can't ssleep.'

'Why is your wardrobe full of paper?'

'I had to keep it somewhere.'

'Can I?'

'Yeah.'

She steps forward and picks up the nearest pieces.

I want to tell you that you are beautiful and that I do think at times that my heart will fall out my chest
  I want to tell you so many things but the words taste of bitterness
  Words that are like vinegar?
  I think about the taste of you
  Curiouser and curiouser
  How can I ever touch you?
  When all I do is burn
  Gwen says they taste as bitter as ~~slows~~

SLOES

These are poems/Nobody sees them/Except me/And the page/And the pen/But they are poems I write/For you/As odes to your skin/And valentines for the shape of your mouth/These are words/I wake up with them in my mouth every morning

Emma Morgan

/They taste as bitter as sloes

I think that you might taste of the lunar flux of tides
and the swirl of biting winds

I would want to make you feel safe with me, like here was safe,
that I could lock the door and I would

I don't know write you things and tell you things
and whisper and sing and stroke you

Sleep with me, sleep with me, sleep with me,
sleep with me, sleep with me

'Bloody hell,' he says. 'You've got it bad.'

She passes the papers back to Popper who carefully sticks them back inside the wardrobe with some bits of dried-up Blu Tac.

'Who's this about then?'

Popper takes off his coat and chucks it on the bed. He rolls up his t-shirt sleeve.

On his arm is tattooed: *ALYS IS MY WONDERLAND*

It looks sore.

'Well, I never. Who's Alys?'

'She works with Nic.'

'Oh yeah, Nic says she's a pain in the arse. Will suit you then. Does she know?'

'No.'

'And you've got that tattooed on your arm?'

'Yeah.'

She looks at Popper who is rubbing at his tattoo with a finger.

'You need to stop with that. Have you put Dettol on it?'

'Yeah.'

'Some sense for once.'

'I can't help it Nat. About Alyss. I've tried but I can't. It's driving me up the fucking wall.'

'What further up than normal? When did you last get any sleep?'

'Can't remember.'

'Maybe you should try to get your head down.'

'Aren't you going to?'

'Nah, gone off the idea.'

And it's true, she doesn't have the taste for death. Never did really.

'I'll ssay ssorry to Gwen.'

'Fucking right you will. I'll let it go because I'm putting it down to stress, but you'll make it up to her in any way she wants.'

'Yeah. Courssse.'

'What about Alys then? You're going to have to show her.'

'Can't.'

'I don't think I'm giving you the option. Call it the price to pay for hurting my girlfriend.'

She can't tell if Popper looks terrified or relieved. Who's to say? The differences between emotions seem as fragile as moths' wings to her tonight. This morning. She needs to go home. That's what she needs to go. See what Gwen has to say.

Nat

Her mobile goes from its place next to her bed and she comes up out of a deep sleep to answer it.

'Yeah?'

'Nat's in A and E,' says Popper and puts down the phone but the call was from Nat's mobile.

She flounders up and goes into the other bedroom to get Gwen but no-one's in there. No-one's anywhere in the flat. Fuck. What's going on? She rings Nat's number back, but the phone's been switched off. She rings Gwen's mobile but that's switched off too. In a panic she rings Lola.

'What the fuck?' says Lola.

'Is Gwen with you?'

'No! What time is it?'

She rings off. In the hall she puts on the nearest coat over her tartan pyjamas and shoves her feet into trainers. Thanks be to God the car keys are on the hook; she hasn't driven for years but she's not getting back into a taxi again tonight. What the fuck time is it anyway?

Her driving is appalling and far too fast, but she manages to find a place to park up towards Kenny. It's 6 a.m. She legs it down to the Royal.

Nat is sitting on a wall outside, smoking a cigarette, white as a sheet. Her coat is crisp with something. She looks like a ghost. Her head feels like it might explode. She marches up to her.

'Don't you never, not never, you fucking idiot wanker, do that to me again. 'Cos I will fucking kill you.'

'Heh Nic.'

'I've been fucking murdering the Mass for the frigging dead all the way here and here you are fucking alive. I thought that little bastard prick had killed you or at the very least inflicted some serious fucking damage. What the fuck is going on?'

'You really wanna know?'

'Try me.'

'I fell over a loose pavement slab on the way out of Popper's and gave myself a massive nosebleed. And it wouldn't stop bleeding. Remember I used to have them? When I got stressed. Well, I'm stressed like Nicola. I know I should just have got in a taxi, but I couldn't bear one on my own.'

'Me neither. I drove.'

'You what?'

'It's OK. I didn't crash. Car's parked up the road.'

'Jesus.'

'Heh,' says Popper, walking up, 'alright?'

She goes over to him and decks him with her best right hook. He falls to the floor.

'And if I've broken a nail, you fucking bastard...'

'Can your rent cubicles by the night?' says Nat.

'Fuck. My nosse,' says Popper, holding onto it with both hands.

'Well, you'll know better than to mess with the big girls now, won't you?' says Nat.

'Fuck.'

'Stop whinging on,' she says. She crouches down next to Popper and gets him to sit up. She inspects his face. He's not bleeding. 'You'll be fine. And it was no less than you deserved.'

'I'm ssorry Nic, I'm ssorry I tried to hurt Gwen.'

'Fucking right. But I'm not the one you should be saying sorry to you, am I?'

'I will. I'll say ssorry, I will.'

'Stop mumbling you idiot. Stand up.'

She gives him a hand up.

Into the street, the sun up now of a Sunday morning. The air is fresh and there is a breeze, one of those Liverpool breezes that gets down the back of your clothes and into your mouth.

'Do you want a lift, Popper?' she says. 'Out of the goodness of my heart.'

'Nah. You're alright,' says Popper. 'Gonna walk. I like the wind.'

He slopes off into it and she watches him go.

'So what did you say to him?' she says to Nat.

Nat looks at her and shrugs.

'Just told him like it is. He fucked up. But haven't we all? Gwen? She didn't want to come with you?'

'I have no idea where Gwen is.'

'What? She's not in the flat?'

'She was gone when Popper rang me.'

'Lola's?'

'No. I rang there.'

'Shit.'

'What are you going to do?'

'I don't fucking know.'

She pulls out her phone.

'Seven thirty... maybe she's gone, you know, home.'

'Yeah. Maybe.'

'What are you going to do about it?'

'I've completely fucked it up Nic. I can't make her stay, can I?'

'Why are you giving up?'

'I'm not giving up. Just...'

'What?'

'She's better off without me, isn't she? That's the reality of the situation. I'm a fuck-up and she's not. She deserves way better than me.'

'The woman loves you. Anyone can see that. And you love her, although you might want to pretend you don't because it suits you that way.'

'What do you mean by that?'

'It's convenient for you, isn't it, that's she gone, if she's gone.

Because that way you don't have to pull your finger out. That way you don't have to actually make any effort to change.'

Nat stops, leans against a wall, doesn't look at her. She stands next to her and waits.

'It's a mess,' says Nat.

'You've got that right.'

'I'm an awful person.'

'Well, I wouldn't say awful. Selfish yes. Arrogant maybe. And your roast potatoes aren't up to much but still, you're the only sister I've got so I guess I'll have to put up with you. And the other thing is…'

'What?'

Nat looks at her straight and they stare at each other for a while.

'I don't want to be without her. And you don't either. You're just faking it. She'll have had to get a train to get home, won't she? I doubt the woman's going to hitch. Let's go down the hill. Just to see like.'

'It's a waste of time.'

'Cos your time's so precious. You can't even be bothered to walk down the fucking hill to look for the only woman you've ever loved. And yeah, I used that word on purpose.'

She takes hold of Nat's hand and Nat, although reluctant, lets her. She starts dragging her down the hill towards Lime Street.

But in the almost empty Sunday morning concourse there is no Gwen to be seen.

'What are we going to do now then?' she says.

'I have no fucking idea.'

'Stop repeating yourself.'

Nat sits down on a bench. The place is nearly deserted and, as always, freezing. Why are train stations always so bloody cold? Nat puts her face in her hands. She hasn't seen her this upset for many a year. She puts her hand on Nat's back, but she doesn't move.

'Natalie?' she says.

Gwen

The train is going to take a hundred years. She is in love with a drug dealer. Never home. Serially unfaithful. Dangerous. A fighter. A killer probably. It's so obvious as to what she should do. She will eradicate her from her life completely. She will never see or speak to her again. But how do you do that? When you still love someone so fiercely? How do you just walk away despite the geographical distance? And the distance in worlds come to that. And then there is Nic. It would mean giving her up too and she's promised not to. It would be terrible. The thought of never being able to see either of them again is almost unbearable and not just that, impossible. She doesn't even know who she would be anymore without both of them. Some soft southern girl with a load of complicated memories of a life that wasn't hers to start with. She feels appalling, worn out, on the verge of weeping. She thinks that she might be going to be sick into her lap. She puts her hand over her mouth and looks out of the window at the passing fields, pretends she is going on a normal visit to see her parents. Normal. What is normal anyway? Right now, she can't bear to think about what she's left behind.

She's so tired by the time she gets there that she can hardly see straight but she walks home from the train station anyway. She packed almost nothing and so her bag is easy to carry. That's the world's smallest consolation. One you could fit on a pin head. Where is home anyway? She thought she knew where it was but now she has no idea. It can't be Liverpool anymore so it's going to have to be back here for now. She is slinking home with her tail between her legs, defeated by the city and its sharp spikes. Nat and Nic. Nic and Nat. What is Nat doing? Where did she spend the night? With that woman perhaps? The thought of that makes her heart gulp. Or one of the other women. The many, many women. It matters less than she thought it would when it was finally admitted. Because she had always known and pretended not to? Perhaps she believes her, that it doesn't matter. But if they don't matter, maybe she doesn't either. Maybe she's one more disposable woman in the long line of them. She isn't loved any more than any of the others are. There is an equality in that at least. Not that that is a consolation. Because she has always wanted Nat to be hers and not everybody's and has always known that that was impossible. And what about Nic? What does she really feel about her? What is Nic doing right now? Will she panic when she wakes up and finds that she isn't there? She should have left a note. Maybe she should text her? But then she is supposed to be going cold turkey on the Shaws. What the fuck is she going to do about work? God, this is going to be absolutely awful; already it feels like a wrenching that runs through her whole body.

She doesn't know whether to knock or to let herself in with her key. It's pathetic that she still has one, like she always knew she was going to crawl back home. She stands on the doorstep shivering which reminds her of Nic standing on hers, having that asthma attack. She feels like she is only a step away from one herself. She rings the bell. After a minute, someone comes towards her down the hall, she can see the shape of it through the stained glass. It is the ample figure of Veronica. She opens the door, and when she sees her, her mouth is a wide o of shock at first and then a huge smile. It's the smile that does it, that tips her over.

'Oh Gwen darling! What a lovely surprise. Come in! Come in! Why didn't you use your key? Why didn't you call from the station? I would have come to pick you up.'

'Because this isn't my house,' she says, and puts her bag down and starts to cry with her hands over her face. Veronica puts her arms around her.

'There, there,' Veronica says, 'there, there. Come on. Tell me all about it.'

So she does, standing there in the hall, in their middle class hall with its overflowing shoe rack and its sanded floorboards and its pictures on the walls of trees and fields. What she tells Veronica is so out of place there that it is almost a fairy story. Quite unbelievable. And it has never been real to her until now. She feels out of her own body telling it, it sounds so strange and far away from this life that her parents live. And there is no going back from this, she knows that, this admitting of the truth is the closing of a door, a slamming of one. Her mother listens carefully without interrupting and eventually sits down on the stairs. She sits down herself, two steps below, not looking at her mother, and goes on talking, it all rushes out of her, a torrent of it until she has run out of words. She's not a Scouser then. They never run out. Nat and Nic. Nic and Nat. She stops and leans her head on Veronica's knees who strokes her hair gently like she did when she was a child and had a nightmare. Perhaps this has all been a dream.

All Veronica says is, 'You should have a lie down darling.'

There is a cup of tea and some cereal and a shower, and then there is bed and a surprisingly long sleep since she had thought she might never sleep again. But no, she lies down and is out of it in seconds. She comes to in her childhood bedroom with its posters of Jimi Hendrix and Stevie Nicks on the walls. Its silk scarves draped over the chest of drawers. Its wooden jewellery box with the ballet dancer inside it. She knows that if she opens the wardrobe that it will be still full of her teenage clothes. She should never have left. She should have stayed here, tucked up and safe. She doesn't have the energy to get up. She turns over and sobs into her pillow until her nose is blocked and she has to look for something to blow it on. She settles on the nearest scarf. How disgusting. Her eyes feel swollen and her mouth like the inside of a bin. She should have brushed her teeth harder. She is home. She is safe. The twins are lost to her. She expects that everyone will say it's for the best. And maybe, if they say it often enough, it will come true. Someone knocks quietly on the door.

'Come in,' she says.

It's her mother with a cup of tea.

'Thank you,' she says and sits up and takes it from her hands.

'I've thought about what you told me,' says Veronica, sitting down on the edge of the bed. 'They are lovely those girls, really lovely, and I know now from what you've told me that they haven't had an easy life. I'm sorry for that, it seems such a shame. But their lives are also messy and complicated, and it seems that living with them both has been an enormous strain on you.'

'Because I lived with a drug dealer and a prostitute? Well, an ex-prostitute.'

'No. Because you lived with people whose life experiences are so different from your own. Natalie may have a reason to behave the way she has, who is to know? And you have choices that perhaps neither of them has and that isn't fair. But you do have choices. The question is not whether living with them is wrong or right. The question is are you making the most of your life?'

'My privileged life?'

'Yes, if you want to name it like that.'

She bites her lip.

'I'll get out of bed,' she says.

'I'll make you something to eat,' says Veronica and gets up. 'Stay as long as you like. This is your home.'

It makes her want to cry again. She gets dressed in an old skirt and t-shirt. Perhaps Lola can go and get her stuff back? And then what? Send it to her? There was a fair bit of stuff. But would it be better to just chalk it up as something else she needs to leave behind? If only she could go backwards, re-teenage herself.

'Gwen,' shouts Veronica up the stairs.

She goes down the stair and she can see Veronica standing on the threshold and then, past her, are two tall figures.

Nat is paler even than usual. There is what looks like dried blood encrusted on her good coat. She looks like a ghost. Perhaps, and this is entirely possible, given her mental state, she is a ghost. She looks at Nic to see if she can see her too. And sees that they are the same. They're not identical, but today they are the same. Pale ravaged beings from another sphere. Twin suffering angels. Terrifying angels. Maybe none of them are actually here. Maybe this is all a dream.

'Why have you got your pyjamas and my coat on Nic?' she says. It's the first thing she can think of. This may be shock.

'Fuck, I'd forgotten.'

'How did you get here?' she says.

'We drove,' says Nic. 'We fancied a day out. Natalie has something to say to you.'

Nat looks at her, but it's a shy look, out of the side of her eyes, not a look she thought she had in her. She wants to reach out and put her hand on her arm like her mother did to her. Say, 'there, there.'

'I'm really sorry Gwen. I'm sorry I fucked up. I'm sorry if this is inconvenient and you'd much rather not ever see me again and I can go now if you want… we can go now…' Nat seems to run out of words.

She stares at them both for a while, chewing her lip. None of them say anything. Nat is looking down at her own trainers. Nic is looking at a flowerpot next to the door.

'Veronica?' she says turning round and there is her mother standing behind her, and she knows that, although it's never come to this before, that her mother would do anything to protect her. She feels nervous then, like she is about to ask for the moon.

'Could the twins come in?'

'Yes,' says Veronica.

'And could they have cups of tea?'

'Yes.'

'Nat likes hers virtually black and Nic likes a huge amount of sugar.'

Veronica nods and goes off down the hall. She looks back at the twins and they both seem scared, which is not something she would have ever thought them capable of.

'Don't be scared,' she says.

'All very well for you to say,' says Nic, crossing her arms.

Nat puffs her chest up and it makes her want to laugh, the pride and the foolishness of it.

'It must have taken you a long time to get here.'

'Yes,' says Nat.

'Too fucking right,' says Nic.

'Come in then,' she says.

'Are you sure?' says Nat.

'It's only a cup of tea.'

'I'm ashamed of my pyjamas now. Although they are yours really. What must your mum think?' says Nic.

'I'll find you something else to wear.'

'Nothing you give me is going to fit,' says Nic, and smiles.

'What have you told your mum?' says Nat.

'Everything.'

'All of it?' says Nat.

'Yes.'

'And she'll let us in the house?' says Nat.

'Your mum is lovely,' says Nic.

'Come in.'

She backs away and the twins step over the threshold, Nic tentatively as though entering a magic castle, Nat with her brow furrowed as if she needs to wrench herself through a wall of thorns. She feels that she should throw out a trail of breadcrumbs to get them to the kitchen. Perhaps it is unwise to let them in the house. Probably. But she was brought up to be polite to guests.

Veronica is nowhere to be seen when they enter the kitchen but there are three cups of tea steaming on the stripped pine table.

'Which is which though?' says Nic. 'Sorry. Should be grateful we've got tea. If I was your mum, I wouldn't have let us in. No way.'

Nic sits down at the table, but Nat remains standing, like she's about to make a break for it.

'You can sit down Nat,' she says but instead Nat gets down on one knee next to the table, by her feet.

'A civil ceremony,' says Nat, looking up at her in the eye for the first time. 'Just your mum and dad and Rosa and that. Nic. That's it.'

'Are you asking me to marry you?' she says, confused.

'Yeah.'

'Nice that Natalie. Did you think of that on the way here?' says Nic.

'I don't believe in marriage,' she says, and she can't tell if Nat looks disappointed or relieved. Nat gets up and sits down at the table so that she's got a twin on either side. She wants to hug them both to her and yet she mustn't, she mustn't.

'You should have asked her mum and dad first,' says Nic. 'What are you going to do next Natalie? The stations of the cross?'

'There's something else,' says Nat.

She watches her to see what she will say. It feels better when they're in the room. So much better. It shouldn't but it does.

'I've got some money put by. If I did my A'levels and if I passed them…'

'Course you'll bloody pass them,' says Nic.

Nat glares at her.

'I dropped out in the middle last time. After Mum died.'

'She lost it.'

'Thanks for that Nic. I was going to go to university. I had a place.'

'Where?' she says.

Nat mumbles something that she doesn't catch.

'What she's trying to tell you is that she had a place at Oxford,' says Nic. 'To do English.'

'What?' she says.

'Yeah,' says Nat.

'But then Mum died,' said Nic.

'Yeah,' says Nat, 'so I gave up. But now, if you want, I could try again.'

'Mind you, I doubt if Oxford will have you. You're probably stuck with some bricklaying college,' says Nic.

'So, I thought, well, if you wanted, if I got a place somewhere then you could come with me. Get a teaching job wherever. If you wanted. If you fancied it like.'

Nat looks down at her tea as though it is going to provide her with support. Everything has been a series of shocks, but this seems even bigger, and she can't get her head around it at all.

'Would that mean you'd give up dealing?'

'Probably.'

'And you'd go to university?'

'If I can.'

'And you want me to marry you?'

'Well to be honest... I just put that bit in on the spur of the moment. Just in case you wanted to.'

'I don't.'

Nat breathes out and looks at her.

'I'm bored of it all if the truth be told. And I love you. I want our lives to be better.'

'Got that off your chest now, have you?' says Nic.

'Thanks Nicola. Yeah, I have. So what do you think Gwen?'
'What about Nic?' she says.
Nat turns to her sister.
'Nic'll come too,' she says.
Nic raises her eyebrows.
'Not Manchester,' Nic says.
'There are limits,' says Nat. 'So, what do you think? Would you be into it?'
'Do you want to change because you want to change or are you just doing it for me?'
'Both maybe.'
'That's an honest answer. And what about what I want?' she says.
'What do you want?'
'Lots of things.'
'Like what?'
'I don't know yet.'
'An honest answer. Well, have a think about it all. No pressure. We'll have our tea and then we'll make a move.'
'You've only just got here.'
'I'm trying not to crowd you,' says Nat.
'Good luck with that one,' mumbles Nic. 'And I love you too Gwen. In case you thought I didn't. But no pressure.'

After that no-one says anything for a while. The three of them sit quietly, drinking tea, looking out at the garden. Her head is a muddle of thoughts and her body a muddle of feelings and it's all too much, all of it.

Nat

She looks at the vegetable patch she helped to dig in the summer. It's so quiet here. She wonders where Veronica might have got to. It was generous of her to let them in her house. They didn't deserve it, or at least she didn't anyway.

'I'm knackered,' says Nic, eventually.

'You could have a lie down in my bed,' says Gwen.

'Could I?'

'Course.'

'Your mum won't mind?'

'I don't think so. Come upstairs with me. Do you need a sleep too Nat?'

'No, you're alright.'

'Oh, I forgot you're a vampire for a second.'

Gwen smiles at her but it's only a tiny smile and that makes this all worse somehow.

Gwen takes Nic out of the room and up the stairs to her bedroom and she wishes then that she had said yes, she likes Gwen's bedroom, the posters on the walls, the hippy bedspread, the safety of it all. She is tireder than she would like to admit, and her hands are shaking slightly. Veronica comes back into the room, and she goes back to red alert, waiting for the lecture or the ejection.

'Are you hungry Natalie?' says Veronica and she realises that she is.

'Yes,' she says.

'I'll make you a sandwich. Cheese?'

'Yes, please. But I can make it myself if you show me where the stuff is.'

'No, you're my guest.'

'I'm sorry,' she says, and is reminded of Popper apologising. She doubts Veronica is going to knife her though. 'Really sorry. About all that I've put Gwen through. She's told you about all of it, she said.'

Veronica cuts slices from a chunk of cheese. She sips her tea. It's gone cold.

'Ultimately,' Veronica says, 'it's not for me to judge.'

She can't work out if this is generous of her or stupid. What would she do in her situation? She'd have ejected them by now.

'It's Gwen's decision,' says Veronica, and hands her a plate with a sandwich on. She takes a bite. Stilton. It tastes good. She tries to eat slowly and keep her elbows off the table.

'You know the treehouse that's at the end of the garden?' says Veronica, who has her back to the kitchen units now, looking at her.

'Yes.'

'Harry built it for the girls when they were tiny. And Rosa, being the oldest, taught Gwen how to climb up to it. One day Gwen climbed up there on her own, up past the treehouse into the highest branches but then she couldn't get down again. And Harry went outside and tried to coach her down, but Rosa stopped him. She told him that Gwen knew how to get down on her own, it was just that she didn't trust herself. She told Gwen to come down because there was ice cream on the table that she was missing. But to come down slowly, to take her time, test each branch out with one foot, just to make sure it would hold.'

Veronica stops talking then and there is silence, it's so quiet that she feels she can hear the floorboards expanding and contracting.

'What happened?' she says eventually.

'I had my heart in my mouth. I was convinced we would end

up in the hospital with her. A broken leg. A broken arm. Or worse. She was up so high. That's what being a mother is like Natalie – that constant fear was encapsulated in one moment. But I realised then, that you have to trust your children. I know that's not fashionable anymore, that idea. Everyone is so scared nowadays about the dangers their children face, even when they're grown up. All the bad things that can happen. And I am too, of course, I'm not immune, but I trust my daughters, both of them, to work things out for themselves.'

Veronica comes towards her, and she automatically rears back but Veronica just pats her on the shoulder.

'Gwen will work it out. But whatever she decides, you need to respect that decision. Will you promise me that?'

'Yes.'

'Good.'

Veronica leaves the room, and she can hear her going back up the stairs. She lays her head down on the table. She traces her fingers over the grain of the wood.

'I'm sorry Gwen,' she says, 'I'm so sorry,' and there is wet under her cheek. She must fall asleep there.

Gwen

As she goes up the stairs with her, Nic slips her hand into her hand. Her nails and longer and sharper but the hand is the same shape as Nat's. They go into her bedroom. She pulls back the covers on her bed and Nic gets in. She pulls the covers back over her. Nic looks at her.

'What you going to say to Natalie?'

'I don't know.'

'We shouldn't have come.'

'I'm glad you did.'

'Are you?'

'Yes.'

Nic closes her eyes, and she reaches out and strokes her shiny hair back from her forehead.

'We came to get you,' says Nic. 'Like you did for me. Except you don't need getting, do you? But we couldn't not try. We couldn't not try.'

She sees that Nic's face is wet, and she reaches out with a thumb to wipe the tears. She sits down on the edge of the bed and watches her fall asleep.

Nat

'What college were you supposed to go to?' whispers a voice into her dream.

'Magdalen,' she mumbles into the wood.

She raises her head off the table. Gwen is sitting next to her with her hands in her lap. She looks exhausted but beautiful. Why didn't she notice before how beautiful she was? Because she's an idiot, that's why. She wipes drool off her chin with her sleeve, but Gwen doesn't seem to notice.

'How did you get down from the tree that day you climbed too high when you were a kid?' she says.

'Very slowly indeed. It's the re-immersion that will kill you.'

'The bends.'

'Exactly. I know you can't change people Nat; I know that. But the question is, do you want to change? And your word for the day is: refulgent.'

'What's that mean?'

'Shining very brightly. From the Latin for 'shining out'. Would you like to borrow a t-shirt? Or would you prefer a kiss? I don't think it will be as good as the one in the park was, but I've brushed my teeth for the second time and…'

So Nat kisses her hard and wraps her arms around Gwen's back. It is the best kiss she has ever had in her life. It may well be the ruin of her if she wasn't already broken.

Nic

She lies looking at the ceiling in Gwen's bed. There are cobwebs. Someone needs to have a go at them with a duster. She's waiting for something to happen. Not her best skill. Not a skill she has at all really. But if Nat tries to change then maybe she could too. She can't stand it any longer. She gets up and tiptoes down the stairs, although they creak. Her feet will be filthy and all. She goes along the hall and into the kitchen. Nat is sitting at the table kissing Gwen, and yes, a part of her is jealous, will always be jealous, but another part of her is ridiculously happy, as though she had been to the funfair and won the biggest teddy going. She thinks that, for once, it's all going to be OK. They come up for air and Gwen sees her.

'Hi Nic,' Gwen says. 'Would you like a kiss too?' And she smiles at her, the best smile she knows.

'For fuck's sake,' she says, 'Don't you bloody start.'

Gwen	*Nat*
She thinks that that is the end of it, or that is the beginning. Or both of those things. This is home now then, they are home.	She thinks that that is the end of it, or that is the beginning. Or both of those things. And some of it hurts, but not all of it, no, not all of it at all.

Gwen

The trees sway outside, making shadows on the curtains, as she wakes up in their bed, in the cold light of dawn. There is someone else in the room. Nat is asleep next to her. Must be Nic then.

'Nic?' she says.

'Nat said to come back with her sso I did. I wanted to say ssorry, but you were assleep. Hope you don't mind Gwen. I wass on the couch but I had a nightmare. Ssorry. I don't ssleep good. Get sscared like. My mum. Sshe comess after me ssee. And other sstuff. Don't like it.'

She sits up.

'Come here,' she says.

He stands right next to her, too close as always. And she realises what he reminds her of, with his small skinny frame and his shrunken t-shirt and his too big eyes – one of her children when they've done something terribly wrong.

'I'm ssorry Gwen,' he says. 'Going for you and that.'

'I said some pretty nasty things.'

'It's true though. Never had much of a home. Gwen?'

'Yes.

'I've not got no one elsse.'

There is a silence for a while. The trees shake outside and somewhere a bird starts up.

'There was this big tree in my garden when I was little and we had a swing in it and you could have come round and gone on the swing,' she says. 'And we would have played all day long until it was time for tea. And then you would have gone home to your house and your mum would have cooked you sausages with baked potatoes and beans and your dad would have read you a story before you went to bed and tucked you in. And they would have loved you very, very much. Very, very much. I'm sorry you didn't get that. I'm so sorry. If I could spare any of you any of it, I would. I can't make amends for the stuff that happened to you. Nobody can. But you're not there anymore. It may feel like it but you're not. You can switch games. You just have to want to stop. What did you play when you were little Popper?

'F... f... f... f...'

'Footie? I understand the offside rule. I think.'

'If I'd known you Gwen, we could have played footie in our back garden,' says Nat, from next to her. 'And you could have come to Formby with us, run down the beach yeah, collected sticks and pebbles. And our dad would have told you stories about when he was a kid. And our mam would have filled you full of cake. She made a great chocolate cake. And if I'd known you then Pop you could have come too. I'm sorry lad, I'm really, really sorry too. I don't know nothing do I really? I haven't got a fucking clue.'

She puts her hand up to Popper's cheek and strokes it.

'This is home for you, "h" is for home, and we are your home now. Don't leave us. Don't let us go. We love you. You are a fucked- up psycho mess but we love you anyway.'

'"Volatile," says Popper. 'On your t-shirt. What they play?'

'You tell me,' she says with a catch in her throat.

'Dunno them, do I? Never heard of them. Are they from down your way like?'

'They're from inside my head. They're an imaginary band. I've got some others. There's "It's Not Rocket Science!" But I think they've disbanded because of all the acid. And there's "Pedro". They're a four piece from New York. They play kind of folky

Mexican Jewish pop. But this is my favourite. Nic made me the t-shirt. What do you reckon they play? I don't really know.'

He looks at her, thinks.

'Kinda heavy. Metally. Thrasshy. Pssychedelic. Rock. Primal Scream. The Captain. Jane'ss Addiction. Motorhead. The Mondayss. The Rosess. The Verve. Metallica. The Pixiess. The Classh. Kinda like that.'

'Sounds good. Popper, can I ask you something?'

'Yeah.'

'What's your real name?'

'Mark. Mark Michael Dempssey.'

'That's a nice name.'

'Would you tell me a poem?'

She stares at him for a while, and he stares back. Eventually she says:

> *Out of the ordinary*
> *Are the curves of green gloss park benches*
> *And the ironwork of fencing*
> *As elaborate as jewellery;*
> *Before long, if you watch,*
> *Everything is ornamental.*
> *Not to mention the tulips,*
> *Those surprises the colours of lollipops*
> *And the way the gardener*
> *Ordered his annuals*
> *Like the most meticulous of men*
> *And expressed his admiration for the lawns*
> *In the language of pansies,*
> *And once,*
> *Just once,*
> *I got up so early of a May morning*

> *That I saw a fox in the dew*
> *Admiring*
> *The begonias.*

'Ssound. That's ssound that is.'
'Would you do something for me?' she says.
'Coursse. What do you want me to do?
'Would you please make me some breakfast? I'm starving.'

She's eating toast and Marmite at the kitchen table.
'You know "Volatile"?' Popper says, standing looking out the window.
'Yes.'
'Could I be in it?'
'Of course you could. You'd be great at that. You could write all the lyrics.'
'Like a real band? Not jusst an imaginary band?'
'Can you sing?'
'Of course he can fucking sing Gwen. He's a Scouser. It's our birth right,' says Nat from the doorway, taking a cigarette out of the packet. Her red hair is around her face, and she is sure then, exactly then, that she loves her completely and the only other person she will ever love as much as that is Nic.
'And Alys?' Popper says.
'Who's Alys?' she says.
'Works with Nic,' says Nat.
'Oh her. Nic hates her. What about her?'
'Dunno.'
'Popper?'
'He's in love with her,' says Nat.
'No! Really?'
'Dunno,' says Popper.

'Go on Pop, show the girl,' says Nat.
Popper rolls up his sleeve and shows her his tattoo.
'Bloody hell! Has she seen that?'
'No.'
'Exactly,' says Nat.
'You're in love with her?'
'Dunno like,' Popper says.
'Try to say something coherent lad,' says Nat.
'Yeah, I'm in love with her. I'm fucking ssoft. But sshe ssaid…'
'What?'
'Sshe can drum. Sshe likess to drum.'
'Oh, I see. So you're thinking?'
'Yeah,' says Popper.
'Like mayhem bottled,' she says. 'Better speak to Lola then. She knows about bands.'

'I ain't never assked no one this before Gwen but could I? Could I have a hug?'
'Of course you can.'
She gets up and he goes over to her. She hugs Popper. He is rigid in her arms and only lets it last for a few seconds before he steps away.
'Ta Gwen. Never been hugged by no girl before,' says Popper, looking out the window again.
'Jesus Pop. Why did you never tell me that? I could have prevented all sorts of demented outbursts. You're like one of those disturbed baby monkeys suffering from tactile deprivation. Would have hugged you every day if you'd asked. Do you need a manager, Mark?' says Nat.

Nat

She sits at the back of the rehearsal room watching, just watching. It's not like she's not good at that. It's a bit like being at a zoo to be honest, only with a bit less mauling.

'Just don't like "Volatile," says Lola, doing stretches while watching Popper pace. 'It sounds like some kind of hair restorer. It's not giving people the right impression.'

'What impression is that?' says Amy who is the laconic to Lola's exuberance and is concentrated on rolling a spliff.

'That we're any bloody good,' says Lola.

'"Turmoil?"' says Popper, stopping near enough to Lola to be heard but not near enough to be punched.

'Too punk,' says Lola.

'"Hard graft?"' says Popper.

'An upper not a downer mate. Something vibey. Something to rock out to,' says Amy.

'"Caned?"' says Popper.

'I am not being in no band called "Caned". It's bad enough being in a band with you bunch of scallywags,' says Amy.

'Scallywags? Thank you very much Amy love for your contribution but I really don't think so,' says Lola who it touching her toes with an easy grace.

'Excuse me. I thought this band was um you know like a democracy?' says Alys, still sitting behind her drumkit. Alys's playing isn't bad but the drumkit, bought with some 'inheritance money' from her grandmother is way better than she is.

She raises her eyebrows and waits for Lola to kick off.

'Course it's not a democracy!' says Lola, putting her hands on her tiny hips, 'What are you on about? This is my kingdom. Mine! And I will be obeyed. I. WILL. BE. OBEYED.'

And, of course, Lola isn't really joking. She is a good match for Popper's intransigence at least.

Alys looks abashed.

'Alys got you lot a gig by the way,' she says to calm things down.

'Where?' says Amy, now smoking the spliff.

'Some mates at LIPA doing some charity sort of thing. We're like the third support or something. It's going to be fierce. If you want to. Is that OK? It's a week Friday,' says Alys, addressing herself to Amy's ear rather than looking directly at her and twiddling with her drumsticks.

Apparently, this Alys kid went to Merchant Taylors, a fact that they all find hilarious.

'I just hope there's plenty room,' says Lola, directing her laser focus onto Alys who visibly flinches. 'Have you told them about Popper and his propensity to crash into things? By the way Alys? Nic says you can sew.'

'Yes. Quite well actually. I used to do some of the costumes for the plays at school and we did like this one thing? It was really amazing, it was...' Alys says in a tumbling rush.

'How are you with sequins? says Lola, rolling her eyes.

'Um. OK I think. We made this sort of queen costume with a sequinned...'

'Good 'cos you'll be sewing until your fingers bleed.'

Lola crosses her arms and looks satisfied. Alys looks at the floor.

She hides a smile. It's like managing an anarchist group.

"Beggars would ride?" says Popper, with his back to everyone.

'What did you just say Popper?' says Lola.

Popper turns to her, 'Beggarss would ride. If wishess were horses, beggarss would ride. My mum used to ssay that.'

'Hmmm,' says Lola approaching Popper who, unlike Alys, stands resolute. Lola might be about to touch him, but she obviously changes her mind before she gets there and diverts towards Amy who hands her the spliff.

'I like that,' says Amy.

Lola is inhaling deeply and with concentration.

Everyone waits.

Lola exhales and so does the room.

'OK,' says Lola. 'Now we're talking.'

Popper smiles, although it's more of a gargoyle grimace. Alys does a Paul McCartney thumbs up which doesn't seem to be ironic.

'Well done, Pops,' she says.

'Good one mate,' says Amy.

LOLA'S SET LIST

First (and possibly last) performance of BEGGARS WOULD RIDE (because I am the one in charge)
Decade (that rank heavy metal thing about wars and stuff)
Bomber (ear bleed drums)
Chicken Neck (check shirt rave thing)
Tasmanian Devil (Ace of Spades backwards)
It's a Soul Thing (soul thing)
Shakedown (Stockport grunge)
Should Not Be Legal to Play (really bad comedown)
No Me Llamaste (you didn't call me – I'm not fucking surprised)

Nat

That daft girl Alys comes down the corridor towards her, all in black with big biker boots and long silver earrings swinging like the claws of some long extinct beast. Lee, in a red shimmery ankle length dress stretched over his large frame, and Lola, in a sequinned black mini, are holding hands behind her which is quite sweet. Lola is dwarfed by Lee in heels, even though she is wearing heels herself. Lee looks like everything is great, Lola is perturbed, she can see that, and she can't blame her for that. Anything could happen this evening. Anything at all.

'What's happening guys?' says Alys. 'Is Popper being sick? Oh the poor thing.'

Alys tries to enter the toilets, but Lee prevents her with a gentle hand.

'Oh! No! No! No! No little Alys, come with me love, you cannot see such a dreadful sight.'

'It's alright. I don't mind sick. Or blood. Or even poo,' says Alys.

'As you would say posh girl, that's - like TMI,' says Lola. 'Go with our Lee and check with the crew. We'll be there in a minute.'

'Oh OK.'

She and Lola, despite both their reluctance, go into the toilets. Gwen is leaning against a sink with her arms crossed and Petey is next to her, drawing with a biro on his hand. A sweat slicked Popper comes out of the toilet naked from the waist up. He puts his head in the sink and turns on the cold tap, water spraying out onto the floor, and everyone steps away.

'Jesus,' she says. 'I've got déjà vu.'

Popper comes up for air. Gwen passes him some green paper towels from the dispenser and Popper pats himself down.

'Popper?' says Lola.

'Yeah?'

'What's with all the scars anyway?'

'Ever been cut with a knife and then pisssed on?'

'I don't like those kind of clubs,' says Lola. 'I'd always thought you'd you know… That you cut yourself up for kicks.'

'Yeah, ssome, but mostly thesse were pressentss.'

'I am wrestling a temptation to give you a hug now,' says Lola.

Gwen hands Popper his safety pinned t-shirt and he puts it on.

'What am I doing in this band? Me, Amy, who should know better, a bleeding sociopath, and some posh kid who learnt "percussion" at school. It's not what you'd call a normal assortment of people is it?' says Lola. 'We should have stayed a two-piece.'

'It might work,' says Gwen.

'Yeah,' says Lola. 'What does the boss say?'

'It might work,' she says, and Lola sighs.

She tucks Popper under one arm and Lola and Gwen and Petey follow them out of the toilets and down the corridor to the door where Lee is standing next to Amy, and Alys is fidgeting with her drumsticks looking even whiter than normal.

'You look beautiful Lee if I may say so,' she says.

'Thank you,' he says. 'Do you like my new eyelashes?'

'He used to get them from Claire's Accessories,' says Lola, 'but these ones are handmade in Japan. Probably from the price of them by virgin geishas.'

'Would you begrudge me?' says Lee.

'I would begrudge you nothing,' Lola says.

Lee kisses her.

'But now I've got lippy on me.'

'Are you alright Popper? Do you feel better?' says Alys.

'I'm alright ta.'

'Good,' and Alys touches him on the hand which is probably not a good idea because he wrenches back and starts shaking again.

'Sorry,' says Alys who looks like she might cry.

'Ssorry,' says Popper, 'bit wound up like.'

She winks at him, and he looks at the ground. If this thing goes any slower between them, it'll be Victorian. She's going to have to force him into it somehow or other.

The door opens and Nic comes through it. She's looking good now, meat on her bones, spring in her step. Nice to see.

'They're baying out there,' says Nic. 'Better get on with it.'

Popper looks like he's going to have a full-on panic attack. She puts her hand on his shoulder and Gwen puts hers on the other.

'Ladies and gentlemen,' she says. 'All for one and one for all.'

She stands aside and Lola kisses Lee and puts on her best smile and goes through the door, followed by Alys, who doesn't look at them, and then Amy. Then there's only Popper. Both she and Gwen let go of him and then she takes his head in her hands and kisses him on his forehead.

'If you don't fucking tell her right after this gig, I will,' she says.

Popper nods and then goes through the door, out into the light.

'Welcome to Liverpool,' says Lola, at the end of the gig to the crowd. Popper is dripping sweat, as is Amy and Alys but Lola looks like she has just come fresh out of the shower. 'We are Beggars would Ride. That was a very small and fragrant example of our upcoming album which we have charmingly titled ALL THE GOOD BEATLES ARE NOT DEAD It's out on Friday if you wanna download it. Or you can get it for free off some dodgy bloke's server in Seoul but then you know, your karma's gonna get you. And no, that bit's not on there 'cos there are copyright issues with Yoko. Alright Yoko? I always liked you. And just so you know we pray to John on a daily basis.'

'And Bill Shankly,' she shouts from the crowd.

'And to Tori Amoss,' shouts Popper.

'You what?' says Lola, turning to him with a look of disgust.

Nic

For fuck's sake. That was a hell of a racket they made. Sort of good though. Sort of terrible as well. Her and Nat and Gwen and Petey stand at the bar. Like a gang of thieves. Like a sort of family.

'Dear dirty city. I'd miss it if we go,' says Nat, signalling the bartender.

'I'd miss the wind,' says Petey, leaning his skinny elbows on the bar.

'I'd miss the Anglican too,' says Nat.

'I'd miss my own fucking accent,' she says. 'Do you get homesick here Gwen?'

'Sometimes. Which is why I fraudulently redid Nat's UCAS form in case she prefers to keep taking her whiskey in The Phil and not The Eagle and Child.'

They all turn to stare at Gwen.

'What? I'd miss Anfield. You can go where you bloody well like Nat, everyone wants to give you a place what with all the diversity points you emit. You might need a different form though to go to The Sorbonne.'

Nat is speechless. Petey is laughing. Gwen has her beautiful smile on. I love you; she wants to say I love you I love you I love you. Gwen's wearing a dress that she made her. Colour of the grass in the park in May, when it's proper green. Knee length, fitted, with cap sleeves. Raw silk which costs a fortune but no matter. Instead of a poem. Way better than a poem she reckons. But she would think that, wouldn't she?

'I love it when Natalie shuts up for a bit,' she says.

'Yeah,' says Petey. 'Nice and quiet.'

Nat tousles the top of Petey's head but she's laughing too now.

And that's the end of all the shite they've gone through to get here.

Or the beginning of another completely different story.

THE END

Acknowledgements

Thank you to everyone who has supported me and encouraged my writing over the years. Thank you to Andrew and to James and the team at Northodox. Thank you to New Writing North. Thank you to my family and friends. Thank you to Paul.